Books By Aya DeAniege

Contracted
Contract Taken
Contract Broken

Coming Soon:
Contract Renewed

Coming Next Year:
Masked Intentions
*Prototype**
At Death's Door

Contract

Aya DeAniege

Front Cover Design by Christina Quinn

ISBN-13: 978-1542985109
ISBN-10: 1542985102

While the idea of sub-space in this book does reflect, in some part, the way the mind reacts in an abusive relationship, it has been altered in some chapters from its true form to suit a means to an end

Introduction / Preface

They split my story.

Now they're bickering about some movie deal. I don't get it. I haven't had enough popularity for that. Perhaps it's that age old cliche of books being made into movies that has suddenly taken off. Popular culture has been remaking movies of old and turning books into movies of late.

None of them are worth the time.

Certainly not this. How much could even be shown on the big screen? Porn and smut and not being able to capture the genuine feeling. Or perhaps it's simply to drive the readers out and into the public.

I'd threaten to beat all three of them, but two would take it as an invitation and the third? Well, I don't want to try his temper. He takes after his grandfather—nasty, beast of a man—I think is his problem.

Fantastic publicist though.

They didn't tell me until *after* it was published that they had broken up my story. It is their right to do so, I suppose. It will make me more money, they claim. Not that I need the money, mind you.

Editors like to change things on me, however. After the first edition was a hit in the community, I was convinced to publish the book at large to the public. To do that, I sent it to a proper editor, someone with years of experience. He came back and told me that I had to change the 'cleave.' Almost everything could remain the same, but I had to change what happened to me those two weeks I was away.

It was unbelievable he said, poor writing, he said.

Of course, I had submitted the book under a pen name.

After several emails back and forth where he told me to change it and I told him where to go and what to do in the politest way I could, I got fed up. How dare the man tell me I couldn't tell my story the way it happened. I walked into the office he held so dear and asked him if he knew who I was.

He had no idea.

Colour me surprised.

I explained who I was and he very carefully explained why he wanted it changed. Because no one reacts well to that sort of thing. For about two seconds I considered what he said, then I dismissed it entirely.

I have seen so many subs abused by Doms because the sub didn't realize. They thought it was normal and acceptable behaviour. My book was so popular amongst the community that all new members were 'strongly encouraged' to read it. We saved several subs from bad Doms when they came to me, trying to tell me it was all wrong. I told them it was, then sat them down and talked about what they should watch for in their chosen partner, the red flags if you will, of a bad relationship.

Predators walk amongst us, using the community kinks as a way to hide. Do not fall into the trap of a predator, but if you do, know that you can get free, no matter what he tells you. You do have a choice, and you're not selfish for having cravings of your own, or for asking why in a situation that you don't understand.

Safe, sane, consensual, I cannot stress that enough. And being true to my story has helps us illustrate that point. It was an extreme, after all, the community had been built to keep Nathaniel's father from hurting more people, but it is still a very real possibility.

The first portion of my story revolved around my signing a contract for the Program and spending two weeks with Nathaniel Edwards in his estate. We played a few times, had fantastic sex, and then something really confusing happened where his father came in and then took me away.

If the man hadn't been provided with photographic evidence, he wouldn't have been able to take me away. If someone hadn't been loyal to him, even though Nathaniel and Mr. Wrightworth both believed Elaina was loyal only to herself? I would have been fine.

I would have remained with Nathaniel because, despite everything, he did know his father very well. He knew that his father was spouting nonsense and hoping to catch him or me in a lie.

We did very well. For all that was said, all that was done, until that image arrived, we were in the free and clear. Nathaniel's father would have eventually left empty handed.

I don't recall a great deal of what happened afterwards. Perhaps that was one reason for the break, to explain the sudden change. Some have complained about not understanding, to which I've given them polite instructions on where to go and how to get there.

Nathaniel's father took me to one of his buildings. It was sound proof and rather small, it really only had one purpose. There were cameras everywhere so that he could watch everything over and over. As much as he liked doing what he did, Nathaniel's father could not make someone disappear whenever he pleased. The government kept a very careful watch on everything and everyone.

Rich people were excluded from the constant surveillance because they paid to be excluded. They also recorded everything in their homes in order to keep the servants trustworthy and to catch their own family doing whatever illegal things they did.

At any time the government could, and had before, demand access to that footage. Anyone who signed a contract, or inherited one, immediately signed over their rights for anything to do with the one poor person who signed the contract. This meant that at any time Mr. Wrightworth, or any other person from the Program, could log into a rich person's security system and watch anything to do with a poor person.

If that poor person happened to help Nathaniel undress, if that poor person happened to be engaged in sexual activities with a rich person.

If they were strung up like an animal waiting to be slaughtered.

The Program saw it all.

The problem they had with me was that after being removed from Nathaniel's home, they had no idea where I went.

Rich people paid for anonymity. Until they are found to be in possession of a contracted debtee, they cannot be watched short of a court order.

No one saw me go in with him, no one even saw him go in.

Mr. Wrightworth tried, I know he did. I saw the files and the favours he called in, in his attempt to find me. Not because I was special, not because he liked to hear me scream in pain or because my terror put a particular heat to his blood, but because I was a poor person who had signed a contract. He had sworn to protect us all, to care for us and, if need be, to step in when we should have withdrawn consent.

Nathaniel's father was very good at what he did. I was not the first person to disappear into this building of his. I might not have been the last either. We don't know for certain.

The moment I left Nathaniel's sight, I went numb. I dropped emotionally. The effects of discipline had been put off while he had been speaking to me, but with him out of sight the world was suddenly very real. What was done to me was real. I was in a state of numbness as I was pulled through and then out of the estate. I didn't put up much of a fight as I was stuffed into a car.

I don't... I don't really remember arriving. But some nights I wake, almost certain that I could feel it still, could see it still. The terror grips me tight and there's nothing I can do but rock myself as it passes over me and my mind fully wakes up, as I realize that I am no longer there.

Sometimes I'll see his face. You can't exactly make a man like that just disappear. Can't lock him away forever or rid the world of his image. When I see his face, it always takes me back and once more I am terrified and I am weak, afraid of what will happen to me and of all that has been done to me since then. The world appears all too large and I swear the very ground will simply open up underneath my feet and swallow me up.

Once a year on the anniversary of my being taken I ...

well... I pretty well lose my mind. Each year I hold onto just a little more sanity. Each year I try once more for freedom and am reminded of how much control he still has over my life and actions because once, decades ago, he had me caught for two weeks in a secluded location where no one could hear me scream.

As part of my rehabilitation I had to watch some of the tapes. To come to terms with what was done to me and to fully understand that, yes, this did happen. I wasn't imagining it, I didn't make it up and I didn't want what was done to me.

Some have said that because I was a part of the community, that I submitted to Nathaniel, that it was all right for me to be treated like that, that obviously I wanted it. To those people I asked how, or why, they believed that it was acceptable to do that to someone when they clearly said no, stop, begged and pleaded for their lives?

As I was raped the first time, I screamed. It wasn't pain, it certainly could not be mistaken for pleasure. The sound of my voice wasn't that of a victim suffering. It was the sound of an enraged woman. I had fought him for days but that was the point where I broke.

He did as he pleased for two weeks, give or take.

And then like clockwork my period started. Thank goodness he was so utterly disgusted at my bleeding and him not being the cause, because if it weren't for that, I never would have been left alone.

I never would have escaped.

Chapter One

The following is mostly transcription from phone records, mingled with the small fragments I recall and what sounds I picked up on in the audio recording. I've never watched the tapes on Mr. Wrightworth's side of things because it's just never felt right to do so. I viewed the phone call on my end, but it was in a numb fashion and years later. It's as if anything to do with that call has been completely erased, or like I wasn't really there for it.

Perhaps I wasn't. What kind of crazy person escapes their bonds and then picks up the discarded cellphone of their captor to make a call when they expected him back at any moment? If I had been caught on that phone... I still shudder to think about what might have happened to me.

"Hello?" Mr. Wrightworth demanded.

"Mr. Wrightworth?" I whispered.

"Izzy, Izzy, where are you?" he said, I could hear the furtive sound of his fingers being snapped. I can picture it in my head, having been in that room myself, the flurry of activity that was going on in the silent moments as I struggled on the other side of the line.

Just trying to hold on a little longer.

"I...I don't know... he took me somewhere."

My voice was breaking. There was no denying that my stability was slipping away. The sound of my voice was thicker than normal, like my throat was closing up, or my tongue was swollen. In reality, it probably sounded like that because I had been strangled more than once, and had been crying on and off before the call. I was on the verge of tears once more and that, in itself, can change the sound of my voice.

"I'll come and get you, I—"

"He hurt me, Mr. Wrightworth," I said, sobbing into the phone.

"Darling, listen to me," the concern was gone, only a commanding tone, then a moment of hesitation to allow me to comprehend that what he had just said went beyond the words. "Are you listening?"

"Yes, Mr. Wrightworth."

"Are you alone right now?"

A sniffled, the phone shifted as I wiped my runny nose with the same hand that held the phone. "Yes, he left some food and didn't tie me well enough. He could be back any minute."

"How much food did he leave you?"

"An apple and a sandwich."

"Okay, you've got a bit of time, breathe."

It didn't occur to me until years later to actually ask how Mr. Wrightworth knew the man wasn't going to be back for some time. Even after the events that were to come in the following months, I never asked Mr. Wrightworth about it. I should have, I should have known better.

Nathaniel's father had left his cell phone outside of where I had been tied up, but still just laying around. Rich people can be a little stupid like that, not thinking about the expensive items they can replace at the drop of a hat.

"I just—"

"You're doing fine, Darling, listen to me. I can come and I can get you, but I need you to do something for me and I'm not allowed to tell you what to say."

There was panting, then a sudden quiet. If he had told me what I had to say, law enforcement might see it as him coercing me into saying something that wasn't true. I'm sure I struggled to figure out what he wanted, but it came to me eventually.

"My name is Isabella Martin," I stopped to sniffle as my voice broke. "I've been taken from my contract holder. I've been raped and tortured."

And then just tears from my side. Little sounds from his

as he was moving and people were running around him. I believe he told me later that he had me on speaker phone. Everything's recorded no matter what call you make, so that wasn't even their concern.

"Good, good, now I need you to do something else, for your safety."

"What?"

"I need you to delete this call from the phone, in case he does come back early. Then I need you to put the phone back where you found it and go back to where he had you. However you were restrained, put it back on. Can you do that, for me?"

"Please don't make me go back there."

"If you don't go back, he'll know what you've done. You'll be gone before I can arrive."

"Please, Mr. Wrightworth."

"Darling," a frustrated growl through gritted teeth. "That's a command. Do you understand me?"

Another sniffle, then, "Yes, sir."

"Good. I'm coming, Izzy."

It took them sixteen hours, between that phone call and them finally arriving. I screamed at them all, wouldn't let anyone touch me. Perhaps I thought Nathaniel's father was making good on one of his many threats. The man had an active imagination and a way of convincing you that what he was thinking about doing to you was very possible, that he had a list of men, dogs, and whatever else he could possibly want to fuck you with.

Not because he was into those things, but because he loved to see women degraded. Anything that disgusted me suddenly caught his attention.

I still didn't know his name.

Mr. Wrightworth had to force his way into the room. He wouldn't let them wrap me in the blood soaked sheet. I remember him snarling something about it not being a photo opportunity. Instead he slipped off his tailored suit jacket and dropped it around my shoulders.

He took my chin between two fingers and lifted my face. My whole focus was on him as I almost sniffled, but ended up shuddering and letting out a little sound instead.

"You need to hold yourself together until we get you to Medical. Understand?"

"Yes, Sir."

And then he picked me up and carried me out of there because I wouldn't let anyone else do it. I wouldn't let them put me on a stretcher or in a wheelchair either. They walked me out past Nathaniel's father, talking to two police officers as if he were innocent. I keened and tried to get out of Mr. Wrightworth's arms. I wanted to run away.

"Damn it, Nicole, where have you been?" he snapped as something pricked me.

"I'm sorry that my life didn't stay on hold for sixteen *fucking* hours. Some of us can't just sit around fantasizing. It should kick in in just a ... there it goes."

They kept me sedated for three days, performing their tests while I was out. Even Mr. Wrightworth said that the trauma I had suffered was enough, and I didn't need to be awake for the rape kit.

He's a firm believer that everyone should be awake for everything that is done to them. In his defence though, I probably would have just screamed bloody murder through the whole thing and no one wanted to hear that.

When I finally did fully wake up, I was restrained to the bed. I don't recall it, but apparently it wasn't the first time they tried to wake me. Mr. Wrightworth had a scratch on the side of his face, Nicole a black eye. Both were there when I woke up, and they didn't mention that I was the cause of the bruise or the cut.

Mr. Wrightworth sat to my right, Nicole stood to my left, her hands on the railing of the bed.

"Good morning, Isabella," Mr. Wrightworth said, reaching down to take my hand. "How are you feeling?"

Weak, tired, that was the first almost lucid moment I had since Nathaniel had sent me to write in my journal. There was a cloudiness to my mind that didn't seem to want to lift, making it hard to think. I couldn't seem to recall how I had ended up where I was, or why I was there.

For me, one moment I was with Nathaniel, the next I was waking up in medical.

"Did I break the contract?" I asked weakly.

"No," Mr. Wrightworth said with a shake of his head.

"No, Darling, you didn't break the contract," Nicole said, patting my left hand. "Do you remember what happened?"

Perhaps out of stubbornness, I shook my head. Looking back at that time and trying to piece together when exactly I knew for certain is difficult. I denied it so long, and for good reason. Over the next few days the pair of them would gently nudge me in the right direction and ask questions. It took years for me to recover enough to have some sort of coherent understanding. I still don't remember most of it, but that's for the best.

Pictures, which had been taken while I was out and the damage was still fresh, were taken again four days later to show the progression of healing.

Throughout the entire process, either Mr. Wrightworth or Nicole was there. I wasn't left alone for seven days. Not even to go to the bathroom. Nicole was a cheerleader about the whole thing, Mr. Wrightworth stoically silent. He didn't appear to enjoy my pain any more than I did.

At some point it came back to me in fragments. At least for a little while. When I couldn't handle it any more the memories just seemed to disappear.

I knew the gist of it from the fragments and what the doctors said, from the damage to my own body.

My nails had been ripped out, several of my fingers broken. I had been beaten to the point that a rib had been cracked. Burned, cut, stabbed at leisure.

And of course raped.

All in a bid to get me to give Nathaniel up. It wasn't even loyalty that kept me from telling his father all about our playing. At some point he had offered me an out, told me that once he knew what he wanted to know, I would be free.

Not free to go, just free.

I didn't want to die. Suppose it's a bit ironic, I had gone into the Program looking to die but when presented with that very option, I refused.

There isn't a doubt in my mind that the moment I told him what he wanted to hear, my fate would be sealed. I didn't believe he would keep his word and that I would be immediately free. To believe that would simply be insanity.

"Don't worry," Mr. Wrightworth said, drawing my attention to him.

His face had that mask, the same one Nathaniel had had moments before his father came into the room. The only part of Mr. Wrightworth that seemed to be alive were his eyes and they were unreadable. To me—at the time—he was hiding something. Afterward, a long time after, I would learn that the mask hid his reaction to my confusion and pain. His eyes were a mingling of pity, sadness, and growing rage.

When Mr. Wrightworth was not with me, he was watching the tapes. It was his duty as head of the Program to review the evidence before it was presented to court. Some arbitrary law that stated as head of the Program he had to know the worst to happen to those who fulfilled contracts under him.

Don't pity him for that, he quite enjoyed most of it.

"There will be time later to come to terms with what happened," he said, patting my hand gently.

"Where's Nathaniel?" I asked.

They were both silent. Nicole shifted awkwardly on the edge of the bed as Mr. Wrightworth tried not to make eye contact with me.

"Why isn't he here?" I asked.

"Nathaniel is..."

A million things ran through my head. I didn't fully understand why he had given me up, but the person I was then was unable to look past my own flaws. As far as I could tell, Nathaniel had been given a choice between his money and me. Of course he had chosen the money.

Rich people always chose the money.

How could I expect a man who I had only known a few weeks to choose me over a lifetime of money? No one would choose me over money. My own family had chosen money over my very life!

Who could ever love me?

"Busy," Nicole said, filling in for the suddenly flustered Mr. Wrightworth. "Nathaniel is busy."

She glowered at Mr. Wrightworth across me, causing the sadist to stiffen ever so slightly and turn his hazel eyes to her. There was a furious anger to both of them, as if they thought they could carry on an argument in silence. I thought they might come to blows, they were silent so long.

"Why don't you give her the item?" she added finally.

Mr. Wrightworth sighed out through his nose. It was a sound that would later make me run from the man. His final nerve was pushed, he would not take any more hints or 'suggestions.' Yet still he reached to the side and picked up a book, which he showed to me, then set back down again.

"Your journal, from Nathaniel's, and a pen," Mr. Wrightworth said to me. "I or Nicole will watch you write your entries, but we won't read them."

I frowned at him, then looked at Nicole.

"There's some concern about previous behaviour, mixed with your outbursts when we woke you earlier," Nicole said quietly.

"What outbursts?" I asked.

"Again, there will be plenty of time later to discuss," Mr. Wrightworth said sternly. "Right now, you need to focus on getting better and getting real sleep, not medically induced. I don't care what they say, medicine cannot provide a better sleep than that which nature provides."

"I am tired," I murmured.

Nicole cleared her throat and looked away. I glanced at her, then turned my attention to Mr. Wrightworth as the man shifted, suddenly uncomfortable.

"We do need you to get up and go to the bathroom first," Mr. Wrightworth said without meeting my eyes.

"No scat," I said, and almost laughed.

They both stared at me. Then they both frowned *at the same time.*

"You do it," Mr. Wrightworth said, then stood and left the little curtained area.

Nicole took in a long, slow breath, then offered me a hand. She helped me walk the short distance to the bathroom. In the relative privacy of the toilet, Nicole leaned against the bathroom door and eyed me as I dropped onto the toilet and groaned.

Things hurt that I hadn't expected to hurt.

"Besides toilets and Mr. Wrightworth's rooms, the whole of the Program building is under video surveillance," Nicole said quickly and quietly. "The community cannot be mentioned, we cannot know each other besides when I drew your blood."

"Oh," I said. "I do have to go."

Nicole sucked in another breath. I sighed and looked away.

"It's good that you aren't completely ... broken..." Nicole said.

"Fuck you," I said.

"Although it's probably just because the one who broke you was male," Nicole muttered, pushing off the door suddenly.

The nurse was gone, suddenly there was a domme in a nurse's outfit, glowering at me as I stared up at her with impudence. I get the whole nurse fantasy some men have, nurses are hot, even in regular scrubs. The Program enforced the whole perfectly fitting uniform of a dark brown-grey.

I didn't think she'd hit me, I was so bold as to believe that a woman wasn't capable of causing me pain. Her hands dropped to her sides, the right one curled just slightly and seemed to twitch, as if there were a crop in it.

"You are going to relieve yourself and you aren't going to cause me problems," she said.

"Then let me have privacy," I said, motioning to the door.

"The concern of previous actions being repeated is very real," Nicole said.

"With what?" I asked, motioning around the tiled bathroom. "The mirror isn't even made of glass. The... there's no toilet seat to pull up, this is a piece of... it's not even a proper toilet! Everything is made of plastic."

"You used to be a labourer," Nicole said.

"And?"

"Is tile sharp?" Nicole asked in a tone.

It was the tone of voice a person uses when they believe you think they are stupid. It also, somehow, implies that you're actually the stupid one, even if you were completely innocent in the first place.

"Yes."

"Go to the bathroom," she snarled.

"Could you at least turnaround?" I asked.

"No."

"Please?"

With an eye roll and a shake of her head, Nicole turned around. She faced the door while I did what was necessary.

The reason they insisted was to make certain everything worked. I'm not going to get into the details of the damages in that part of my body, but only say that they were concerned and had good cause to be concerned. I glean over the whole thing of my being in the hospital, but really that would be a lie. My coming to terms with what was done to me, and my recovery over that time played a huge role later on.

Recovery after abuse is not simply bed rest and then you're magically better. It takes a really long time and there are moments where you're alone and...

Everything just falls apart on you.

I was lucky, I had Nicole and Mr. Wrightworth there at every turn. They devoted weeks of their lives to getting me through the physical stuff. They picked me up when I fell, they wiped the tears away when I cried, they helped change the bandages, and when I wouldn't go to the bathroom because it hurt too much, they were there to help me then too.

Healing hurts. And you don't really have any other option. It just does. Pain is a part of getting better and getting stronger. The only choice you really have is whether it's going to win, or if you're going to persevere.

That day?

That day the pain won.

Chapter

Three weeks after my arrival, I was released from medical and into the general population. I was given a room which was large enough for a bed and a desk, with a small bathroom about the size of a closet but it was private. All the fixtures were new.

The bed's frame was made of that fake oak stuff, its blankets and pillows a lavender colour. I might not have been allowed purple in Nathaniel's home, but the Program didn't know, or care about purple being claimed.

Inside the bathroom was a small stall shower, just big enough for one person, a toilet that was almost built into the wall, and small sink. There was one door into the bathroom.

My room had cheery blue walls and a thick grey carpet that all but silenced footsteps. Under the bed were two drawers filled with clothing in my size, which had been provided before I arrived. The bed itself had several blankets on it, with an extra one over the foot of the bed.

It was as small as my bed back home, in the slums.

I almost started crying at the thought of sleeping in such a small bed. It wasn't that I was spoiled, but that it reminded me of what had happened.

Did I mention private?

Most of the Program building still had public washrooms. I had been given a private one because I was what was referred to as 'recovered.'

What that meant was that I had been in a contract, but had been pulled out due to a breach of that contract. Whenever there was a breach, the one who was wronged was treated

, were the most fragile thing in the world. The ȝram even had some sort of insurance which would pay .or a second contract of the same amount to the contractor if the poor person was the one who caused the breach.

It was also the first time I had been alone in three weeks. I wasn't completely recovered, but they had needed the bed I was taking up. Mr. Wrightworth had even gotten into an argument with a doctor who had suggested I be taken to a slum hospital if I needed medical attention so badly.

The doctor was right. I didn't need medical care any longer. Bones and fingernails take weeks to heal. A majority of the flesh damage was healed, though it would be months still before I was back to to my old self, physically.

After looking around and peering out the one window, out over the slum that the Program building stood over, I sat on the bed and stared at the wall just over the desk. There was a glossy black circle, like the one that had been behind the desk of the other Program building I had gone to for intake. Another camera, watching my every move. I stared at the camera for a very long time before I stood stiffly and walked to the bathroom.

There, I closed the door, sat on the closed toilet lid, bent over and started sobbing. I wept about what was done to me, about Nathaniel abandoning me. In the end, I cried about being useless yet again. They hadn't even told me what to do with myself, just shown me to the room.

Eventually, the tears stopped coming.

When they did, I went about the process of giving myself a sponge bath. My fingers were still throbbing, though most of it was a phantom pain, but I didn't want to step into the small cubicle shower. The idea of being locked into such a small space was no kind of comfort.

After my sponge bath, I shuffled to the bed naked, no longer caring if someone watching me saw me naked. I climbed under the blankets, dragged them over my head and slept.

A great deal of the Program building was automated. There wasn't just a bed and a desk. There was also a screen built into the wall. The curtains were automated and opened upon an alarm that was set by the controllers of the building.

No one ever worried about not setting their alarms, because they had no control over the action.

My curtains opened at seven in the morning and sunlight spilled in. That damned room faced east, I'm pretty certain I was put in that side of the building on purpose. It's nearly impossible for me to sleep when there is direct sunlight on my face.

The television turned on and trilled several times. A news broadcast started, telling me all about recent events. Nothing was said about me or Nathaniel, let alone his father. It was all about rich people getting married and I just didn't care.

I rolled over and dragged the pillow over my head until the broadcast ended. Then I had to get up and drag the curtain closed, before going back to bed, not even caring that I probably flashed someone outside the window.

I slept through the day, getting up several more times when the curtain opened and the television turned on with news broadcasts.

No one brought me food and I didn't bother trying to go out looking for it. I stayed in bed the entire day and then the next day as well. The next day the broadcast was louder, the curtains wouldn't close, and the lights stayed on despite my flicking the switch by the door. In the end, I climbed back under the blankets and dragged them over my head, resolute to ignore everything.

When my door opened sometime in the afternoon, I sat up. Mr. Wrightworth stepped in without knocking. He stopped just inside the door and glowered at me with his hands in his pockets.

"This is not a romance novel from just before the collapse," he said sternly, approaching the bed as I struggled to get my body to work. "You don't get to pine and act like your world is ending because a man isn't here to save you. He's not coming, no matter how much you fester in bed."

He came to a stop at the head of the bed as I cringed away and hid in the corner. I turned away from him, afraid he would strike me in his anger.

Don't poke the sadists. That's good advice in and out of the community.

When the strike I expected didn't come, I peered out from

under my arm.

He was frowning at me. It was a puzzling sort of look like he knew what he was seeing but couldn't quite make the connection. I probably had the same look on my face, not understanding why he hadn't struck me. He was obviously angry with me.

Mr. Wrightworth stiffened and pulled away ever so slightly. "This isn't about him."

The man swore and crouched, opening one of the drawers, then the other. He pulled out some clothing and almost threw them at me. I saw the twitch of his hand, then the way he seemed to pull away. In the end Mr. Wrightworth placed the clothing very carefully on the edge of the bed. He even smoothed out the wrinkle from where he had gripped it tight when he had been about to toss the item at my head.

"Dress. Now."

"I don't want to," I said, though I have no idea where the courage to say no came from.

"That is a command, Darling. Dress."

He moved back to the door, then stopped and walked into the bathroom. A moment later he came back out.

"Better plan. Shower, then dress, now. If I need to shower with you to make certain you wash, I will be very unhappy."

Mr. Wrightworth barely finished speaking, I bolted past him so fast. There wasn't enough space in the shower for two people to stand separately in the stall. I certainly didn't want to be crammed into the stall with an angry sadist.

I showered, whimpering the pain that every motion of washing brought out in my body. My fingers ran through my hair, not understanding what had happened to it. Yes, I had been around plenty of mirrors, but I had avoided looking at myself in the mirror.

By the time I was washed, the dead feeling inside had turned to an anger.

I marched back out of the bathroom, ripping the clothing out of Mr. Wrightworth's hands as I went. I pulled on the black underwear and threw the bra at his head before I dragged the dress over my head. The dress was a dark grey colour, form-fitting but not too tight. It covered from shoulder to knee, and had no sleeves.

"Now take it off," Mr. Wrightworth said, then threw the bra back at me. "And put on the entire outfit. I don't give a damn if you were gifted with a pair of perky breasts that any woman would kill for, you wear a bra while in this building."

"No one would kill for these things," I snapped back, stripping the dress off.

I put on the bra and then pulled the dress back on over top. Suddenly it fit differently. Suddenly my breasts weren't just there, they were right there and I swore I could use them to set a cup of water on without spilling any of it as I walked. Even when I had worn something, it had been a binding to keep my breasts as close and tight as I could, to get them out of the way. This felt weird and different in a weird and different way.

"Your orientation was supposed to start yesterday morning, but when you didn't get up, they cancelled it and contacted me this morning when you ignored yet another wake up call. Good job getting your camera shut off, by the way. They don't appreciate looking at that much of any woman unless they're auditing."

"That's off?" I asked, motioning with my head to the camera.

The man smiled that Cheshire cat smile of his, it was my only warning before he grabbed me and thrust me onto the bed by the back of my neck. I struggled as he fumbled, then squealed at the sound of leather striking flesh. Mr. Wrightworth's hand remained on my neck for a moment as I whimpered against my blanket.

"Would I do that if it were on?" Mr. Wrightworth purred, bending down over me.

"No," I said.

"Good," he said in that tone that Nathaniel was such a fan of, his hand running down my back and hesitating just above my backside. "If you prove petulant, I will strike you again. Do you understand?"

"Yes," I said.

I understood that doing wrong would result in pain. What I didn't understand was why I was wet, why there was a sudden tremble that seemed to be a throb between my legs.

I wanted him to strike me again.

"What's the matter?" he asked.

I writhed against the bed, embarrassed to say. His belt had hit the left side of my backside. It burned and hurt, but there was nothing on the right. I felt as if everything was unbalanced.

"Darling, if you don't tell me, I can't see to it."

"Please, Sir, the other side?" I asked, lifting my backside off the bed.

Mr. Wrightworth shuddered out a breath. "That was discipline. But this one time, I'll do as you ask. Keep your backside up."

The second strike made me cry out again, but in relief. Everything seemed to recenter. Everything was balanced. I had asked for something and received it. The strike of the belt was a a pain more than what Nathaniel had shown me, but a great deal less than what had been done to me by his father.

I found comfort in being beaten at my command.

What is wrong with me?

Mr. Wrightworth's hand slid over first one, then the other hip, roving over the burning flesh. The pain seemed to dissipate as his hot hand flowed up my back, to grab a fistful of hair. I was dragged off the bed and bent backwards, but Mr. Wrightworth's other hand slipped around my waist and held me up as those hazel eyes seemed to bore into my soul.

"This can't happen," he said sternly. "You are still recovering. You don't want to be struck, your body is going through a type of withdrawal." He released me, stepping away as I almost stumbled. "You will behave. If you don't behave you will be subjected to the same discipline as others in the building."

"What is even going on?" I asked.

"Orientation would have explained that," Mr. Wrightworth snapped as if it were my fault.

"No one told me that orientation was even happening," I snarled back in a similar tone.

His hand clenched as his eyes closed tightly. There was an inward struggle. After a very long moment, the hand relaxed slightly, thumb running over index and middle finger. His hazel eyes drifted half open, staring at my desk as he seemed to consider.

"I will do your orientation," he said finally, turning to me.

"All right," I said with a shrug.

"They probably couldn't face you anyhow," Mr. Wrightworth muttered before he made a motion and left my room.

It took me far too long to realize what that motion meant. I finally stepped out of the room and closed the door behind me. Mr. Wrightworth motioned to the black square on the door, just above the doorknob.

"Fingerprint access, no one else besides myself and the cleaning staff have access to your room," Mr. Wrightworth said, motioning again as he walked away.

With a sigh, I followed him. Suddenly I wasn't certain I wanted Mr. Wrightworth giving me my orientation. I wasn't certain he'd actually give me any answers, or if he'd just leave me more confused than when he started.

"I've worked out a job for you in the auditing department. You don't have to deal with rich people or poor folk coming into the contracts. You'll be reviewing contracts, then calling both the rich and poor person involved to ask them questions about their time with the Program.

"The purpose is to check on people who were once in the Program. To hopefully draw the rich folk back in and get quotes from the poor folk to use for advertisement in the slums. You will end up having to deal with people, just not face-to-face.

"You will need to learn a great deal, most of the contracts are written up in legalese, meaning in the language lawyers use, really. It's annoying and hardly makes sense.

"Tomorrow morning you will be taken to the archive rooms. From there you will learn the system and pick a file. The point is to pick at random. No names are on any of the files. Everyone has been given numbers and contact ids. You won't know who they are and they won't know who you are. If you encounter someone who you met while you were with Nathaniel, please be as discrete as possible. Phone calls are monitored and anyone that the Program knows you had contact with has been notified."

"I'd like to go to church," I said.

We both came to a stop in the hallway. Mr. Wrightworth turned towards me and almost frowned.

"You cannot have contact with Nathaniel until the review has been complete. But it is my understanding that you found the church to be ... eye opening, and I will see what can be done. It will still be several weeks before you can leave the building. We need to make certain you are more stable before we let you out of the safety net. Come along."

My stomach grumbled as we went along to the elevator. I looked down at the floor. A grey carpet with a single blue line leading to the elevator. On the elevator, there was a blue line up the wall and to a particular button.

"Where's that go?" I asked. "Fire exit?"

"In the event of a fire, the ceiling will light up, leading you to the stairwell and then out of the building," Mr. Wrightworth said, then pointed at the blue line. "That leads to my room. I have a closed circuit system, like a rich person, but also have no real privacy. My rooms are supposed to be sound proof, but I haven't mustered the courage to ask my neighbours about what they can hear. I have few visitors, though."

"Oh," was all I managed to say.

The doors opened on another floor. I frowned at the buttons, then looked at Mr. Wrightworth.

"The whole building is under the control of a couple of people. They control the alarms, the elevators, and various other things. The point is to have a security system, but have a thinking system. Our computer systems are coming along nicely but it's not exactly unhackable yet. You step in, it will take you to where you need to go. For the first few times it may be best if you speak out loud what you want. Once they know you better, everything will just seem to work even if you aren't certain what you want."

"That's creepy."

"They are very good at what they do, and I love them to bits for what they do for us," Mr. Wrightworth said quickly. "It's also the only way they can function. If you're worried about giving them dirty thoughts, you can't. People say they suffer from something, but it makes them incapable of making such a connection. They wouldn't even understand that they were bring bribed or that someone else wanted something.

"Where they took us to now, is the cafeteria."

I stepped off the elevator with him, into a huge room. There were people sitting at tables all over, they came to a stop as Mr. Wrightworth stepped out of the elevator. Then their eyes roved over me and suddenly everyone turned back to their own tables.

As I said before, I hadn't seen myself in a mirror yet. I avoided it and any and all reflective surfaces.

"You need to see a stylist," Mr. Wrightworth said as he motioned towards the line. "Our plastic surgeons did a marvellous job stitching up the cuts on your face. In a few more months it will be almost impossible to tell you were cut. They did that work all over, not just your face."

"Which was why I had three stitches removed from—"

"Which is why," Mr. Wrightworth said sternly, giving me a warning look, "they kept you for so long in medical. To give the flesh as much chance to mend as possible. Work may pull at the new scar tissue. That hidden by your clothing isn't that big of a deal, it could take years to fade. It was the visible scars they were concerned about. But apparently another two weeks was too much time."

The surgeons did a marvellous job, as he said they did. The scars were visible for about a year afterwards, but fading constantly. I don't recall if Nathaniel's father had been particularly focused on my previous scars, or if the surgeons had taken it upon themselves to fix the marks on my wrists from my previous suicide attempt.

Rich folk had some fantastic plastic surgeons. They could fix almost anything, given the right conditions.

"Here you will find a great many foods to choose from. You will choose one meat, two vegetables, one starch, a piece of bread, and a serving of dairy. Either pudding or milk or cheese, I don't care how you get it, you will get it. If you don't know what a food is, you will ask. Today you will eat a salad. She will have a salad, Mark, the spring greens with the chicken breast and balsamic vinaigrette. Have the same delivered to my office in two hours, except in wrap form and Havarti instead of whatever it is you're serving that with. Is it even cheese?"

"Just because you think you know cheese, don't mean what I serve isn't cheese," Mark responded gruffly.

Mark was a big man. A big, big man. He had a barrel of a chest and was wide at the shoulders. Mark was also a recovery, though he had been recovered when his contractor was caught forcing homeless people to fight to the death. Mark had turned his contractor and the contractor's friends in, forcing him to work in the Program building because of death threats. He loved his job though, and Mr. Wrightworth made certain he was never lacking for fresh ingredients.

"I'm going to put a sausage in a bun on the side," Mark said, adding exactly what he described to my plate before he handed it over to me. "Girl looks like she needs meat on her bones and you don't get meat from salads."

"Just for now, Mark," Mr.. Wrightworth said, then shook his head as we continued on.

Somewhere along the way he picked up a tray and made me put my plate on it. To the tray were added a banana, which almost made me laugh, and a glass of milk. Mr. Wrightworth took me over to the windows, where a table cleared out at the sight of him, and sat me down. He watched me eat every bit on my plate, not saying a word.

"I don't like the black stuff," I said, poking at the remaining vinaigrette at the bottom of my bowl. "Tastes bad."

"You don't like balsamic vinegar, there are many dressings to choose from," Mr. Wrightworth said quietly.

"Are you going to show me where to go for work?" I asked.

"No, not today. But tomorrow morning I might take you there. No, today I want to discuss the expectations. You are not to speak to others about your work, except those in the archives or those you need to ask about certain terms. No visitors are allowed in the archives, those you contact—the ones you are auditing—are not allowed to ask you questions about specific contracts, not even the contracts you are auditing. Everyone who participates in a contract is provided a copy, they can refer to that document. If they demand to speak to a supervisor you are to put them on hold, then press the star button and one-one-nine. That will direct them to who they need to talk to. No one will have a way to call you directly. You shouldn't be receiving any phone calls from outside of the building. Do you understand?"

"I do," I said, fidgeting as the cafeteria seemed to empty out suddenly.

"Lunch is over for them," Mr. Wrightworth said quietly. "You will come here each meal period and eat a meal, then return to work or your rooms. Weekends off, your work day will be nine to five. This is interim work while we find a solution and review your contract, so there's not really a pay of any sort.

"Once your case has been reviewed, we will talk again about your future and your options. But you should know that I will fight for your every right, just as Albert will fight to get you back. He's already begun the process of suing the Program for illegally collecting on a contract."

"Who's Albert?" I asked.

"Albert Edwards, Nathaniel's father. He didn't tell you his name?" Mr. Wrightworth asked.

"No, we never spoke... I think."

"I wonder if his behaviour has changed," Mr. Wrightworth muttered. The man sighed and looked out the window, then back to me. "As to Nathaniel.

"You will find no one in the Program willing to speak to you about him. Not how he feels about you being taken away, or how he is doing. They won't say where he is, or if he has a new ... whatever role you played for him. You are to have no contact with him and him no contact with you. Can't have him getting his claws into you."

"He didn't really do anything wrong," I said.

"We can discuss that later," was the soothing response.

Always later, they would always want to talk about Nathaniel later. No one wanted to talk about him right then, or even when I was finally ready and strong enough to face the truth. It was like a break up, except the people around me were truly committed to making certain that I got over him.

"Each morning you will rise, you will go to the gym and you will work out. There are personal trainers there, they have been notified of your conditions and health record. You will do exactly what they say. Once a month you will go to a stylist to have your hair cut. You will also go to medical once a month to have a full examination. Once a week you will see a therapist who I have chosen. It is my understanding that she is well versed in the sort of proclivities that Nathaniel is interested in."

"So you trust her?" I asked.

"I see her three times a week, so yes, I trust her," Mr. Wrightworth said. "I will take you to the stylist now, and you will have your hair trimmed. You will not have a fit when you see your face. Those marks will disappear, and anyone who brings them up should be referred to me because I will give them similar markings for throwing it in your face."

"Why do I need to see a stylist?" I asked, reaching for my hair.

My fingers had been bandaged for so long, I didn't have a full grasp of what had been done to my hair and scalp.

Suffice to say, an hour later I was weeping as the remainder of my long hair was being chopped off into a short pixie cut. I loved my long hair, it was the one feminine thing about my looks that I had kept, even as a labourer. Mr. Wrightworth assured me that the cut looked good on me, as did the stylist. Their reassurance didn't help me any. Nor did hearing the two of them make the plans for it to grow back out.

It would take two years to get any good length back, three before I had my full head of hair again.

Three years I would carry the physical mark of Nathaniel's father on me. Long after all the scars faded, there would still be something there physically, reminding me of what had been done.

It was only then that I realized the invisible marks, those on my soul and mind, would remain with me for the rest of my life.

Chapter Three

For a while, my life was...well, boring. I went to work. I sorted files, I ate, I went home. I learned who not to so much as make eye contact with because she'd just keep talking and talking and talking.

I didn't exactly make friends. Mr. Wrightworth was right about the marks on my face.

Others would get a look on their face and then start acting like I was about to break down sobbing at any moment. The only thing that ever made me want to cry was seeing that look on someone's face. Rich or poor, it didn't matter. The moment people heard I was a recovery was the moment they treated me differently.

So I kept to myself, mainly.

The only person who didn't treat me like I'd break would never shut up. It was like she had no filter, and she thought she had lived a sad life, but she hadn't actually. One of those one-uppers was what she was. When it somehow got leaked that I had been raped, she immediately had to tell me about how she had been raped by three men.

She never was, I saw her file.

It wasn't even the lies that bothered me, at that point in my life I believed her when she told me things. No, it was the fact that she never stopped talking, but in the same breath complained about how they expected too much of her and didn't give her enough time.

Which wasn't hard to do, I suppose, as the woman never seemed to breathe. She also had no time to work because she spent it all in the archives talking at me. Not to me, just at me. I couldn't get a word in edgewise and if I did, somehow the conversation to a dark turn.

Finally, I reported it to Mr. Wrightworth and poof. Her clearance was revoked. I finally had peace and quiet.

At least while in the archives. While outside of them I still had to put up with her nattering whenever she cornered me in the hallways or the cafeteria.

It took me two months to work through my first contract. During that whole time, no one told me anything else about my job unless I asked them about it. No timelines were given, no goals. Unless I specifically went out of my way to ask the others in the archives a question, they asked nothing of me.

They didn't even work in the same areas as I did. Their computers were logged into a giant mainframe in one room, and I was down the hall with a small computer and all the hard copies of the contracts. Almost a decade of contracts, thousands of them, were stored in three locations in physical form as well as two separate hard drive systems on opposite ends of the country.

Rumour said that some rich person had tried to destroy the contracts once, to get out of paying a poor person when he broke the contract. I had no idea if it was anything more than a rumour.

I would find out later that this was because I wasn't being paid by the hour for my work. So no one wanted to give me a deadline like I had a real job. Auditing contracts was supposed to be busy body work, something to keep me busy until the review was done.

Which no one told me how it was going.

I went to the gym every morning, and they put me on a workout similar to what Nathaniel had assigned me. Even in two months, I saw a difference in my body and my stamina. I just felt better, I didn't ache over all, and I spent more and more time on my feet. I was on my feet because my hip no longer hurt, it was a novelty to be able to stand and walk without constantly trying to ease the pressure in my joint.

After a month working in the gym, one of my trainers mentioned a night class to me. The class was on self-defence, geared towards teaching women how to take down a bigger opponent.

He would bring it up every single day until I finally gave in to his suggestions and attended.

Once a week I went to a therapist. Our sessions mainly revolved around us sitting there and her asking how my week had gone. She never really pried into anything or insisted we talk about something. If it did come up in conversation, she'd ask if I wanted to talk about it and I would say no.

I didn't want to share with this woman, even if Mr. Wrightworth trusted her with his secrets. To me, she seemed like a predator, and that made me uncomfortable. She wasn't open about her relationship with the community or about how much she knew. I only had Mr. Wrightworth's words to go on.

Once a month I would go to the stylist, then I would spend the entire next day in medical. They would check everything from my toes to the top of my head. I was not the only one to receive this treatment. Every other worker in the Program had a mandatory checkup once a month Nicole did most of my checkup for me, or was with me as the doctor was there.

The first month she frowned, the second month she asked me about the bruising on my shins.

I had gotten clumsy suddenly. I'd forget I had a drawer open and run into it. I'd take some skin off my arm where I hit the edge of a table. Smack my head on a table when I bent to pick up a pen. Little things, things that had never bothered me before. Most of the time I didn't even remember what I had done to earn the bruise. I'd find them when I showered, or the next morning as I dressed.

The entire time there was a building pressure under my skin. I didn't know what it was but suspected it had something to do with not knowing what was going on. In those two months, I hardly saw or spoke to Mr. Wrightworth. Only when I requested a meeting or we happened to pass one another in the hallway.

I learned that both the men and women of the Program whispered about him whenever he wasn't around. They didn't seem to care that everything they said was recorded and could be viewed at his leisure later on. The whisperings revolved around his sexuality and who they thought he was favouring at that moment. There were sidelong glances at me whenever he walked into the same room as me.

I didn't know then, but apparently Mr. Wrightworth has a tell. He would ignore those who were doing well, or who he was keenly interested in. Even if that interest was because they were recovering from a bad contract. Publicly he was always watched. It seemed everyone wanted to catch him playing favourites, to find him giving preference to someone he liked. They all wanted to be the one to find Mr. Wrightworth's flaw because he appeared too perfect.

Little did they know, the man's dark secrets were played out in his apartment.

When not working or at a mandatory event, I spent my time in my room watching whatever the controllers put on the television. I made certain to wear clothing at all times while in the sleeping portion of my room because I had no idea how to control the television without them. It was almost comforting to know that they were watching over me, but remained faceless.

I'm not sure how they managed the whole building. Possibly they simply loaded up a random playlist of videos for each apartment with the television on.

One day they put on Vikings vs. Zombies: An Erotic Tale and I ended up sobbing my eyes out at the reminder but didn't ask them to turn it off. I cried through the entire movie. As the credits rolled there was a knock on my door and then footsteps running away.

With a sniffle and a frown, I approached the door cautiously and yanked it open. There sat a large, floppy, stuffed animal with a piece of paper taped to his nose.

'Sorry we made you sad.'

As it turned out, the controllers didn't just control things. They did learn about everyone in the Program and a little about people in general. For the most part, they didn't react to what they saw. We were just people going through the motions of life.

They didn't like to see someone crying alone, though, and would do whatever they could to cheer them up.

I dragged the new item into my room, kicked the door

closed and dropped onto the bed with it in my lap and my arms wrapped around it.

It was so soft and squishy.

And then they chose then to put cat videos on my screen. What is it about cat videos that make them so timeless? The videos changed a little each time a new one started until I ended up watching baby pandas tumbling over one another. I had never seen a panda before, they went extinct long before I was born, but they were also so adorable. I flopped over as one of them did and was out like a light.

I snapped awake when the door opened. Though, I lay perfectly still to not give away the fact that I knew someone was in the room. I waited until the person was right at the edge of the bed. The element of surprise, my self-defence teacher said, was a powerful weapon.

If he didn't have such a unique form—which I recognized in the light cast by the tumbling bundle of puppies playing on the television screen—I would have used my self-defence training on Mr. Wrightworth. As it was, he reached past me and turned on the light attached to the wall above my bed.

He frowned down at me, then looked at the stuffed animal. With a glance, the television shut off. Mr. Wrightworth seemed to stare off for a moment, then turned back to me.

He was a bit like a god in the Program building. The controllers were willing to do whatever he wanted and anticipated his every need. He had hired them, he knew them so intimately, and they knew him so well that sometimes he'd only open his mouth to say something and the room would change to his desires.

"I was alerted to some odd behaviour, are you all right?" he asked quietly.

"Fine," I said.

"Ah, the explosive 'fine' answer," he murmured.

He reached for the blankets and dragged them up over me and the stuffed animal, effectively tucking us both in. Then he sat on the edge of the bed and set a hand on my shoulder.

"How about I read to you until you fall asleep, and we can discuss everything else in the morning, hm?" he asked, pulling out his phone.

“I’m not a child. I can put myself to sleep,” I said, trying to sit up.

His hand, still on my shoulder, suddenly turned to stone. I couldn’t sit up, and it remained that way until I stopped resisting and settled back down onto the bed. It didn’t seem commanding so much as firm. Perhaps a little exasperated, it was the middle of the night, after all. Mr. Wrightworth never did well with sleep deprivation. His patience was short as it normally was.

At two in the morning, however, he had absolute no time for prideful whining.

“I never pegged you for a little, but I suppose playing at the different titles is a part of exploration,” he murmured in response. “You will lay there and listen to this story. Ah, here it is.”

Mr. Wrightworth had a way with the verbal arts. He was gifted with a deep voice and years of being Nathaniel’s aide, and then working with rich folk, had given him an accent unlike any I had ever heard before. I swear he liked reading people to sleep, but he’d never admit it.

I’m not certain when exactly I fell asleep, but the new sleep was a great deal deeper than that of before. When I awoke again, Mr. Wrightworth was gone, and the curtains had been pulled back. I had the stuffed animal in both my arms, hugged close with my nose buried in the top of its head right between its ears. It was so fluffy, and it smelled a little of plastic and a lot of clean fabric. I brushed my face against the soft fur of the bunny and considered staying in bed.

Then the television turned on. Some happy woman from a children’s show was talking about greeting every day with a smile and a song.

With a groan, I threw back the blankets and dragged myself out of bed. I tossed the blankets back to where they belonged. Then I set the stuffed animal on top of the bed.

Going through my day was almost painful. I wanted to stay in bed, and in that moment of the night before when Mr. Wrightworth started reading the story. It was the safest I had felt in months. It was the first night I hadn’t dreamed of my time with Nathaniel’s father.

At breakfast I dropped a knife on my foot, thankfully it

was only a butter knife. I very nearly dropped my tray when I tripped over the tiles on the floor. I was completely out of my rhythm. Every table was full, I had to wait awkwardly for someone who had finished, and clearly had been for a while, to notice that I was waiting, and to get up and move.

Then the elevator didn't work. Not, as in the controller didn't open the doors, but the elevator was literally broken. I walked up ten flight of stairs and ended up huffing and puffing at the top.

"Need to do more stairs," Mr. Wrightworth said as he held the door open. "I need to see you at some point today. Will three hours from now work?"

I could only shrug as I panted. I had nothing going on in the day, having just closed my first audit and about to start my next one.

"You're right, I'll bring you lunch, and we'll eat in the archives as we talk," he said, tugging at his tie. "See you in four hours."

I walked into the archives and had just slid the glass door into place when Kathy walked in.

Yes, her name was Kathy, and she was the chatty one.

I spent an hour just trying to get her to shut up about her dog. First off, I didn't understand her keeping an animal that didn't listen and chewed everything and pissed all over everything. And yet she refused to train the thing. That is not something to talk about. That's something to deal with on your own. She was almost always talking about that dog.

Unless she was one-upping you.

Kathy was just about the only annoying thing about the Program. While in the building, I never understood how she got hired in the first place, or what she did. Everyone knew her, but no one knew what she did besides wander the hallways bothering people.

Like it was some creepy social experiment.

After Kathy had left, I hurt myself no less than six times. Hitting my knee on the file cabinet, slicing into my finger with a file, as in the thick manila sheet that holds the files. Until that point, I thought papercuts were bad. Getting cut by something thicker than paper somehow hurts worse.

Slammed my hand in another drawer, ran forehead first

into a pole, and—just as Mr. Wrightworth walked in—somehow managed to stab myself in the finger pad with a letter opener.

I had been playing with it idly, and he startled me. I don't care what he might have said about what he saw, I did not stab myself on purpose, I was not, at any point, trying to hurt myself.

"Who gave you a letter opener?" Mr. Wrightworth asked as he finished placing the bandage.

"It was in a drawer," I said, motioning with my free hand.

"Mm," he responded, sounding very much like he didn't believe me. "I brought you a book. The church book club will be reading this in a month or so, and I thought perhaps you would like to join the book club."

I perked up at the mention of the church. The book he handed me was some silly thing that was relatively simple. It wasn't even very thick. Frustrated, I looked up at Mr. Wrightworth, thinking that he was trying to pull a fast one on me. During my visit to the church, I had heard the group discussing *Canterbury Tales* by Chaucer. It didn't make sense to me that they'd be reading something by a contemporary author which was a third of the size of *Canterbury Tales*.

The man smiled ever so slightly. "I also brought lunch. It seems you and I need to have a discussion."

"What about?" I asked, setting the book on the table.

Mr. Wrightworth ignored me and picked up a container, handing it to me before he picked up the other one. He pulled out a utensil for each of us and gave me one. Then he sat and started eating as I glowered at him. Annoyed, assuming that Mr. Wrightworth wasn't going to talk until I ate, I sat beside him and poked at my food. We ate in silence.

When he finished eating, Mr. Wrightworth closed his container and placed it back into the bag.

Then he reached out and took my half-eaten container and set it back into the bag as I tried to follow it.

He didn't even say anything to me about it, just did it.

Licking his lips, Mr. Wrightworth sat back in his seat and studied me. There was something so very self-assured about the way he sat. He seemed to enjoy the moment of silence as

I struggled.

"I've had complaints. Not complaints, but comments, really. Perhaps concerns would be a better way to put it. I've had concerns about your behaviour."

"About what?" I asked. "I do my work. I keep my head down. Is this about Kathy? I mean, sure, I don't like her, but I've never been rude to her."

"Kathy? No, she complains about everyone who doesn't agree with her every word," he murmured, sitting forward to entwine his fingers and set them on the table. "The comments I received are about your well-being. It seems you've been hurting yourself more and more."

"I—no, that's not true, I'm clumsy. I guess...?"

Mr. Wrightworth looked pointedly at my bandaged finger before he looked up slowly and met my eyes. "Clumsy?"

His look made my breath hitch in my throat. My stomach twisted as the man waited for an answer that I couldn't seem to form. At least, not an answer that I knew he would accept. As the silence stretched on, Mr. Wrightworth appeared almost amused. I struggled to get anything out of my mouth. If only to get the talk over with so I could go back to work.

"I've been running into things. Maybe there's something wrong with my brain and my balance. I'm not hurting myself on purpose."

"I have yet to accuse you of doing it on purpose," Mr. Wrightworth said. "There has been some who suggest that you are doing it for attention. Do you feel starved for attention, Darling?"

He never uses my real name.

The only name he ever used was 'Darling' and I suppose he wasn't just asking after my well-being then, or my mental stability. He was asking about something else. It had been months and months, after all.

And I *had* been thinking about it, craving it. Like an addict cut off from their drug of choice, I lay awake at night thinking about it, but not daring to touch myself.

"Well, I don't exactly have friends," I said, looking down to my hands in my lap.

I picked at my nails as Mr. Wrightworth watched me silently. I found a snag on one of my nails and picked at it vehemently as the silence drew on. I glanced up once, catching those hazel eyes watching me, then focused back on my lap.

"I told you I don't make friends easy," I said to my lap.

"You did, just as I told you that I don't make friends quickly. What about Nicole? You only visit her for your medical appointments."

"I... didn't know I could visit Nicole."

"I see," Mr. Wrightworth murmured. "Then I suppose I should tell you that you need to make an effort to make female friends. You need to talk to someone about something. Someone besides Kathy. She doesn't count, even if you do talk to her, it's like talking to a wall with that one.

"You can visit Nicole. She's been wondering why you haven't. She thinks that her religious beliefs and yours might align, that you could enjoy one another's company."

We talked like that in public. Anything to do with the community was referred to as if it were religion instead.

"I can maybe, if I..." I sighed. "I don't know where to find Nicole outside of my medical appointments."

"Talk to her during the appointment about doing something else," he said sternly. "And look at me when I'm talking to you, not at your lap."

I sat up and met his eyes. But only for a moment, then I looked away again.

"You should try to make regular friends as well. You need to go to movie night and try to talk to someone else. Not making connections is dangerous for you, you are very closed off."

"I'm not closed off, not at all."

"The controllers feel sorry for you," Mr. Wrightworth said. "They've never given someone something before. If there's a problem, they report it. That's their jobs. I had to write up the controllers for inappropriate behaviour. The only damned reason I knew there was a problem was because I walked in to check on them."

"You wrote them up for having a heart?" I demanded.

The man made a sound that was almost a snarl.

"The rules are very clear. They broke the rules, and they had to be written up. They're damned well lucky circumstances aren't different, or I'd bend them over their desks."

I flushed at the thought.

"Your position with Nathaniel was sexually based," Mr. Wrightworth purred out. "Some of the men have started talking about the possibility that you miss that part of your contract. They may try contact of some sort."

"No, I don't want that!"

I was up out of my seat and had placed the table between us before I knew what I was doing. The extra space was needed. I looked to the exit and wondered if I could make it out the door before Mr. Wrightworth caught me. Would the controllers interfere if he...?

He's gay. I'm afraid a gay man might hurt me.

I dragged in a slow breath and hugged myself. My heart beat hard in my chest. I could feel it in my throat and almost hear it in my ears. The whole world seemed to get smaller despite my reminding myself that Mr. Wrightworth was gay. He wasn't a threat to me.

"That is interesting," he said, standing as I shrunk away from him. "Have you been seeing your therapist?"

"You know everything about me, you can probably see the tapes of my sessions, so you know I've been going to the therapist."

"I'm asking because that's what people do, is ask about each other."

"You seriously watch everything about me?" I asked, shaking my head and frowning.

"Not everything," was the quiet response as those eyes flowed down to my feet and then back up again. "There was one thing that was suggested, by Nicole, as a possible solution for your little accidents."

"Is she one of the ones who believes I'm doing it for attention?" I spat out.

There was a stifled laugh as the man smiled. "Something of that sort."

Each word seemed to be its own sentence. As if he hesitated afterward, trying not to say the wrong thing. I was left baffled as to what he meant and couldn't help but feel annoyed that Nicole thought I needed some attention from a man.

"I don't need attention."

"Said the woman who is gripping her arms so tightly that her fingers are going white," Mr. Wrightworth said. "Through gritted teeth, with red in your cheeks. You look like you're about to attempt to take my balls for suggesting you might need contact with another human being."

"And what would you suggest?" I asked.

Mr. Wrightworth slid his hands into his pockets. He considered the table with a small smile before he moved around the table and towards me. He didn't stop until he was inches from me.

"My place, tonight at six," Mr. Wrightworth murmured. "Don't eat before you come. It doesn't matter what you wear. I won't keep you late."

"What makes you think that I want your sort of attention?" I asked.

"If you're linked to me, we both win. The men won't try anything with you because you will be spoken for. The women will shut up about me and perhaps put their noses back into their files where they belong."

"That's not what I meant."

"You're leaning towards me not away."

"What?" I asked, looking down.

I shifted away from him, arms still hugging myself tightly.

"When a person doesn't want to be touched, or to be near someone, they lean away. They'll lean towards the exit and turn that way. Your feet are facing me. Your skin flushed, and your breath is coming quicker, but not fast enough to be fear. That grasp you have on your arms has changed. That's not anxiety. It's the simmering anger of being caught with a dirty thought."

"Mr. Wrightworth, I don't believe such a relationship would be appropriate."

"Give it a chance, Darling. There are addendums to all contracts, even my contract as head of the Program."

My name, the mention of the addendum? I was caught in thought as Mr. Wrightworth pulled away. He moved across the room and picked up the bag, clearing his throat when I didn't react.

Ever so slowly I turned towards him.

"My place at six," Mr. Wrightworth said with a slow smile. "Let's see if we can't come up with something interesting to do."

"How do I get there?" I asked.

Even though he had explained it before, it had been months before, and I hadn't needed the lines since then. They had melted into the background, were simply a part of the setting.

"Follow the blue lines. Don't be late, Darling. I don't like it when my visitors are late."

Chapter Four

At precisely six, I knocked on the blue door.

Mr. Wrightworth's floor had a great deal fewer doors than mine had. Those doors were further apart down the hallway, and there were maybe a dozen in all. Whereas my floor three or four dozen. I had never bothered to count them before, but looking down that hallway I realized just how many people lived on my floor. People I almost never saw. And if that was one floor down one hallway, there were thousands of people working in the Program building and living there. Each to their little apartment, each with walls and a locking door between them and everyone else.

In the slums, we were six to ten in a two bedroom apartment.

Everyone could find Mr. Wrightworth's apartment, though he lived alongside the higher ranks from the Program. The carpet and walls all had the same quality to them as the other floors I had been on. From the outside, the upper-rank apartments appeared to be the same as those of the lower floors, just a little larger.

Mr. Wrightworth opened the door in pyjama bottoms and a worn t-shirt. The shirt had once had a band's logo on the front but had faded to almost nothing through so many washes. There was even a small tear in the collar of the shirt, which was clearly a size larger than Mr. Wrightworth needed.

My mouth fell open. I was so surprised to see him without the formal wear. At that point, I was almost certain he slept in the suit while standing up. Underneath the suit, he wasn't as lean as he appeared. There was a wiry sort of muscle to him, not quite as obvious as Nathaniel's, but still there.

"You're late," Mr. Wrightworth said, stepping to the side as he motioned into his apartment.

"I'm on time."

"On time is late," Mr. Wrightworth said.

I walked in and shifted to the side as he closed the door.

Mr. Wrightworth's home was a rather large apartment. It had two rooms, not small ones either, a full bathroom, and a living room with a balcony that overlooked the slums but also faced east. The kitchen was larger than my place a few floors lower, and it even had an eating area attached to it.

The walls and carpeting were still the neutral colours of my apartment. Whereas my walls were blue, Mr. Wrightworth's were a purple-ish grey. There was no artwork or photographs on the walls, making it look stark, but then most apartments in the building were bereft of wall decoration.

I gawked about, just looking at the space of the place. Of course, I could only see the front hallway and into the kitchen, I would see the rest of the apartment later.

"Stop gawking," he said, moving into the kitchen.

Suddenly he came back.

Mr. Wrightworth wrapped a hand around my throat and tightened until I gasped. My whole world narrowed to him. I whimpered, I wanted to melt into that touch, but managed to stay on my feet. I did reach up and grasp his wrist with both of my hands. I needed the extra stability.

"I said stop gawking," Mr. Wrightworth said in a commanding tone. "Understand?"

"Yes," I said, a shudder rolling through me.

Why do I react like that every time?

The roiling in my belly and sudden moist feeling between my legs didn't help matters. I certainly didn't understand then the sort of comfort one can find in submitting to another. I was still very new to the whole thing.

Many don't realize that it's not submitting to just anyone that does it, it has to be the right person. Being forced to submit to Nathaniel's father hadn't enticed me in the least.

But Nathaniel would never hurt me without cause. Mr.

Wrightworth would never cross a line, at least not once he knew where the line was.

"Yes, Master," Mr. Wrightworth corrected.

"Yes, Master," my voice shook as I spoke the title.

Patrick wasn't just there to tease Mr. Wrightworth. He was there to make a point.

It was only then that I realized that Patrick played a larger role than being subservient because of the rift that was developing between the Program and Nathaniel's company. A Master was different from a Sir. I understood that even then. They had even told me as much during that day at church. The two had been dropped into the same category, however, as a dominant. We hadn't had the time to get into the actual differences between the two titles.

He released me and walked back into the kitchen.

"There are cameras here, but only I have the password to access the network," Mr. Wrightworth murmured as he pulled a pot off his stove. "The walls are supposed to be sound proof, but I've yet to test that. As much as I want to hear you scream, we will end up using a gag. Don't need to get arrested for—what's that look for?"

"I don't like gags," I said.

Mr. Wrightwroth shivered and set the pot on the counter by two bowls.

"You will get used to them."

"Nathaniel used a ball gag on me because I didn't say something when he wanted me to," I said, the fear blooming in my belly. A cold flooded through me as I recalled that I was supposed to have told Mr. Wrightworth about it the first time I saw him. "I was supposed to tell you the next time I saw you."

"Given the circumstances, I doubt anyone would blame you," he said, opening a drawer and pulling out a spoon.

"But he said if I didn't—"

"No harm, Darling," he said, raising his voice slightly. "Come here. This is dinner. It's just mashed potato with some ground meat and peas. My mother's favourite thing to make when the pay didn't stretch quite far enough and rations ran low. Although this has more meat and peas than she put."

I took a bowl, happy for the slum food. It was comforting

to see and smell something I recognized.

"My mother used corn, and the meat was usually stuff she strained off her broth," I said, accepting a spoon.

"I remember those days, then my brothers and sisters went to work but still lived with us. That was some good eating. For about a year before they all moved out."

We moved to the eating area, and he sat. I sat across from him and immediately began to eat. He smiled slightly as he ate a bite of his food.

Again, we ate in silence.

When Mr. Wrightworth finished his meal, he stood and picked up my bowl, waiting just long enough for me to place my spoon into the bowl before he walked to the kitchen.

The dishes went into a dishwasher, along with the pot and spoon. He hadn't made any extra, had wasted no food. It was a mark of a poor person long into life. Waste not, want not.

"Come," he said, walking off.

Almost sighing, I stood and moved through the kitchen and followed him deeper into the apartment. The bathroom was right by the door of the apartment. The two bedrooms were along the outer wall of the building. Both had windows, and both had curtains on regular rods. He took me into the room at the end of the hall.

I have no idea how he managed it, but Mr. Wrightworth had smuggled in play furniture. Perhaps he had the items labelled as something else and shipped in their pieces. Attached to the ceiling in the middle of the room was a chain through a hoop. The chain went through the hoop and then connected to the floor, where it was locked into place in another hoop.

"Strip," Mr. Wrightworth said.

I stripped off the work dress I had tossed on. I didn't have anything else that appeared formal enough to wear on this imaginary date of ours. Besides the clothing I used to work out in, all I had were the work dresses. I wasn't even certain where to go if I wanted new clothing.

Mr. Wrightworth looked me over, then motioned to the bra. Hesitantly, I took it off and dropped it with the dress.

He approached me as the fear returned. I was almost naked, in front of a man, and it wasn't for medical purposes.

It felt so wrong.

"Anything that isn't covered is available for being struck," he said, motioning down as he stepped ever closer.

I pulled away, putting distance between us as I crossed my arms over my chest to hide my breasts.

"Mm, those," he said with a small nod. "Those aren't exactly appealing to me. But if the bra is on, there will be a band across your back. That will interfere with what I want to do to you." I shivered again. He smiled in response. "You, of course, know that I don't play with women except as consensual discipline. This is an exception. We are not that sort of pair. I will never fuck you, or have you. If sexualization is brought into the play, we will use toys on you. Never on me.

"This isn't about me, though I'm sure I will derive pleasure from it in some form.

"Come over here."

He moved to the chain hanging from the ceiling. I edged towards him, and he snapped his fingers, jabbing at his feet. Afraid that he might hurt me otherwise, I rushed to the spot.

"I'm going to tie you with this," he grabbed the chain and the manacles attached to them. "Tonight, that's all that's going to happen. Raise your hands," when I did as he told me, he slipped the manacles on each of my wrists and tightened them. "I'm going to sit by the door there and turn on some music. You will hang here until I let you go. You will trust," Mr. Wrightworth took my chin in his hand and lifted my face so that I had to look into his eyes. "You will learn to trust me, Darling."

He walked behind me and music began. The music was soft, almost peaceful, but it didn't quite override the panic that was quickly overwhelming me. Of course, I hadn't been tied since my time in medical and that had been only a little while. To a bed no less. Nathaniel's father had strung me up like that, he had even used a chain and manacles just like that.

I stiffened at the thought as I caught a whiff of a familiar cologne. Trying to get in a breath, I turned towards Mr. Wrightworth, half expecting Nathaniel's father to be there.

"Face forward," Mr. Wrightworth snarled.

I turned back, my heart thundering in my ears. The smell seemed to get stronger. I tugged at the manacles, needing to get away.

He was there. I swear he was there!

"Banana!" I shouted.

"What?" Mr. Wrightworth asked, his confusion plain in his voice.

"Banana," I sobbed. "Please let me down."

The man came around me, frowning as he cocked his head. "What's that? What's banana for?"

"It's my safe word," I said between sobs, still struggling to get out of the manacles.

Mr. Wrightworth's hand darted out, grabbing the chain and holding me almost still as he stepped close to me.

"Why would he use that word? Most use red so that you can call yellow as well. Hold still. Stop. Stop, Darling." I came to a sudden stop, still crying. "I'm going to let you out, but you are not to run, understand?"

"Yes," I cried.

He pulled me free of the manacles.

Of course, I ran.

I made it out of the room and almost to the front door before Mr. Wrightworth slammed into me. His body impacting with mine forced the air from my lungs and thumped me against the door. Almost naked, I struggled against his hot body as he grabbed first one, then the other wrist. He pinned my wrists to the door above my head. I shuddered to a stop as he pushed himself against me, pinning me with his body.

And that was how I learned I liked being restrained physically.

I half expected a flood to come from between my legs. I pushed against his body, and Mr. Wrightworth responded by snarling. The fear came flooding back at the anger in that snarl. I struggled again as he yanked me from the door, dragging me into the kitchen. He thrust me over the counter, narrowly missing the upper cupboard with my head. I struggled harder, crying out when he thrust against me, pinning me with his body once more.

What does a man do to a woman who disobeyed him and

was then pinned to a counter? I thought he was going to rape me. The wound was far too fresh.

I struggled harder.

Mr. Wrightworth growled again and sat up, one hand very firmly placed between my shoulder blades. The other hand moved and I thought he was pulling himself free. It didn't help things a moment later when he yanked down my underwear.

"Please don't!" I cried.

"You should have thought of that before you ran," he growled back.

I flinched. The stinging impact didn't seem to register fully. It was not the sort of stinging I expected, certainly a lot higher than I expected. Even if he was going a different route. The second strike made me whimper as the sting turned to pain. The third strike was followed by yet another heated flood as my hips ground against the counter.

"Are you..." Mr. Wrightworth stopped. His free hand flitted between my legs. "Well, that's..."

There was a thumping at the door. An annoying sound as I writhed against the counter.

He leaned close, sighing out.

"I think I'm going to have to alter that sexualization comment. Get to the bathroom and stay there. Now."

He pulled away and threw a tea towel at me, to cover myself. I stepped out of my underwear, which had been around my ankles on the floor, and left the kitchen, headed for the bedroom, not the bathroom.

Mr. Wrightworth answered the door as I went around the corner.

"Mr. Wrightworth, we're part of the patrol, just received a complaint about thumping and a female voice. We need to check your apartment. It is policy."

"I have a visitor," Mr. Wrightworth said quickly. "What was heard was not pain."

"We still have to check. It is policy."

"I have a female guest one time, and everyone thinks I'm raping and murdering her in my apartment?" Mr. Wrightworth demanded.

"Sir, it's policy," the other man said, sounding a bit

desperate. "Of course we don't think you've done anything, but we have to check."

"Mr. Wrightworth?" I called out as I walked around the corner. "Who's at the door?"

I lifted the tea towel as Mr. Wrightworth stood to the side and pulled the door fully open. Holding the two corners up near my breasts, the fabric draped down, barely covering me. Thank goodness Mr. Wrightworth liked big tea towels. Otherwise, I would seriously risk showing a nipple or the very edge of my sex.

Two men in policing garb gaped at me.

"I'm sorry, who are you?" one managed to get out, reaching for a notepad and pen in his pocket.

"Izzy," I said with a hesitant smile.

I wanted to run away.

The two men weren't moving and—while Mr. Wrightworth was between them and me—it was dawning on me that he might not rape me, but that wouldn't necessarily stop him from inviting the other two in to do the job. I wanted to get rid of them as soon as possible, but neither seemed interested in leaving anytime soon.

They even stepped into the apartment, and Mr. Wrightworth closed the door behind them.

I took a step back. Mr. Wrightworth, behind the pair of them, shot me a scathing look and jabbed sternly at the floor. My feet became wooden. I couldn't seem to get them moving.

"Izzy?" the man asked.

"Isabella Martin, recovered fourteen," Mr. Wrightworth said quickly, stepping around them.

"Recovered fourteen isn't supposed to be alone with men," the man's partner said quickly, pulling out his walkie.

"I'd rather not have that discussion in front of her," he growled back.

"What do you mean I'm not allowed to be alone with men?" I asked, turning my attention to Mr. Wrightworth. "You never told me that."

"You came here willingly, the point was to keep others from cornering you before you were ready," Mr. Wrightworth said to me quickly before he turned to the policemen. "I'm sure the controllers can confirm that I invited her here, and she came over. I've done nothing untoward to Izzy. Besides ravaging her as she begged me to. Would you need proof of that as well?"

"You know they may require proof, and a check up with a doctor," one of the men grumbled. "I'm sorry, Mr. Wrightworth, it's policy to make certain no one can abuse anyone else. Most especially for the recovered members of the Program. You wrote the rules. We're only enforcing them."

"I don't want a check up just because you don't believe him!" I all but shouted back at them. "You are making me very uncomfortable. Mr. Wrighworth, I don't want to do this!"

"Go to the room, I'll speak with them," he muttered, motioning as if he were trying to calm me down. "Darling, please, go make yourself comfortable."

I bolted down the hallway and out of sight. Into the playroom, I slammed the door and sunk to the floor, tears welling up at the very thought. Doctors could tell if a woman had sex, I knew that meant that something would end up happening, to cover our tracks because I hadn't done as I was told. I couldn't very well let him be accused or charged because I hadn't listened.

My tears were almost dried when Mr. Wrightworth walked back into the room and closed the door. I skittered away from him, holding the tea towel tight against me as I moved. When he came towards me, I whimpered but didn't dare say anything because obviously the room was not as sound proof as he had been told. He reached and yanked me to my feet, then thrust me against the wall and pinned me with his body.

"Do you like this?"

"What?' I asked, barely holding on.

"My body against yours, do you like this?" he asked.

"Yes."

He pulled me off the wall and to a spanking bench. The bench sat at hip level, for Mr. Wrightworth. There was a step, then a long flat surface. He bent me over the side and pressed against me.

There was no denying the heat of the man pressed against my back, of his hot breath against the back of my neck and shoulder. The things I would have been willing to let him do to me at that moment were obscene. I felt comfortable being touched like that.

Nathaniel's father never came that close, not after the first time I bit him, or the time I had kneed him, then kicked him in the head.

At that thought, the realization that I found it comfortable and that it was a thing that hadn't been done to me, the wonderful feelings curdled into nausea.

"And now?" he asked.

"Please don't," I managed to get out.

With him pressed tight against me, it was hard not to feel the way his whole body stiffened. The man pulled away just slightly.

"I'm sorry, are you afraid I'm going to rape you?" he demanded.

"They're going to want proof," I said, the tears welling back up again.

"No, they aren't. I've dealt with it. Answer the question. Have you—at any point tonight—been afraid that I might rape you?"

"Yes."

Mr. Wrightworth snarled. "I'm still gay."

"I know," I said, and then burst into a fresh bout of tears.

"You enjoyed being pinned and my pressing against you," he said through gritted teeth.

"I know," I said, crying harder.

He released me and walked off.

I sniffled and stood, hugging myself as he walked towards the door and picked up a book from the table beside the door. He walked back to me and opened the book, pulling a pen from the spine.

"Rape sensitivity," he muttered, scribbling on the page.

"What's that?" I asked.

He handed me the book. I blinked the remaining tears from my eyes and read the page as he stripped off his t-shirt.

The book appeared to be a list of terms, most of which I didn't quite recognize. There were little marks beside certain items. One or two of the items had already been scratched off, but I didn't know what the terms meant, so I didn't ask about them.

"No anal," I said to him, finally recognizing something I knew.

"If we do have sex, let's face it, that's the way it'll be," he said, holding out the shirt as he reached and took the book with his other hand.

I took the t-shirt and pulled it on, grateful for the covering. He made a motion to me and left the room. I followed him out and to the living room, where he sat on the couch and motioned beside him. So I sat beside him as he opened the book and placed it on the coffee table.

"These are things I want to work on with you. They all lead to the point of you being comfortable enough to move onto another. I know you enjoy submission, that it's something in which you are very interested. Obviously, we have a lot to work on."

"Like my not panicking when you tie me."

"Not everyone is looking to hurt you the way you were hurt. And if whoever you move onto takes advantage of you, I know you'll tell me. Then I'll come in. I'll tie him up and beat him. See how he likes that. Oh, this could be very fun, come to think of it. It's been a while since I had a man."

"And you added rape sensitivity to that?" I asked.

"You feel like every man wants to rape you, that can't happen. You're taking self-defence classes. You don't go out after dark. You never talk to anyone, and you lock the door to the archives even though no one has ever tried to go through it except for me."

"So? I'm being safe."

"You're being a victim. You're letting him win."

"He hasn't won."

"As long as there is fear in your life, he is winning," Mr. Wrightworth snapped, causing me to flinch away from him. "As long as the smell of him makes you want to cry, he is winning. As long as you can't live the life that you want to live, he is winning.

"Before him, you wanted to be tied up. You wanted to be pinned and had at the pleasure of a man. You were very interested in orgasm control, which is on that list, by the way. You aren't the first victim I've taken on. There's something about you lot that just delights me. You know real terror. You know that I'm not crossing a line.

"When I play with some vanilla tit from either side of the debt line, they're just terrified and revolted at everything I do to them. You, however," he leaned in just a little closer, "you like it, even as you're trying to get away from me."

"You've had another victim?" I asked.

"Yes, he claimed that he wasn't a victim," Mr. Wrightworth paused to smile as his eyes seemed to fog over. He gave himself a little shake and focused on me. "I tied him with the chain and manacles, as I had you tied this evening, and I beat him until he told himself the truth of the matter. Saying that you aren't a victim doesn't change the fact that you are. Facing that fact is usually the only way to move on from it. You were a victim. You were attacked, and your weaknesses were used against you. That doesn't make you weak. Pretending it didn't happen, that it didn't affect you? That makes you weak. I don't like it when my subs run from their problems. It makes things complicated for me, and I like uncomplicated."

"I'm not running from anything," I protested, but only half-heartedly.

Mr. Wrightworth had been right about me more than once before. Him simply saying it set me on the path of wondering if it were true or not, onto the path of questioning myself.

"We can go over these," Mr. Wrightworth motioned to the book, "tomorrow evening. In the meantime, you should consider what I've told you. Carefully consider your boundaries and limitations. I want you to prepare yourself to have those boundaries crossed, or at the very least pushed. I will not settle for simply tying you up and beating you until I get bored."

"Normally your play sessions end in sex," I said.

"Normally yes, but I'm making an exception for you. That exception may change, as I'm told sexuality is fluid. Nicole counts herself as heterosexual, but for the right sort of woman, she will play at bisexuality. Which is why she is still with Mary after all these weeks."

"You're saying that to tease me," I grumbled.

"I am, yes," Mr. Wrightworth said with a small smile. "At the end of the day, I am still very gay, and I'm fairly certain we'd be chasing the same bed partners. While flattered by your reaction to me, it does little for my cock."

"Ew, you call it a cock?" I asked.

"There it is," he said with that Cheshire cat smile.

"You did that on purpose!" I exclaimed.

"Of course."

"No mindfucks."

"That wasn't a mindfuck. It was manipulation. Learn your terms."

"You learn your terms," I grumbled in response.

Mr. Wrightworth's hand twitched against his leg. His eyes narrowed ever so slightly as he considered me as if wondering if I realized what I had just said. Looking back, I know how ridiculous it was to bait a sadist, but at that moment I was just snarky and sarcastic.

"You should leave now," he growled out finally.

"Fine, what time should I be here tomorrow?"

"Six, don't eat before you come. Wear whatever. It won't matter in the end."

Chapter Five

It was a standing command.

Almost every night, at the same time, I visited Mr. Wrightworth. I have no idea how he always managed to get off at the same time and get everything he did in a day done, but he did. I strongly suspect that when people discovered that he had taken an interest in a woman, everyone dropped what they were doing to make certain he could get off in time.

The next night he fed me noodles and fried vegetables in an Asian style. Again, dinner was eaten in silence. I finished my plate before Mr. Wrightworth for the first time.

Food was a bit of a control issue with him. No one could eat unless he were eating as well, even going out. He had difficulty walking past people who were wasting food. I did ask him about that little tic eventually, though I don't feel it would be appropriate to include his answer.

Suffice to say, it was something he dealt with for years and had great difficulty overcoming.

After dinner, we moved to the living room and sat where we had the night before. He pulled out that little book and set it between us, facing me on the couch.

There was a list of items that we went over. These are items that are on nearly any fetish list. It wasn't that he wanted to know if he could do all those things, but he asked instead for a number between one and five, to indicate how I felt about them. After going through the list, he turned the page and scratched an item or two off his list, then set the book between us once more.

"Starting at the top here, which I was writing as it came to me, anal training," Mr. Wrightworth tapped the page, then looked up at me. "Normally anal training is some extreme nonsense, fitting a fist into your anal cavity or some insanity like that. The training I'm interested in is pleasure training. I'm going to prepare you for the feeling and then tie it into orgasm training so that you can come from anal. It's quite easy to do once I have you trained for the one, and the other will follow shortly."

"Why?" I asked.

"Because any Dom you go to will likely demand it, especially after finding out that you're from the slums. Rich folks don't even care. Anal is like the spiced up sex for them. It hardly phases them at all. While I want to get you ready to move on to another Dom, I also want to make certain you can gain as much pleasure from the interaction as possible. I don't want him scarring you for life over a sexual act which is simple enough to train for."

I shifted on the couch, uncomfortable about the idea. Nathaniel hadn't started the training as Mr. Wrightworth had suggested, but then I had been with him such a short time. When would he have brought it up?

"Protocol, this is how you will behave towards me and I towards you. You will refer to me as Master, not Sir. You will thank me for everything I do to you, whether it is discipline or play."

"Why?" I asked again.

"Everything I do to you, you consent to, you agree to my doing it to you. I want that in the forefront of your mind as I do it to you. You allowed this, in many cases you wanted it to be done to you. Perhaps you even begged me to do it, but it is consensual, and there is a safe word. So you will thank me, to remind you that you wanted this to be done to you, and you agreed to it."

"I haven't agreed to anything yet."

"I'm almost entirely certain that you will."

"Almost?"

How could he not know for certain? He knows everything!

"Almost," Mr. Wrightworth responded quietly. "Next,

you will learn formal care. This will include how to help a man dress, how to dress yourself, how to eat at a rich person's table, some dance and on down that list as far as we get while you are with me.

"The next line item is masturbation. After each play session, you are to return to your room and masturbate, unless I give you the go-ahead to skip it. That will be an exception, not the rule."

"But the controllers see everything!"

"Not my problem, doesn't change the protocol in the least. I'm looking into getting toys for you, though I do know that you are perfectly capable of using your hands. You will do so. If I ask you in public whether or not you had fun last night, that is code. You are to respond yes, if you did, and no if you did not. As we play more, I will add more to your plate."

"More to my plate?"

"You will have to come more than once."

"How can you do orgasm training if you aren't creating the orgasms?" I asked.

"This isn't about orgasm training, which I will—what is the term—suck it up for? This is masturbation, which is entirely different from orgasm control. That comes later and is only for your future partner. I want you to masturbate to help lower the stress level during play."

"Will you be doing the same?" I asked.

"What did you think I was doing behind you last night?" he asked.

He hesitated, his hazel eyes flowing over my face as I attempted not to show my interest in that statement. The reason he had told me to turn around wasn't just for training purposes. It was because he had been in the middle of something else entirely. Aroused by my terror, even though all he could see was my back. How good, I thought, he must have been at reading body language to see what I was feeling just by the muscles of my back.

"I will restrict my activities to outside of the play session if I can. Not mixing play and sex is new to me, and it seems I link it to great orgasms. That in itself is a sort of orgasm training. Most end play sessions with sex, I've always been one to intermingle sex with play."

"How exactly do you intend to bring in orgasm control?" I asked.

"That will be linked to the masturbation, I've done this before, except the end game was to have him beg me to fuck him," Mr. Wrightworth paused to smile slightly. "And beg me he did. It was so glorious to get to that end."

"Aren't you afraid that if we did that you'd end up—" I motioned between us.

Mr. Wrightworth shrugged.

"But you're gay."

"The point isn't straight or gay, it's going into play with an open mind," Mr. Wrightworth said. "I'm not going to deny every sort and thought, just as I expect you to have an open mind about what I plan to do to you."

"You're being very confusing," I said.

"Perhaps because I'm confused," Mr. Wrightworth grumbled. "No other woman has done to me what you have done, as you no doubt picked up on when you attended the church."

"They seemed surprised you would feel that way about me. Like they didn't see what all the fuss was about."

"Mm, on that note, lift your skirt," Mr. Wrightworth said, reaching over the couch to pick something up off the side table. "Come here, sit on my lap."

I moved to obey, settling in his lap, my back against his chest. He was so warm, so strong. I melted against him. For the first time in months, I relaxed, pressing closer to his chest than was necessary.

"What's this?" he asked, wrapping his arms around me. "Oh, my dear, Darling. Did we just find a reward for you?"

I made a small sound and adjusted against him, bending my head to look up at his hazel eyes. The man watched me, his arms tightening just slightly as he smiled. I swore the heat multiplied as his strong arms tightened around me protectively. The smell of the man, the promises he was making? My heart skipped a beat as our eyes were locked, breath sighing. He could have asked anything of me then, and I probably would have done it without question.

I knew he wouldn't ask anything of me. That was one of

the reasons I would have done it if he had.

It was one of those moments that seemed to last forever, yet was over too quickly, ending when he spoke.

"I think we did, and this is a reward I can deliver happily."

He held me for another minute or so, warmth oozing slowly into my body, then reached over me and pulled my skirt up further. With a pen that looked oddly familiar, Mr. Wrightworth wrote on my right leg.

I am beautiful.

I didn't believe it at all. It made me feel awkward and weird, that it was written on my leg. Having to read it every time I went to the bathroom made it all the stranger.

'I am beautiful,' it's a fact that few women believe about themselves. Beauty is in the eye of the beholder, so they say. Mr. Wrightworth and Nathaniel were the first ones to make such a comment. Even my fiance back in the slum had never called me beautiful or even pretty. Ours had been an engagement of debt and convenience, not about love and passion. While we had come to care about each other over the course of our engagement, it hadn't been deeper than a puddle of piss left by a drunk on the road.

"Another trick of mine," he grumbled, sliding me off his lap.

Is everything Nathaniel does, something that Mr. Wrightworth taught him?

"Next item on the list," he said quickly, picking up the book again. "Play won't start until you are comfortable being tied. You are not allowed to come until we play."

"I haven't since I got back anyhow."

"No masturbation," Mr. Wrightworth said sternly, even shaking a finger at me. "Your safe word is banana, though I don't know why he'd choose that."

"Banana," I said, then laughed.

"Oh..." he said in response and suddenly focused on his book.

"What's that mean?" I asked.

"Nothing, it's nothing," Mr. Wrightworth grumbled. "Plugs, let's talk about plugs. Do you know what that is?"

"To plug a sink?"

"Think something like that, except for anal instead," he responded, smiling slightly when I edged away from him. "I will place the first one, then after that, you will be responsible for putting them in. You will wear the plug during play, but we won't start for a few weeks. It's a part of anal training.

"Next vibrators, I'm trying to find you one. I may bring it into play, but in that instance, you will control it and use it on my command."

"You've only really talked about sex stuff," I said pointedly.

"Well, I'd rather ease into the other items. Most blanch when I bring up the pain portion."

"Like a bandage, just rip it off."

"Speaking of bandage, how is your finger?" Mr. Wrightworth asked.

"It's fine, get on with it."

"I use floggers, paddles, whips, hands, belts for smacking. I also use needles, deal in some knife and fire play, use tooth and nail."

"Tooth and nail?" I asked.

"Give me your arm and I'll show you."

I held out my arm and Mr. Wrightworth took it gently, drawing it—and me—to him. He turned my arm towards him, which turned my wrist towards the ceiling. Ever so slowly he bent down and took the meaty part of my lower arm in his mouth.

And then he bit me.

Some Doms bite fast. It's more like a nip, like they're afraid of it. Doing it that way hurts and doesn't feel right in the least. Biting down slowly, putting more pressure until it starts hurting is much more pleasant. Nipping fucking hurts and the Doms think they're being all Domly, but they're just dicks. Might as well stab me, for all the good it does, but they think they've done me some great favour.

It's been years since, of course, I've played with others, though.

When Mr. Wrightworth released my arm, I shivered. I didn't pull away. I stayed stuck in place as he straightened and watched me for my reaction. His hand flowed over the teeth marks on my arm, making me shiver in delight as the flesh tingled.

"As I said before, anything that isn't covered can be used as I see fit."

"My mouth isn't covered," I said, concerned about the idea.

"I face fuck, which is not what Nathaniel prefers."

"How do you know what he prefers?" I asked.

Mr. Wrightworth seemed to struggle for a moment. I could see him debating whether or not he wanted to tell me, whether he should tell me. The information he had might have crossed the line of what should and should not be said about Nathaniel, to me.

"We've had a threesome," he said finally. "I don't think he liked the balance I brought in, but he did lose a bet, so I had to make certain it was worth it. Point being, I face fuck."

"You keep saying fuck like it means something to me."

In response, he turned and picked up his remote. It took several minutes for him to find the video he wanted, and then he played it for me. The video scared me, but mainly because I thought that kind of video was illegal. Once it ended, I turned to Mr. Wrightworth with wide eyes.

"You have the option," he said. "But no, I've no interest, at this point, in doing that to you."

"I thought that was illegal."

"Very illegal, it would be counted as rape, even though you saw her give consent beforehand. She loves doing that, especially with strangers."

"No, the video!"

"Oh, that's a home movie. We have several floating around, all on encrypted drives."

"Nathaniel said those didn't exist."

"Because Nathaniel doesn't know they exist. Just like he doesn't know that his old Master has hours of footage of him. On that note. I'd like to remind you that, yes, everything here is recorded, but only I have access to it. Everything everywhere is recorded, but like rich folk, I have control over who can view my footage."

Nathaniel's Master is rich.

I couldn't help it, even three months out from having seen

Nathaniel, he was the last thing I thought about and the first when I awoke. Everything was compared to him. I slipped him into the conversation whenever I thought that I wouldn't be admonished for it. Still, no one talked to me about him, and it drove me absolutely batty.

The problem was that I still didn't know what was going on. He had tried to make his father take "him," whoever the unnamed man was instead of me. It still gave me hope that he might want me.

"Why doesn't he know?"

"Sometime in the future, I might show you the videos, I do have access to those. You might even enjoy it, Nathaniel mentioned you might be part Domme, and you might enjoy tying up Doms yourself. That's an interesting premise. Not many Doms would let you tie them up, though any strong man might do. Even Nathaniel, but we can discuss that later, once the review is complete."

"It's not done yet?"

"We can discuss that tomorrow at your three months sitting," Mr. Wrightworth growled. "Now, we will use almost all the furniture in the room there. We will start off testing your limits. I know you can take a harder beating than Nathaniel was giving you because his father rarely holds back and you're still standing. I won't go that far, but I will hurt you, I take far too much enjoyment from it."

"Aftercare," I blurted out.

"Right, you drop, and you drop hard," Mr. Wrightworth said, flipping to a clean page. "The expectation is that we are in a relationship, to those outside. Which means that you will end up spending nights here, we will sleep in my bed. Both clothed, of course. Baths can be a part of aftercare, and we will eat a little more. Massages help, I find, sex as well, which is part of why I want you to masturbate. If you spend the night, you will have the bed to yourself for about an hour as I clean the room and shower.

"Which means, of course, I will have to place toys in my room. You will have to use them and clean them yourself."

I blushed at the prospect and looked away.

"Orgasm is not something to be hidden away. Doing as I command you will show you that, it will help you come in the future."

"I have no problems coming," I snapped back.

"For Nathaniel, perhaps me as well. Did any of the others at the church bring that reaction out in you?"

"No," I said slowly.

"Which is why we are doing the training that we are doing. I don't want there being a mental block because the other Doms are lacking some spark, or whatever it is that you see in Nathaniel and me."

"You're both very attractive, and command a room."

"Maybe it's the sadist thing," Mr. Wrightworth said quickly.

"I don't think Nathaniel is a sadist," I said.

"Not fully, just half on his mother's side."

"I'd say it was his father's side," I grumbled, then laughed despite myself.

"Let's talk about your needs."

"No sleep deprivation, I don't like gags at all, they scare me. I like the feel of a man, so not touching me isn't an option," I paused and pulled my legs up, hugging my knees as I realized just how quickly those words had come from my mouth. I hadn't even hesitated, and I suddenly felt self-conscious. "How do I explain the marks at checkup?"

"There's a reason why Nicole does most of your checkup," Mr. Wrightworth said quietly. "The plan wasn't for me, but after last night, I think any other would be a bad idea. Nicole insists on sex with her subs, she would probably strap something on for you and you might enjoy it, but I think it's important not to push sex after what happened. Letting it come out of you until you can take it no longer, that's the best way."

"Yeah, except if I come begging you for it, you won't give it to me."

Mr. Wrightworth hesitated. The man looked genuinely baffled.

"I'm going to have to come up with a solution for that," he muttered. "When you come begging for it, I'll have a solution. It's months and months away, I suspect, that's plenty of time."

I adjusted in my seat, feeling such an urge, but only for a

moment. "How do you plan on working on that?"

"Once you're comfortable with me, I'm taking you back to church. You will wear yellow, and I will talk to some Doms. They will pin you in sexually suggestive positions, but you will trust that none of them will try anything, and if they do, I will crack their skulls."

"That makes me uncomfortable."

"In most cases, they aren't going to be interested in you at all."

"It's also the skull cracking that makes me uncomfortable."

"I've only had to do it once, everyone listens and obeys since then."

I stared at Mr. Wrightworth. The man chuckled in response.

"The point of that is to get you comfortable with other men so that you know that even if you feel like you are in a sexual position, you are safe. By the time you're ready to move on to another, you will trust me enough that, were they to hurt you and tell you not to speak of it to me, you still will. I will deal with them then and there."

"I suppose..."

"Oh, and you are taking self-defence classes," Mr. Wrightworth said, scribbling something on the page. "So we will have sessions where I fight you. If you win, I will reward you. If you don't, I will discipline you. I want you to be able to get out of nearly every sort of hold a man might take on you. Once you can, we will work on you fighting while tied up. You'd be surprised how easy it is."

"I suppose..." I said again. "How long until we play?"

"Why?" he asked.

I was suddenly thinking of my arm, of how the pressure under my skin had alleviated a little when he had bitten me. Until that point, I hadn't realized just how tense I had been.

"Darling, tell me why," he said when I didn't immediately respond.

"There's been a pressure in my flesh for a long time, and after you bit me, it doesn't feel as bad, yet is worse all the same," I said, rubbing at the spot.

"But last night when I spanked you, that didn't help?" he

asked.

"A lot happened just after and before," I said in my defence.

"I was more of thinking, you had spoken your safe word just before that happened," Mr. Wrightworth murmured. "I think that's why it didn't help. You had withdrawn consent. Technically I shouldn't have spanked you at all, but when you disobey, you need to be disciplined."

"But I'm very aware of it now."

"Listen to that desperation," he purred out. "Almost makes me want to tie you up and give you what you want."

"This isn't funny, Mr. Wrightworth!"

He slid across the couch, closing the distance between us. Draping an arm around my shoulders, he pressed me tight against him. His warmth only reminded me that, yet again, the pressure was building.

"I've already told you that we won't play until you are willing."

"I am willing," I snarled.

"You need to be tied, shall we try that and see how you react to being tied?" he asked.

I snarled in response, no actual word, just an annoyed sound. Mr. Wrightworth took my chin in his hand and pulled my face towards him.

"Let us go to the play room. If you can stay tied for an hour without panicking, I will play with you tonight. If not, it will wait. You do not get to play with me, or be spanked, or have impact play unless you obey my rules. And if you continue to hurt yourself during the day, you will regret it. Do you understand me?"

"I do," I said with a quiver.

Anger was roiling through me. The fact that he was forcing me to submit before he gave me what I needed was infuriating.

He led me to the room and tied me. I made it twenty minutes before I called the safe word. Mr. Wrightworth would repeat the process over the next two weeks and each day I'd make it just a little further. As much as it infuriated me, him making me wait gave me something to aim for. I wanted to make it through the hour to get what I felt I needed. He had dangled a carrot in front of me.

And it worked.

Chapter Six

The next day was a three-month review, which no on told me about beforehand. Mr. Wrightworth had mentioned it the night before, but he hadn't gone into detail as to what the review encompassed.

Or where it was happening.

Or the time.

I suppose that he assumed I knew all those things because in real life people don't just list the same thing over and over. He had only mentioned the review in passing because it happened to come up, not because he had wanted to talk about it.

The review started at ten in the morning, just as I was trying to decide which contract to audit. The boring one, or the long-winded one? They sent Kathy of all people to get me, and then she dared to admonish me for being late to my own review. I had to listen to her nattering all the way from the archives, across the Program building and to the room that my review was being held.

The Program building was not even close to small.

As I stepped into the room, I was furious. My hands clenched. I was angry about everything that was going on in the room—from the way most of the men gave me an exasperated look, to the twitch of Mr. Wrightworth's lips. I made the leaping conclusion that he had sent Kathy to get me, thus it was his damned fault I had to deal with the woman's impudence.

"Miss Martin, please, have a seat," one of the other men said, motioning to the desk chair that sat in the middle of the room before them.

I marched to the chair and dropped into it. When I glowered at Mr. Wrightworth, he made a motion as if straightening a skirt. Instead of being furious, I was more annoyed as I snapped down my skirt to fix it. Then I glared at the other men at the table as they shuffled papers.

"I wasn't told this was happening," I said through gritted teeth, trying to remain polite.

"That doesn't matter. You're here now."

It does matter.

I clenched my hands in my lap. Instead of glaring at the men at the long table, I glared at the wall behind them.

"Just to be clear, Miss Martin, this is not about the job you've taken on," Mr. Wrightworth said. "If there were any problems with that area of your life, we would bring it to your attention right away."

"Like this review was brought to my attention?" I asked sarcastically.

"...Uh..." one of the others made a sound, and my eyes darted over them, trying to pinpoint who it was. I didn't figure it out until he spoke. "That was a one-time error, surely you don't plan to hold a grudge against us?"

"You forgot to tell the person being reviewed about their review," I said back, trying to be as calm as possible. "And it's not the first time. I was also not told about orientation, or what was expected of me once I left Medical. The ones in charge of my orientation didn't even show up. So don't you sit there and tell me that this was a one time, small error."

"Recoveries are still few and far between," Mr. Wrightworth said, a cold edge to his voice suddenly. "There are kinks in the system that we are still working out. Patience is required."

"I was taken from my contractor, raped, tortured, and very nearly murdered. You don't get to tell me to be patient. I already have to be patient about my recovery, about my emotions, about relearning things that should be simple tasks. You don't get to tell me to be patient while you figure out why your people aren't doing what they're supposed to."

"Obviously you are doing much better," one of the other said quickly, scribbling something down on his paper.

"No, she's not," Mr. Wrightworth said, turning his attention to them. "When I realized our error, I sent Kathy to fetch Miss Martin. I thought if she were a little annoyed, she wouldn't end up crying. Obviously, I misjudged her reaction to annoyance."

"She's standing up to authority."

"She's being a brat," Mr. Wrightworth said sternly.

He kept slipping in words that meant one thing to the others in the room but had so many other connotations.

"I'm not a brat. A brat would tell you to suck it. You did something stupid, and I'm calling you on it. I'm tired of slipping through every single crack in your supposedly almost perfect system. You don't get ignored and missed this often if the system is almost perfect."

"Let's just get to the review," Mr. Wrightworth said through gritted teeth.

"Well, this is about how I'm doing. So. I was shown to a room and given absolutely no expectations or rules. I wasn't told I was expected anywhere the next morning or how anything worked. I thought everything was run by a computer until this one over here informed me that it's run by controllers, as in people. Who he wrote up because they had a fucking heart and gave me a stuffed animal when I was upset when no one else could be bothered!

"Then when he finally does take notice and we..." I fell silent, suddenly struggling for words. "I was finally starting to feel normal, and someone called the police on him. It was like being violated all over again."

"That was Michael," Mr. Wrightworth said, motioning to a man down the line who looked up suddenly and then around the room as if looking for an escape route. "The police were just doing their jobs. Your state of dress didn't help matters. If they had gawked much longer, I would have had to assault them. I've already suggested more sensitivity training for the officers in the building. As much as they are men, they cannot gawk at an almost naked woman. They need to be more respectful."

"They were gawking?" one of the others asked.

"And making excuses to stay and speak with Isabella. They tried to tell me she was distraught, but it was obvious that they wanted to get a closer look at the woman. As a man, I don't blame them. Our officers, however, need to be above that when they are on the job.

"She was distraught because of them, not because of me."

"But a relationship with you of all people, Mr. Wrightworth?" Michael asked. "I think you're taking advantage of her position and that the relationship should be prohibited."

I shook my head as Mr. Wrightworth snarled.

"I finally take an interest in someone, and of course you attempt to get in the way," Mr. Wrightworth said.

"Everyone knows you're gay," Michael said boldly back. "The women might ignore that fact because of your face and your mystique, but you are still gay. There's only one other thing you're interested in, and Miss Marten was recovered from just such a contract."

"I beg your pardon?" I asked.

"Mr. Wrightworth is interested in the same things as Nathaniel. He's taken you on a, what do you people call them? Submissive? Mr. Wrightworth is taking advantage of your fragile state to manipulate you into being his submissive. You have absolutely no obligation to submit to the man."

I stared back at Michael. For a very long moment, I struggled with what to say.

"Fuck you," I said finally.

"Excuse me?" Michael responded.

"Fuck you, for trying to over complicate things. Yes, Mr. Wrightworth is mainly gay. Sexuality is a fluid thing, he wants to explore sex with a woman and...it is a safe bet for me, I suppose because it can hardly be serious, but my needs are seen to.

"As to Mr. Wrightworth's other proclivities, also fuck you. What we do behind closed doors is none of your business. If he were fucking me with vegetables or beating me until I cried, it doesn't matter as long as we are both consenting adults. The moment I withdraw consent, and he doesn't listen, Michael, is the moment I will come to you and tell you so that you can finally have your wish and burn him to the ground. But until then? Fuck you.

"My sex life is none of your fucking business."

There was an extremely long silence as I glowered at Michael.

Then Mr. Wrightworth said, "All right, Michael, I will agree that she has recovered at least a bit."

"I agree with Michael," another man said. "But only in that this could be viewed as you taking advantage of her. She's not speaking to her therapist, she has no other friends, the only person she's spoken to is Kathy, which I think we all agree isn't speaking to someone."

"Nathaniel took me to church; I want to go back there, but Mr. Wrightworth says I can't yet. People there were kind to me, I talked to them, and they talked to me."

"Leaving the building is a bad idea," the man said in response. "Not yet, anyhow. But you haven't even gone to the rooftop gardens. The lights in here are made to help with the fact that we live mainly indoors, but being from a slum, surely you crave the outdoors."

"There's a rooftop garden?" I demanded.

"I'll take you there," Mr. Wrightworth muttered.

"I think at the very least, as part of us not protesting too loudly about the relationship, you should give her a proper tour. Another crack she fell through, no doubt."

"I can agree to that," Mr. Wrightworth said.

"But Miss Martin also needs to speak to her therapist and deal with what happened to her. Albert is proceeding with his civil suit against us to take her back."

"He won't win," Mr. Wrightworth purred out with a small smile. "But I see your point, she needs to be as stable as possible because they will, no doubt, demand she attend. They might even call her to the stand."

"And no one's told me anything about that," I said. "What's the review of Nathaniel, how's that going, what's going on outside the building, why am I in limbo?"

"You aren't supposed to know about that," Michael said.

"Why not?" I asked. "It's about me, and it's about my future and what will end up happening to me. So why can't I know about it?"

"As you may have surmised from us speaking, Nathaniel's father is trying to get you back," Mr.

Wrightworth said. "If he sees you out of the Program building, he will assume you are strong enough to stand trial, and he will force the issue before you are ready. He might even use that information to get you back. If you are caught going to church, he will tell the court you were an active participant. He is already arguing that you consented and then withdrew consent when you grew bored and decided to play the victim to explain your absence."

"That's not true," I said, panic lacing my voice.

It uncurled in the pit of my stomach, threatening to spill the contents of my breakfast even as it seemed to clench so tightly that I couldn't seem to breathe. I didn't want to go back to Nathaniel's father.

"If we were to tell you what was going on in the review, his father might use that information as well. You may not be aware, but Nathaniel signed a contract with his father which allows Albert to use anything Nathaniel owns, or any contractee under him, to the extent of the contract. The blank contract was meant to protect you from that, without the terms written out, there would be no way to hold anything to you besides what Nathaniel told his father was going on."

"You told me that there'd be no rape and no torture, you made me say it to a camera."

"I know, why do you think I did that?" Mr. Wrightworth asked.

"Why is it still being reviewed then?" I demanded.

"It's not what the terms of your contract were that he is arguing," Michael said. "What Albert Edwards claims is that there was no rape and no torture. Simply rough sex and participation in what is referred to as 'the lifestyle.' BDSM often results in scrapes, cuts, beatings, and all the rest."

"But I didn't consent to be with Nathaniel's father."

"Any interest shown in Nathaniel could be construed as you being interested in the contract," Mr. Wrightworth said. "It's for your protection that we keep you in the dark. If you show interest in the contract, Albert will use that information to prove his consent theory."

"Right, like we *just* had drunken sex, and I decided in the morning that I didn't want it," I snarled back.

"That's why we're telling you nothing about the process,"

Mr. Wrightworth said.

"It's not right, I'm stuck in limbo and known nothing about anything because the man who raped and tortured me is trying to get me back and no one seems to be outraged about this except me."

"Trust me," Mr. Wrightworth said.

"He's outraged," Michael said. "*We* are outraged, but we aren't going to let that blur our rational thought. If we allowed that, we would lose you, and we are not willing to lose a single contractee, not if we can help it."

The panic returned tenfold. It wasn't just from fear. It was also from not knowing what was going on. It's impossible to make plans, to make an escape route if you don't know what might happen. When there are too many loose possibilities, I become overwhelmed.

"I can't do this right now," I said.

And then I bolted from the room. In the hallway I stopped, one hand on the wall. I only stopped because I didn't know which way to go or where I could hide. The whole world did a sickening spin as the door to the review room opened and closed.

Mr. Wrightworth slipped his arms around me and pulled me away from the wall. He pulled me against his chest, arms tightening reassuringly as I buried my face in his suit jacket. I wanted to clench my hands, but instead found them clenched against his lapels already.

"Come on, let's get you cleaned up," he said, leading me down the hallway.

"What?" I asked.

My voice sounded thick like I had been crying. Confused, I wiped tears from my eyes and looked at Mr. Wrightworth's suit. I had wept on him without realizing it, creating a splotch of wet right in the middle of his suit jacket but he didn't seem to care as he pulled me into a room.

A bathroom.

The door swung shut, and he pulled me to the sinks, turning on the water before he moved to the towel dispenser.

"I'll have to change, but afterwards maybe after a nap as well, I'll come get you for that tour," he said, dabbing at his jacket with a towel as he grabbed several more. With a sigh, he dropped the one towel in the garbage and approached me with the other ones. "I know this is difficult for you, but it's not just you on the line. Going into the civil suit early is a gamble, but I'm fairly sure I could win. It's also about the community."

"What?"

"Nathaniel signed a contract with his father—"

"I know that. They mentioned it before. And a man or two."

"One other person is involved in the contract. The second man is likely Nathaniel's cousin, a young man of twenty who Nathaniel removed from his father's reach and placed into my care to make the boy disappear. Disappear he did, Albert will never find him."

The second man was mentioned very quickly, as if the entire sentence was just one big word.

"Nathaniel told his father to take the man instead of me."

"That was stupid, Nathaniel should have known there was no choice," Mr. Wrightworth muttered, wetting a towel.

He wrung the towel out and used it to dab at my cheeks and face, wiping away the tears.

"He didn't even hesitate before throwing the other man under the bus," I said.

"For you," Mr. Wrightworth murmured comfortingly. "He threw someone else under the bus for you. Even if he has known the other one for some time. Then again, this other one could probably have survived better than you. It wouldn't be a new sensation for him, let's just leave it at that."

If Nathaniel had saved a cousin from his father, hiding a victim from his abuser, then why would he have thrown the other man under the bus like that? One didn't save a victim to toss them back to their abuser to save a person they barely knew.

"I survived."

"You did, you did remarkably better than I thought you would. Then again, I also thought Albert would take Nathaniel and ship you back here. Never did I consider the fact that his father would be prowling so close to home. That shows escalation and probably insanity.

"I just need you to hang on until the end. Once the civil suit is thrown out, we can proceed with legal charges. The only reason they've put that off is because they haven't quite decided whether or not the contract was broken. If I can prove that, I can have him charged with assault and sexual assault, kidnapping, detaining against the will and numerous other things. You need to hold on."

"I don't like not knowing."

"I know," he said quietly, throwing out the damp towel. "I know you like to know what is going to happen. You like having rules and then following those rules."

"I mean, what's going on with Nathaniel? Why hasn't he called or done anything? Was it me, did I do something wrong? Does he not want me back?"

"Oh, Darling," Mr. Wrightworth said, pulling me into his arms. "You've done nothing wrong."

"And you still won't tell me!" I shouted, smacking Mr. Wrightworth's chest.

"No, I will not," Mr. Wrightworth said, capturing my hand when I tried to slap him again. His other hand darted out, wrapping around my throat as he twisted my arm until I cried out. "How I wish I could tie you up and beat you until you submitted."

"You're hurting me," I cried.

Mr. Wrightworth released my arm, then my throat. I held my arm to my chest, running my hand over the spot where things had been pulled.

"You're tense, is why that hurt in that way," Mr. Wrightworth said. "When you relax your body can move in such a way without damage. You need a hot bath and a massage, both of which I can help with tonight after our session."

"I'm not tense," I said, pulling away from Mr. Wrightworth.

"Does your back hurt?" Mr. Wrightworth asked.

"Well, yes, but I got used to sleeping on the mattress from heaven that Nathaniel gave me. Sleeping on that cot in the room is like a rock now."

"You're tense," Mr. Wrightworth said. "Did you want something to help you settle?"

"Settle?" I asked.

Mr. Wrightworth went to the door and locked it. He returned to me as he worked at his belt. For a moment I thought he was going to ask me to kneel.

I wanted him to ask me to kneel.

Blame Nathaniel or a hundred other things, but the possibility of being that close to a man was almost too much. It was one of those things that Albert hadn't done to me. I had thought it was because he was afraid of being bitten—because I would have bitten it off—but there were toys for that. Special gags which kept the mouth open and he chose not to use them.

The belt came off, and Mr. Wrightworth bent it in half. My breath hitched in my throat as I realized what Mr. Wrighworth had meant. While the idea of oral enticed me, the idea of being bent over and struck by this firm Adonis of a man made me wet instantly.

"You said you wouldn't until I could be tied," I said.

The excitement that coursed through my veins was too much. How long had it been since I had a good, balanced strike to my backside? What *wouldn't* I do for that? Every bit of me tingled with anticipation.

"Come here," Mr. Wrightworth said, motioning me forward with two fingers.

Not quite believing what he was offering, I edged towards him. Mr. Wrightworth took me gently with his left hand, pushing me forward with his right. Supporting me with his left, he bent slightly.

"Mainly, I just want to prove how tense you are," he said. "I think I know the correct measure, but as we've not properly played, my aim may be off. You get one strike."

"No, you have to even it out," I said.

"What?" he asked.

"It has to be even on both sides, or it gets worse very quickly," I said.

"Mm, you really do make that easy, don't you?" Mr. Wrightworth said with a chuckle. "Two strikes then. Let me know if it's too hard."

Mr. Wrightworth's right hand ran over my backside. Not because he was interested in it, but because he knew how to play me. The hand roving over me made the anticipation coil in the pit of my stomach. When the hand left, leaving cold where there had once been heat, I shuddered out a breath.

"Please," I said when the belt didn't fall.

"Ohhh, you are so good at that tone, but it's 'please, Master' or there will be trouble," Mr. Wrightworth said.

"Please, Master, strike me."

Mr. Wrightworth shuddered out a breath. He took a moment to steady himself, and then the belt fell. I pushed back into the swing, flinching forward as the sting bloomed across my backside.

And then I writhed.

Oh, how I wished it would go on all afternoon. How I wanted it. I thought back to the gym in Nathaniel's estate and longed for that afternoon delight once more.

The second strike fell, and I moaned. Mr. Wrightworth's hand moved down my backside and over the flesh he had just hit. Ever so slowly he helped me straighten, then tugged my dress down and smoothed out the sides as I trembled.

"Did you like that?" Mr. Wrightworth asked.

"Yes, Master," I said.

"You need to thank me whenever I do that," Mr. Wrightworth murmured.

"Thank you, Master."

"Good, Darling," Mr. Wrightworth said with a smile, sliding his belt back on. "Just think of that when I have you tied up. Maybe that will make it easier for you to get through it."

"Please, can I have some more?" I asked, biting my bottom lip and smiling slowly.

Mr. Wrightworth went a funny sort of red colour. He frowned ever so slightly.

"That should not have almost worked," he grumbled, then jabbed a finger at me. "You do not get more until you can be tied for more than an hour without panicking."

Chapter Seven

That night I had to go to Mr. Wrightworth's place a little later than usual. I saw my therapist and talked to her a little bit. I don't want to go over what we discussed. She has been kind enough to keep silent, even when the media pressed her for information. Suffice to say, I did end up opening up about my frustrations because they were on my mind when I walked into the room. The one bit I will mention was shown in court, but only after Mr. Wrightworth saw it during an audit of my interactions inside the Program and asked my permission.

I don't recall exactly how we reached that place. We had been talking about the review and she asked, probably for the millionth time:

"How did that make you feel?"

"Frustrated. Angry. I can't even protest because if I protested, it might be construed as wanting to go back and then I'd just... I'd end up back there. I don't want to end up back there. I want to fulfill my contract. No one will even tell me if I'll be able to."

"It upsets you that you can't do what you promised you would do?"

"Yes! He didn't break his word, his father did, and now it's some sort of he said, she said. He says I gave consent then cried rape."

"Did you?"

"No!"

"That was an awfully fast and loud protest," she murmured, pen pausing above the pad of paper. "Do you, perhaps, feel as if you did cry rape because Nathaniel's sexual preferences had trained you to give into such feelings?"

I stared at her for a long moment, frowning as I tried to understand what she even meant. "Just because I agreed to let Nathaniel tie me up and spank me, doesn't mean that every Tom, Dick, and Sally can do the same. I decided to let Nathaniel do that, not his father. That's like saying that just because I'm sexually active, it's okay for any man just to bend me over and have his way with me."

"Some men do view it that way. Do you take their comments to heart?"

"No, but they can't act on that belief."

"You're afraid what he wants will come to be."

I'm afraid I'm weak.

"Mr. Wrightworth says it won't, he also says I should trust him."

"Since when are you two in a relationship?" she asked, stiffening suddenly.

"I suppose since last night or something," I said with a shrug. "How did you know that?"

As it turned out, Mr. Wrightworth would only tell his subs to trust him. Anyone else, he would tell them to trust the Program. His therapist was the only one he trusted not to say something because she was the only one who hadn't. The turn over rate for therapists in the Program was a little high, but they were the only ones who, for whatever reason, couldn't be trusted to keep their mouths shut.

I left her office feeling hollowed out. When Mr. Wrightworth let me in, I managed to hold on just until the door closed.

"I am a victim," I said, and then burst into tears.

"Damn, I was really looking forward to beating that out of you," Mr. Wrightworth said, then smiled that Cheshire cat smile.

Which made me laugh just a little bit. It was a silly thing, but I thought it funny that I had messed up his plan for me. The fact that he seemed to also believe it was funny made the tears stop.

Mr. Wrightworth approached me and set his hands on my

upper arms as he looked me up and down. Then he leaned forward and kissed my forehead. It was just a comforting peck before he pulled away and looked me over again.

"You were a victim, I'm going to help you become a survivor," he said. "I have dinner almost ready. I don't think you're going to put up with being tied today. Too much has gone on. So it's into a hot bath for you, missy."

"I want to try," I said.

"No, not even going to," Mr. Wrightworth said, pulling away and heading into the kitchen.

I followed him, protesting as we went. "Why not? I think I'm up for it."

"You don't believe that you're up for it," he grumbled, shutting off the stove. "You're thinking about the bathroom this morning and desperately wanting more. I, however, am going to stick to my word from now on, and you don't get anything more until you can be tied. You're trying to push your limit, and I can't have that."

"How do you know?"

"It's written all over you."

"No, it's not."

Which is never a good thing to say to a man like him. I should have known better by then.

He paused with a spoon over the pot and eyed me. The silence stretched out as I adjusted my weight and looked at the counter near me. I didn't notice anything on the counter, just looked at the clean faux marble rather than make eye contact with Mr. Wrightworth again.

"You've got one arm across your breasts, gripping your other arm so tightly that your knuckles are white. You've shifted your weight onto your bad leg, and anytime you mention being tied, you look at my knife on the counter. You could try that route, but..." the man sucked in a breath. "Well, that might just be the exception to the rule. Fucking someone who has attacked me and I've bested, is very much a turn on for me."

"I'm not, that's not why I was—" the words came stumbling out of my mouth.

How did he see what I didn't realize I was doing?

I had been glancing at the knife, which was well within

reach, handle facing me. As that dawned on me, I realized that the knife was also clean, as was the cutting board. Mr. Wrightworth was scooping rice with canned chicken into the bowls. Another slum meal which required absolutely no chopping.

He had placed it there on purpose.

I shifted away from the knife, aware that every time I stepped into Mr. Wrightworth's kitchen, I ended up standing in the same spot. The other place I chose was across the kitchen. Mr. Wrightworth's eyebrow quirked up as his hazel eyes drifted to something on the counter, then to me.

A frying pan sat on the counter, handle facing me.

"I'm not trying to kill you!" I protested.

Mr. Wrightworth smiled and handed me a bowl of rice. "I've noticed that you drift towards items which could be used as weapons. You get all giddy in the play room, all sorts to hurt a person there. Hm, maybe I should borrow Michie for you. He's a full on masochist, loves being beaten by a woman."

"I'm a submissive," I said sternly, marching to the kitchen table.

"At the moment," Mr. Wrightworth said. "See, sexuality was explained to me like submission and domination was. In the public eye, for example, Nathaniel is dominant, but for several years he was submissive in private. He quite enjoyed being submissive, but not who he submitted to."

"Because it was a man."

"And because it made him uncomfortable, being underneath this person," Mr. Wrightworth hesitated as we sat, then smiled. "And not just because he was literally under this person. Mayfair is another example. Or Nicole. They both started as submissives, then switched to dommes. Nicole can switch back, but only for the right Dom. Has to be male, has to be sadistic. She and I have a standing agreement, because—as you put it—sometimes the pressure gets to be too much. It makes her itch under her skin and causes her to make mistakes. Then she starts running into things, getting hurt, even falling down a flight of stairs."

"So you beat her so she can resettle and get back to work."

"No one in the community knows that, so don't go blabbing."

"I didn't plan on it, but I'm a submissive," I said. "I like submitting."

"To myself and Nathaniel," Mr. Wrightworth said pointedly. "So far you like submitting to sadists. I think I will, I'll borrow Michie or another male sub. Oh, oh yes. There is a male sub I'd like to borrow for a night. You can have your fun, and then I can have mine."

I poked at my food for a moment, wondering why that bothered me.

"I don't like it when you talk about sex with other people in front of me," I said finally, daring to meet those hazel eyes.

They held no judgment as Mr. Wrightworth said, "Right, you didn't even like the possibility of Nathaniel playing with someone else. We'll have to work on that. I might focus solely on a new sub, but I always end up with multiple partners. I like threesomes. They're so messy."

"I don't like it still," I muttered.

"What if it were Nathaniel?"

I whimpered, then gave my head a shake. "The one time you want to talk about him is a threesome?"

"I've had him before. It's quite exquisite to watch him writhe. There's also Michie, but he's such an obedient one that I hardly derive any pleasure from it. He does struggle on command, but even that lacks a certain quality."

I ate a little food for something to do. Mr. Wrightworth watched me for a while, then lifted his spoon and began eating himself. We didn't speak again until the dishes were cleared away.

"You didn't answer the question," Mr. Wrightworth said, sitting across from me once more.

"What is with you two?" I all but shouted. "He asked the same thing."

"I know he did, you told me about it, remember?"

"You hot for him or something?"

Mr. Wrightworth arched an eyebrow at me. I growled and tried not to sound as irritable as I felt.

"Great, I get the only gay man who's attracted to straight

men," I said. "I thought you two were friends."

"We are."

"Now it's just getting creepy," I said.

I *knew* gay men didn't always fall in love with their friends. Making such a broad comment was like saying men and women couldn't be friends because they ended up falling in love—or at least lust.

"There is a great deal of history between him and I that I will not explain to you," Mr. Wrightworth said. "But I asked you a question, and you didn't answer. You have to answer me when I ask you a question."

"You've never said that was a rule."

"Protocol," Mr. Wrightworth corrected. "But you are correct, I seem to have neglected to mention it before. So I'll trade you the answer for the reason I'm asking that particular question. Only, you have to answer first."

"Maybe if it were Nathaniel, then yes, I'd be tempted into at threesome," I said.

"He'd be the meat, we'd be the bread," Mr. Wrightworth said with a toothy smile.

I opened my mouth to protest but found the words dying in my throat. The image that popped into my head tried to reconcile what I knew about sex and how a sandwich would look. I knew a couple of ways two people could come together, but three was still a little confusing.

When the image finally aligned in my head, I whimpered out a sound.

Somehow that made it better.

Women were always portrayed to me as needing all the attention during sex. The pornographies I had watched up until that point almost always had threesomes, and it was two men and a woman. In those videos, however, the men took turns, there was nothing in them that did what Mr. Wrightworth was describing. The few that had the other balance always lost my attention quickly because two women pleasing one man always seemed humdrum to me. I know it's a male fantasy but from my point of view...

It's a waste of a good time to have two women playing with one man.

"I asked the question because I knew it would make you

uncomfortable," Mr. Wrightworth said, a finger rubbing across his lips as I glared at him. The finger almost hid the quirky little smile he had. "Not because I'm sexually interested in Nathaniel. The man is a Dom on nearly the same level as me, I have no interest in tying him up. That would be an abuse of the trust between him and me."

"What about Nate?" I asked boldly.

"Oh, I'd tie him up in a heartbeat," Mr. Wrightworth said. "But he and I have a standing agreement, just like Nicole and me. Only he hasn't used his end of the deal yet."

"And you've been careful not to use yours?" I asked.

"Finding a willing sub is easier than finding a Dom you can trust. After Nate had been released by his Master, we made the standing agreement. That's not the sort of thing you just walk away from cold turkey."

"How long has it been?"

"Three years since he last had the urge, but even then, I wasn't around. Nathaniel ended up getting drunk and putting himself through a glass door. He's just damned lucky Nicole decided to grace him with her presence because she too was feeling the urge, but I wasn't around for it."

"When do you ever leave the Program building?"

"I leave every six months for one week," Mr. Wrightworth said, standing. "Which will be in one month's time. We will go to church before I leave, and when I get back. You are to ask no questions of where I have been during that week, or what has gone on. Am I clear?"

"Perfectly, but does that mean I can ask where you've gone every other day?" I asked.

"As long as it doesn't involve Nathaniel, yes, you may."

Creepy behaviour.

The warning flashed inside my head. Creepy was the only term I could place to it, but I knew something was up, something was weird about his week off. It might have just been him doing a trust exercise, or maybe he just went off into the woods for a week and slept and drank and got all the dirty, stupid things out of his system. There seemed to be too much perfect about him for Mr. Wrightworth to be real.

He didn't even look rumpled in a faded t-shirt and old sweatpants. He might as well have been wearing a suit, for the way he made that clothing work.

I stood and followed Mr. Wrightworth as he walked away. He went back to the kitchen and to the bathroom, where he immediately turned on the taps of the tub. I watched awkwardly from the door as he added Epsom salt, bubble bath, even a bath bomb, to the water. I don't know what scents were in the items that went into the bath, but it resulted in a mildly floral scent with a bit of citrus. It as a little strange, but somehow it worked.

He lit candles that were pre-placed around the room with a long lighter. The flickering flames cast a low, yellow glow over everything.

Then he produced a washcloth and soap. He turned to me as if expecting something.

"Oh, right," he muttered. "Training time."

"What?" I snapped, pulling away when he approached me.

"Bath is a treat," he said sternly, moving to the side as he motioned to the tub. "When you are getting a gift and you know it, you need to react accordingly. So in this instance, when I turned to face you, I expected to find you naked and willing to accept the treat.

"Because you can't get in the bath with your clothing on, not because I want to see you naked. Which I have, many times."

"I know that," I muttered at my feet as I fiddled with the buttons on the front of my dress.

"Take it off, Darling," Mr. Wrightworth said quietly.

The dress came off, and I immediately covered myself with my hands as I glanced up at Mr. Wrightworth. The man dragged his two front teeth over his bottom lip and made a small, barely audible sound.

"No, that haircut has got to go," he growled. "I don't care what they say. You look like a boy, young man at most."

His words made me choke on the very air as I realized why he had bitten his bottom lip.

In the right light, I look like a man. Nice to know.

"You don't look like a man," Mr. Wrightworth said suddenly, as if reading my mind. "Your face in the candle light doesn't hold onto the feminine beauty. It casts odd angles. Neck down, very much a woman no matter the light. Get in the tub."

"In, in that tub?" I asked, jabbing a finger at the bubble filled ceramic tub.

"Yes, that tub."

Grumbling, I went over and stepped into the tub. The heat was just a little too warm, but oh so pleasant once I adjusted to it. I stepped the rest of the way into the tub and sunk into the water. There was something oily in the water, but not in a bad way. It just made my legs slick as they grazed over one another.

Mr. Wrightworth disappeared for a moment and returned with a book, which he handed to me.

"Wash then read the book. You are not to leave that tub until the water is cool."

"Why?" I asked.

"It's what a bath is."

"A bath is to get clean... never mind, it's a rich people bath."

"Exactly, read the book, soak in the water. I'm going to turn on a little music and sit outside the door. No one is coming in here but for me, understand?"

"Yes, sir... uh, Master. Yes, Master."

Mr. Wrightworth reached as if to pat my head. As his fingers flowed over my hair, to the back of my head, they tangled in the short locks. He yanked my head back until he appeared almost upside down. I tried not to struggle, well aware that ceramic while wet was dangerous. My hands did grip the sides of the tub tightly, trying to take the weight off of my hair.

"A Sir, in my book, can be tested. A Master is the be all, end all of your existence. Which am I?"

"My Master," I whimpered out.

"Don't forget it again."

Mr. Wrightworth released me, which all but dropped me back into the water. I managed to save the book, having at least some thought inside my head, but the rest of me went under the water. If I hadn't seen the difference before, I certainly did at that moment. When I came up for air, Mr. Wrightworth handed me a towel for me to dry my face.

"Don't worry if the book goes under, I can replace it," he said, kneeling by the tub as if he hadn't just yanked me halfway out. "The only ones who can call me 'sir' work for me, you do not. I don't like hearing that come from your mouth."

"It was a slip of the tongue."

"You want Nathaniel, I get that, I do, but he's not here, and you need to respect me."

"I do respect you," I said desperately.

"Are you panicking?"

"Yes!"

"Hm, all right, we can save the title lecture for another night, soak in the tub. Masturbate if it pleases you, but you aren't getting out until the water cools. Or if you have to go to the bathroom, I suppose," Mr. Wrightworth cast a sidelong glance to the toilet, then looked back at me. "Bathroom breaks are never off limits."

"If I have to go, I have to tell you, and if I lie about it, I'll regret it," I said.

"Good, enjoy the bath, most women do," Mr. Wrightworth said. And then just sat there, awkwardly. He bent his head towards me and gave me an expectant look.

I frowned back. Then it clued in. "Is this a thank you moment?"

"It is."

"Oh, I'm sorry. Thank you, Master."

"You'll learn," Mr. Wrightworth said, then stood and left the bathroom.

Thanking him every time is going to get annoying fast.

With a sigh, I went about washing myself and then tried just to lay in the hot water. It was nice, it was, but I wasn't used to doing nothing with my time. Frustrated by the lack of movement, I reached over the tub and picked up the book, which had, in the end, suffered some minor water damage along the one edge. I opened it to page one and started reading.

By page ten I was hooked but horrified all at the same time. It wasn't just a book. It wasn't even romance. No, Mr. Wrightworth had chosen an erotica for me to read. An erotica. What's the difference between that and my life's story? Well, for starters there was a lot more sex. Like one sex act every chapter, at least. They just got regular sex out of the way in the second chapter. And the chapters weren't that long, a few pages. There was barely any plot to it.

"Darling?" Mr. Wrightworth asked as he knelt beside the tub again.

I jumped in place, splashing water everywhere and dropping the book into the water.

"You seemed engrossed," he muttered, then reached over and picked the book out of the tub, watching the water slough off of it. "A little too engrossed. When was the last time you masturbated?"

I blushed at the question. For a moment I thought it was no one's business but my own, but then I remembered that it was Mr. Wrightworth's business and that he had just asked me a question.

And I was still staring at him stupidly a full minute later.

Maybe this is why he doesn't like female subs, because we all just get embarrassed and won't tell him what's going on.

"Not in, um," I frowned and looked away as I tried to recall. "Not since Nathaniel's place."

"You haven't even made certain that all your parts still work?" Mr. Wrightworth asked, giving me a look as if I were crazy. "If you were a man you would have done it with people watching, just to be sure nothing was damaged."

"Well, I'm not a man and a man probably wouldn't have ..." I trailed off as I struggled to say what I wanted to say.

"Wouldn't have been raped, is what you were going to say," Mr. Wrightworth muttered, reaching between my feet to pull the plug. "I've got my hands on something I'm told all women enjoy."

"Does it vibrate?" I asked, my belly doing a twinge as I thought of the last vibrating toy that had been used on me.

"It does," Mr. Wrightworth purred out. "Male subs don't like this, they believe it to be unfair and some scream bloody murder. They can't get their heads wrapped around the sensation. Come on, there's a robe on the back of the door there, put it on and come to the bedroom."

"Why?" I squeaked out.

"Because I told you to," he called out as he left the bathroom.

I stepped out of the almost empty tub, wiped my feet on the bath mat and headed out of the bathroom, remembering at the last moment to grab the robe. The door to the bedroom was open, and I peeped in but didn't take the final step.

"I said you could come in," Mr. Wrightworth said, sitting on the edge of the bed.

The rest of the apartment was sparse. It barely looked lived in. The bedroom wasn't really an exception, besides a digital photo frame that faced the bed from the table on the side closest to the door. I stepped in, and Mr. Wrightworth motioned to the door behind me. I turned awkwardly and closed the door, then looked to him for guidance.

"Take off the robe and lay face down on the—" Mr. Wrightworth hesitated, eyes flowing over me. "What exactly did he do to you?"

"Nathaniel did," I squeaked out, surprised words made it out of my throat.

I was thinking of the night Nathaniel called me to kneel, of my reward afterward. Mr. Wrightworth stared back at me, mouth partially open and a finger pointing towards the bed. He frowned ever so slowly, then gave himself a shake.

"Vibrator, right, this isn't about the vibrator, just do as I asked you."

I moved to obey, walking around the bed to the other side. Sliding onto the bed, face down, I moved my hands under the pillow and groaned. Mr. Wrightworth had a good bed in his room, one of the perks of being his rank. It wasn't hard like mine was and didn't feel weird. It felt amazing and comfortable but firm at the same time.

Not too hard, not too soft, just right.

"Hopefully the heat did some of the work," he said, straddling me.

"What are you doing?" I asked, suddenly tense.

"Getting a better angle, what did you think I was doing?"

He has his pants on and is gay. There's no candlelight either.

I forced myself to relax.

"Darling, what did you think I was doing?"

"I was afraid you might do something," I said, burying my face into the pillow.

"I couldn't hear that, because you muffled it by face planting into my pillow, so I'm going to assume you said that you thought I was going to give you a massage," he hesitated and bent over me, then returned a moment later.

I heard the distinct sound of semi-liquid coming out of a tube.

"Nope," I said, turning as best I can. "No, that's not going to work."

Mr. Wrightworth blinked at me, then held out the tube. It was hand lotion, not lubrication like I had thought.

"Most people use oil," he said. "But you just washed, and I don't want oil all over my clean bed. What exactly did you think I was squeezing out?"

"Lubrication."

"Just because I'm gay doesn't mean I'm automatically going to..." Mr. Wrightworth trailed off, seemingly connecting the dots. "This is hand lotion, Darling. I'll get a pump version for beside the bed, for next time. This time, you can see it with your eyes. May I?"

"I suppose," I said, dropping face first onto the bed again. "But I don't see what's so—oh."

Mr. Wrightworth's strong fingers worked their way into my flesh. They found every knot, every pressure point on my back and some sensitive spots I hadn't about which I hadn't known. He worked on my back for I don't know how long. And then loose and relaxed as I was, he pulled me against him and shut off the light. The heat from his chest just made it all the better.

Just before I fell asleep, I recall looking up at the ceiling and seeing the stars for the first time. It's against the rules to alter the apartments in any fashion, at all. Tape on a wall was allowed, but no tacks, no nails or screws or new paint jobs. Everything had to be approved, and if anything was spotted, it was removed immediately.

Mr. Wrightworth had painted the Milky Way on his ceiling in glow in the dark paint. The paint was invisible when the lights were on, during inspections and the like.

No one else ever reported it, because no one else had ever been in his bedroom before.

But I remember seeing those stars and just thinking about how comfortable I felt, and how I never wanted to get up again.

Chapter Eight

Almost two weeks later, I made it through Mr. Wrightworth's little test. I hadn't called him to stop, but the fear was still there and writhing inside of me as he came around and unbound my hands. He rewarded me with a little kiss on the lips, and a piece of dark chocolate, which I hadn't had before.

Dark chocolate is so much better than milk chocolate.

And the kiss was just lacking.

There's one thing Nathaniel didn't learn from Mr. Wrightworth.

I wasn't certain if the little touches and caresses he had shown me were because he was training me, training himself, or making an effort to give me something to talk about, if anyone to ever ask about our relationship.

"Would you like to negotiate a play session?"

"Yes, please, Master."

The skin all down my back tingled as Mr. Wrightworth smiled. He handed me the clothing I had shed, and I pulled the items back on, then followed him out to the living room.

"I will introduce the plug to start," he said as he sat down. "I've also been sorting through the Doms and talking to some few that might catch your eye. They understand this is a slow and hesitant process, but they've agreed to attend the first meeting you will be at, just so that you can see them and they can see you."

"I'm not ready yet to move onto another Dom."

"And I'm not saying you are, but I'd like to introduce the idea of you being ready."

"Is this the same meeting where people will just pin me down whenever it pleases you?"

Mr. Wrightworth smiled again. "Yes, it is. I still feed off of you being terrified, even if it is a very real, very wrong reason that you are afraid. I can't help my reaction."

"Well, then you know..." I said as I pointed towards the play room.

"That you were terrified? Yes, that was just delightful. Carrying that edge while I hurt you more is, well, it's practically a dream come true for me. If only you were male, I'd keep you all to myself. The point wasn't to get rid of the terror entirely. That could take years. Neither of us has the patience to wait years. The point of the exercise was to get you to the point where you wouldn't call out your safe word because being tied no longer crossed the line. It's a type of immersion therapy.

"Not everyone in the community has suffered, but some have, and they've had great success rehabilitating themselves with play."

"But can we wait on the plug?" I asked, shifting uncomfortably on the couch.

Mr. Wrightworth watched me for a long time, so long that I thought he'd say no, before he answered.

"We can wait for one session. We both desperately need this, if you think the plug will be too much, it will be."

"I do have to see the actual doctor, this time, Nicole said, it's the start of my six-month gynecological health or something?"

"That's in a week, isn't it?" he asked, then hesitated as I nodded. "Perfect timing, I still expect you to masturbate after each session. In fact, it just came in."

"The vibrating toy?" I asked, trying not to sound too excited.

"No, your personal toy," he said, then stood and left the living room.

He returned a moment later with a box. With a frown, I took the box, which was just a cardboard box, nothing fancy, and opened it. From inside I withdrew a silicone toy still in a sealed bag. I gawked at the thing, it wasn't quite a penis, at least no penis I had ever seen. There were ridges and bumps, and the head was practically shaped like an arrow. It also had pastel colouring to it in many different shades.

My eyes shifted from the toy to Mr. Wrightworth.

"This is huge!" I protested.

"It's smaller than Nathaniel is," Mr. Wrightworth countered quickly. "If you need to reassure yourself, you could always put it in your mouth. The mouth doesn't exactly change sizes."

"Why couldn't I have, like, a normal one?"

"You know why."

Because if it was shaped like a human penis, I might fantasize about Mr. Wrightworth?

"I did quite a bit of research and women seem to prefer this model. It is yours, and you will use it to do as I've asked you. There's lubrication in the box."

"But the controllers are watching."

"There are only three of them, they can't watch everything, all the time," Mr. Wrightworth said. "And I didn't say do it where no one can see you, I was giving you a command. You are supposed to thank me for this, and not sound like you're bitchy."

"Thank you, Master," I said, sounding more glum than annoyed.

I had hoped for something more. I certainly didn't want that to be the solution to the sex problem. Using a toy was *not* the same as having a man.

"You need to use that toy in the next week. Doctors can tell if you've had sex. Rumours are spreading that I'm gay, so any oddities will probably be dismissed as my not being able to find the right hole. But there has to be signs of sexual activity or there will be questions."

"Yes, Master," I said, closing the box with a sigh.

It was not what I was expecting at all.

"You do remember how to masturbate, don't you?"

"Of course I do! But I've never used something like this before. Nathaniel did, so I guess it's possible."

"On that topic..." Mr. Wrightworth hesitated as my breath hitched in my throat. I looked up and realized he had hesitated to watch my reaction. "What were the terms he was using, for the orgasm training?"

He did that on purpose!

"He would say, 'come for me, Darling' and sometimes he'd add in a 'please.' Why do you ask?"

"Come for me, Darling," Mr. Wrightworth said in a commanding tone.

To which I shook my head.

"No, it wasn't like that at all. It was like he was begging me to."

"Now there's a tone he knows I can't do," Mr. Wrightworth grumbled. "I will practice on my own and see if I can't find something similar. Once the training has been laid, it's best to keep up on it rather than rebuild from the ground up. And, from what I hear, you reacted quite eagerly to his training in that area."

"Yes," I said with a blush. "I did like it."

"Good, nearly every Dom wants a sub who comes on command, but few have the patience to do the training. So, being a sub who can, makes you a luxury commodity. We'll work on that, but again, not this session. This one, let's see..."

Mr. Wrightworth went about setting up the foundation of the play session with some little input on my part. He explained each term that I didn't understand. I interrupted a few times to ask things be added.

Such as, I like it when, after being struck by a crop, it slides between my legs. Mr. Wrightworth agreed eagerly to most of my changes, which really should have told me that I was playing right into him. Once a Dom knows what a sub does and does not like, he'll either give or withhold depending on his mood and what he wanted to bring out of the sub. That first session, however, was about releasing pent up emotions and giving me pretty well whatever I wanted as a re-introduction into the lifestyle.

He made absolutely no promises to be gentle with me. Unlike Nathaniel, Mr. Wrightworth knew I could take a vicious beating. He had watched all of the videos by that point, though I still didn't know he had even seen them.

We went over everything in great detail. Including the fact that, were the opportunity to present itself and I was good, he would make every effort to 'force' an orgasm. He figured it would be difficult for me to come while strung up. It was a fair assumption, I suppose.

Going through my next day, I writhed in my seat. There was an ache deep in my belly as I thought about the events of that night. By the time the night came, I was practically whimpering with every step.

He rain checked me.

Rain checked! Like it wasn't something I've been begging for!

Our event was pushed to the next night because of an emergency meeting. That was all I was told, in a letter he slipped under my door. I was furious.

And wet and horny.

He hadn't said I couldn't help myself outside of his commands, so I tried that.

The toy was marvellous, but it didn't help in the end. Not because things weren't working, either. I'd hit that edge but not be able to go over it. There was something missing, which resulted in my giving up in annoyance.

It wasn't exactly sexual frustration that was bothering me, resulting in me horny, wet, and a great deal more frustrated.

The next day, I took a strip off of Kathy for wasting my time yet again on a trivial item. I told her that if she ever made an accusation of such a sort again, I'd file a formal complaint. I cannot for the life of me remember what she was talking about.

Work dragged by, I was wrapping up my second audit and was just sitting around, waiting for people to return my phone calls. By the time I got off work, I was so cranky that I marched straight to Mr. Wrightworth's apartment. I arrived as he was unlocking his door and he frowned at me.

Then gave me that Cheshire cat smile of his.

"Dinner is at six. I will see you then."

And he closed the door on my face.

By that time I knew he was a creature of ritual, but that didn't make me feel any better. I had to go back down to my apartment to shower and wait.

And wait, and wait.

I hate waiting around.

When I finally got back up to his apartment, I was

tempted to make myself late on purpose, but I didn't want to lose the opportunity.

I knocked, and Mr. Wrightworth answered the door in a pair of sweatpants and a t-shirt. He stepped to the side, and I followed him in.

"Have you eaten?" he asked.

"No," I responded.

Mr. Wrightworth closed and locked the door. He headed immediately into the kitchen and opened the stove, pulling a casserole dish out of the oven with his bare hands.

"Uh..." I said.

"It's fine," he growled.

"Do you not have feeling in your hands?" I asked, tapping the casserole dish quickly to check the temperature.

"Yes, it is hot."

"With your bare hands?" I demanded, taking his hands in my own.

I had never touched Mr. Wrightworth's hands before. He had grazed my wrists as he tied me, but I hadn't registered the feeling of them. They were calloused and scarred, lacing white lines that ran all the way across the palm. There were little pinpricks here and there. I had never seen scarring of that sort before. With a finger, I traced one of those lines.

Mr. Wrightworth made a sound and yanked his hand out of mine.

"Sorry," I mumbled and turned to the cupboard to pull down some plates.

People pulled away when you crossed a line. I had never crossed a line with Mr. Wrightworth and wasn't interested in damaging our relationship. It worked, whatever in the hell it was that we were doing. I didn't want to screw it up by accidentally crossing a line.

Mr. Wrightworth slid up behind me, the heat flowing from his body made me shudder as I turned awkwardly in his arms, the plates in my hands. He pinned me against the counter with his hips and lowered his head. Since being released from medical, I had begun watching a great many romance movies and television shows. I knew what that head lowering meant, and raised my face slightly.

As our lips came in contact, I shuddered. His tongue

delved into my mouth as his arms wrapped around me. The kiss was vaguely familiar, better than it had been the last time he had tried to kiss me.

He's been practising.

Mr. Wrightworth's hands tightened on my hips as the kiss deepened. I moaned against his lips.

With Nathaniel?

That was what was familiar about his kiss. It was how Nathaniel kissed, but not quite. Like Mr. Wrightworth was trying to learn how to imitate that kiss, but hadn't had enough practice yet.

I swayed as Mr. Wrightworth pulled away and took the plates from me. I leaned heavily on the counter, trying to catch my breath and wrap my head around the idea.

One day Mr. Wrightworth kissed one way. Then he kissed a great deal more like Nathaniel. How, why? A million things went through my mind as Mr. Wrightworth placed food on both of the plates.

When he turned to me, I put a hand to my lips and stared at him.

"Why?" I asked.

Why the sudden change?

"You didn't hurt me. I wanted to make that clear," he said. "It was a strange sensation, like a tickling. I'm not ticklish."

"Oh," I said weakly but gave my head a shake.

"What?" he sighed, holding a plate out to me.

"You kiss differently than you did before," I managed to get out, taking the plate.

Mr. Wrightworth smiled and walked into the dining room with his food. I stood still for another moment before I rushed after him. We sat and ate in silent, then Mr. Wrightworth stood and took the dishes away. He returned and sat across from me.

He hadn't specified when or how the play session would begin, only that it would happen. I took my lead from him and tried to relax as I waited.

"As to the kiss," Mr. Wrightworth said. "I noticed your lackluster response to my last kiss and chose to practice. Nicole suggested it, and she is typically correct about this sort of thing. I think we can both agree that Nicole, of all people, knows how to pleasure not only herself but other women."

"I haven't seen her with other women, so I'll take your word on it."

"Was it better?"

"It was..." I struggled to find an appropriate word. "Familiar."

Mr. Wrightworth's mouth opened slightly, then snapped shut. He frowned ever so slightly as he studied me sitting across from him.

"We are not permitted to talk about him."

"I'm not trying to talk about him, but, well, obviously that's something you didn't teach Nathaniel," I said, then made a face. "Sorry, that wasn't nice of me to say."

"No, he's always had a natural talent for kissing," Mr. Wrightworth grumbled.

Actually grumbled. There was an irritability to that grumble that startled me into a long moment of silence.

I blinked back at him, watching how the man was suddenly uncomfortable.

"Oh my God, you've kissed him too?" I asked.

"Yes, I kissed him."

"You two are so complicated," I muttered.

"You kiss during play," Mr. Wrightworth said, then his face twisted ever so slightly, and he added, "And during threesomes. It's a part of sex."

"I get that," I said. "It's more of, you kissed him, and you've not found anyone else who kisses like him. Damn, that's not a good sign. You've probably kissed a lot of people. I like the way he kisses."

"I'd say you like a great deal more than just the way he kisses," Mr. Wrightworth said. "It's been almost three months. No one has mentioned him to you, but you keep bringing him up."

Panic started to overwhelm me. What if he had moved on? What if Nathaniel already had another sub?

What if he didn't even remember my name?

"Is this the talk where you tell me I need to not bring him up?" I asked. "Because technically I didn't bring him up, you did."

"It's not a bad thing that you ask about him. People just think it odd."

"People meaning..."

"Your therapist, so many others who are involved in your case. They tell me I should be worried about your mental health, so I've chosen to worry."

"How do I be healthier then?" I asked.

"I don't know," he muttered. "You obviously still see him in everything. If I meant to become your Dom, your one, and only Master, I would think that you couldn't submit to me because obviously you are still submitting to him. The whole reason we didn't just wait and pass you off to Nicole for rehabilitation was that we didn't think you'd accept her."

"Nathaniel said you were the addendum," I said, thinking on that for a moment. "Do you think I'm still following the contract because that was the only thing that could have saved me?"

"Maybe, I also think it's absolutely adorable," Mr. Wrightworth said with a small smile. "From a legal standpoint, what you're doing is perfect. You're following all the verbal commandments of the contract and as long as you are, at the end of the review you would be paid handsomely no matter the outcome."

"What do you mean?" I asked.

"If ... if it comes to the end and Nathaniel is found at fault, in breach of contract, or doesn't want to continue the contract, you would be paid an amount that would depend on time served, services rendered and if you followed the contract. Time here at the Program building counts towards time served. If it comes down to it and he is found not to be at fault and chooses to keep the contract, the Program would pay him in some way for the inconvenience."

"Wouldn't it be in his interest to continue the contract, then?" I asked.

"Monetarily I suppose," Mr. Wrightworth said. "He's never been one to do something for the money, however."

"This not knowing drives me nuts. Does he want me or doesn't he? Am I carrying a torch for someone who's already moved on?"

"Ah," Mr. Wrightworth said. "That's a typical woman response, I think. You'll have to simply make do. Breaking the rules is not suggested."

"I know I need to just suck it up."

"I didn't say suck it up, Darling. I said make do. The part of that which I don't like is that you are making do with me."

"I don't know what I could say to that since tonight is supposed to be our first play session," I said. "I mean, come on. Nathaniel was attracted to me. Even if he didn't make that clear right away, he was attracted to women, so I knew there was that possibility. Then I started thinking about him doing it to me because I sexualized him.

"You were off limits basically, and you've helped me, probably a lot more than I realize. But so far you've said you'd do something and didn't do it."

"Fair enough, but I'd counter with, I promised one thing and didn't do it right away. There's still plenty of time tonight to play."

"I know that. But like, I don't know how to even say it," I hesitated and thought, then adjusted in my seat. "You know I've been looking forward to this for weeks. You stated that you were looking forward to it for weeks and now that it's come time, we're sitting in your dining room talking instead of playing.

"On the one hand, as you said, it's never too late to withdraw consent, but if you're withdrawing consent, just do it, so I know, don't drag your feet.

"On the other hand, if a play session makes you hesitate, what would you do if it came to the point that I was begging for it? I'm no expert, but denying a woman who doesn't beg, when she finally does, doesn't seem like a good way to enforce appropriate behaviour."

"I'm not stalling to drag my feet, nor do I plan to withdraw consent," Mr. Wrightworth said.

"Then why are we sitting in the dining room?" I asked.

"Waiting for you to initiate play," Mr. Wrightworth said, smiling slowly.

"You didn't tell me to initiate play. Or how to."

"That's not the point," Mr. Wrightworth said. "The point was to sit here and not to bring it up until you did. I wanted to make absolutely certain that you were willing to go forward with this. I've been sitting here giving you time to withdraw and leave."

A heat bloomed in my belly. Every part of me seemed to shiver at the same time. There seemed to be a flood of heat between my legs. Knowing that he was giving me every opportunity to back out seemed to make everything all the more exciting.

I shuddered again as Mr. Wrightworth stood. He pushed his chair in all proper like, then looked at me as his one hand sat on the back of his chair. The other dropped to his side, thumb rubbing over his forefinger and middle finger.

"Perhaps we should move to the playroom," Mr. Wrightworth murmured.

"Yes, Master," I said, unable to keep the tremble from my voice.

Chapter Nine

Mr. Wrightworth led me to the playroom and closed the door behind us. I watched as he slid a bolt into the door, higher than I could reach even if I stood on tiptoe.

Stupid being short.

He had added the bolt after my attempted escape the first night. There were enough questions about our relationship as it was, without my running away again.

Seeing the bolt didn't disturb me in the least. I trusted him to let me out of the room when the time came. There were times when I caught myself looking around for items that I could use to either reach the bolt or stand on to reach with my hands.

By the door, Mr. Wrightworth had placed a little pink caddy with several items. Those items were used for cleanup or during. They included a small bottle of lotion, lubrication, and even a bottle of hand sanitizer.

"At some point, I will leave that unlocked," Mr. Wrightworth said, looking over his shoulder to the bolt. "Not tonight, but one night. When it is unlocked, I will expect you to call 'blue,' which we will pretend is your safe word. Then you will make for the door. If you make it, you win. If I catch you, I win and can do as I please with any part of your body."

A chill swept through me. From my head, right down to my toes. I wondered if Mr. Wrightworth knew what those words did to me. As I met his eyes, I knew. He also knew that I would be afraid of what he wanted to do with 'any part' of my body and that the fear would make me fight harder.

He wanted a fight.

I swallowed and nodded, then looked away.

"Not tonight, though, tonight is about you," Mr. Wrightworth purred out. "Begin."

"Wait, does the safe word still work for," I motioned to the door behind Mr. Wrightworth, meaning to ask if the safe word would work for that little scenario.

"There is no scenario when the safe word doesn't work," Mr. Wrightworth said, sounding mildly confused as to why I would ask that question.

My dress was off in an instant. The underwear would have followed, had he asked for them as well. Mr. Wrightworth watched as I knelt and presented myself to him. The face down position that Nicole had taught me so long ago in the church.

I hadn't done the position for anyone else. Nicole had seen it, of course, but I had been fully clothed. On the floor, face down with my backside in the air, I could feel the curling feeling in my stomach. I adjusted, aware of the way my satin underwear shifted with me.

Aware of how much I needed to be touched.

It felt so marvellous to kneel.

Mr. Wrightworth walked around me, looking me over in silence. The quiet dragged out as anticipation mounted. There had been no timeline placed on the play. He could have kept me like that for hours before he started the part of the play that I was craving.

"Still no to the plug?" he asked. "Because I desperately want to put something inside of you."

I considered as Mr. Wrightworth walked away. I did consider, and I turned it over in my mind as he returned and crouched down by my head, holding the item out. It wasn't even large, which I couldn't recall him mentioning before. Not even close to large. Not even close to the size of the average man.

Looking at it, my thought was actually:

Will I even know once it's inside me?

The point of it wasn't to be overly large. It was a starter plug, something to start with, rather than immediately inserting something the size of the average man.

Or Nathaniel...

"It would please me," Mr. Wrightworth purred out. "But you've every right to say no. I just need you to say it."

"Yes," I said.

"Well, maybe—wait, what did you say?"

"Yes, Master, I want to please you," I said, peering up at Mr. Wrightworth.

The man's mouth opened, then turned into a smile. "Call yellow if you want it out. If there is any irritation at all, let me know. It's fairly common for those who are just starting out. It may only last a few minutes, and that's fine." As he spoke, Mr. Wrightworth moved away. I kept my head down, where it belonged in that position. My eyes were on the floor, and I didn't see what he did before he walked back and behind me.

"It's not the first thing to be there," I said, the gasped out as he inserted it.

"I don't appreciate bitterness," he said, a hand rubbing over my hip before he pulled my underwear back up. "But I do understand you feeling comfortable enough to talk about that with me. Now shush and be a good sub."

He left me like that for several minutes, returning when I began moving my hips.

"Irritation?" he asked.

"Weird, like I can feel it suddenly," I said.

"That's irritation, let me remove it," he murmured.

We used with the plug every time we played. Mr. Wrightworth instructed me on how to use the plug and had me place it myself, then withdraw. It reached the point that I didn't even think about it. I linked the plug to play, and anything connected to play is just delightful.

After removing it, Mr.Wrightworth placed the plug in the caddy by the door. All the items that entered me, or cut into my flesh in any fashion, went into that caddy. It was where Mr. Wrightworth placed all items that had to be cleaned and sterilized before the next use.

He came around behind me, studying me for a moment. After another drawn out silence, Mr. Wrightworth walked around me, to the items hanging on the wall. I kept my eyes on the floor as he seemed to hum and haw over which he wanted.

Mr. Wrightworth never hums and haws over anything unless he knows a sub is anticipating his choice. I didn't dare look up at him, not wanting to end play before it began.

"Ah," he murmured, plucking an item off the wall.

He returned to me and struck me on one side with a crop, causing me to jump and cry out.

"Keep your voice down, or I will need to use a gag. Don't need any more questions. High pitched whining annoys me anyhow."

"Please, Master, the other side?" I asked, adjusting my hips as I tried not to move.

The second strike brought out a moan. He wasn't striking me hard enough to hurt in the least. Mr. Wrightworth hit me several times in quick succession. Each strike brought out a squeak. Each was a little harder than the last. When I expected another strike, there was a long pause. I tingled with anticipation, biting my bottom lip as I tried not to make a sound. The crop slipped down my backside and between my legs, causing my breath to shudder out as it grazed over me.

"I asked Nicole for some tips," Mr. Wrightworth said, tapping the crop against my wet underwear. "She made it out to be that women are just lumps of sexual energy waiting for someone to caress and touch them. Is that true?"

"Only if it's you doing the touching, Master."

"That's a perfect answer to my question," Mr. Wrightworth purred out. "I want to tie you the way I have been, stand and move to the middle of the room."

I did as I was told. The man frowned at me as he stepped up to tie the manacles.

From what I could tell, he hadn't been looking at me as I stood. I had no idea why he would frown, but I knew it wasn't a good thing to see his eyebrows draw downward.

"I have to ask because I'm not familiar," Mr. Wrightworth said, stepping back as he looked down, at my underwear.

I twisted my hips, trying to hide the crotch of my underwear. He reached out and grabbed my hips, yanking me back as I yipped out. Mr. Wrightworth's nails dug into my flesh as he growled.

"Can women *really* make their underwear that wet, or is it just you?" he asked.

"I don't know."

"Interesting," Mr. Wrightworth murmured, releasing my hips. "You didn't thank me for the crop."

I swore under my breath.

"Because you haven't been trained yet, I will let it go, but you will thank me."

"Every strike?" I asked.

"When I pause," he responded, walking off.

Being chained to the ceiling allowed me to turn all the way around and see everything in the room. I turned slightly and watched as Mr. Wrightworth picked up the paddle. He had said he would use it on me—and he stuck very close to what he told me he would do—but when he had said he would spank me, I had hoped he was going to bend me over the spanking bench.

Mr. Wrightworth returned and smiled at the look he saw on my face.

"Oh, I know," he said, his smile growing larger.

And then he struck me with the paddle on the backside. It was long enough to hit both sides as one. He held nothing back. I cried out as my legs went out from under me. Mr. Wrightworth reached and dragged me back to my feet by my wrists, delivering another blow from the other side.

Pain like that shouldn't have felt so good. The biting sting of the wooden paddle flooded my body with pleasure I didn't have words to describe.

Mr. Wrightworth stepped in front of me as I panted, my mind reeling. He lifted my chin with the paddle.

"Thank you, Master."

He smiled just slightly.

I still struggled with the idea of it. He had hit me hard, perhaps not full force or I would have broken, but he wasn't exactly holding back. Surely I should have been in actual pain, not clenching my teeth to prevent myself from begging for more.

Mr. Wrightworth took the paddle and turned it sideways, sliding it between my legs. He pressed upward, bringing me to my tiptoes.

"Move your hips," he said.

I did as he said, shivering at the pressure. Finally, there was a feeling against my sex, something to stimulate me. Feeling that edge coming up, I stopped. Mr. Wrightworth frowned and pulled away.

"You aren't supposed to stop until I tell you to," he growled.

"But—"

"No excuses," he growled, striking me again.

His hand slid around me, gripping my hip tightly as he hit me four more times.

I hate being uneven, he knows that.

Mr. Wrightworth's hand slipped between my legs, pressing against me.

"Stop," I begged.

His fingers worked awkwardly, but I was already on that edge. I tensed and cried out angrily as I came, my hips pressing down against Mr. Wrightworth's hand. The man held me as my body convulsed, betraying me as I gritted my teeth and moaned at the same time.

It didn't feel right to come during play without permission.

In fact, it felt hollow.

It did nothing for me but frustrate me all the more as Mr. Wrightworth pressed tight against me.

"Did you just come?" he asked, sounding confused.

"Yes, Master," I cried.

"Why are you crying?" he asked, moving around me.

"I didn't have permission to come," I said.

Mr. Wrightworth nodded slowly, his fingers trailing over my stomach. "You did try to warn me, but I suppose some discipline is necessary for not trying harder. I'm going to get the flogger now. You came so eagerly. Let's see if you can't come again for me."

"What?" I asked as he walked to the wall.

He selected a flogger with small tails and moved back towards me, flicking it this way and that to show me how it moved. A flick of his wrist and the flogger struck me gently between the legs, causing me to jump.

"Now I want you to come for me," Mr. Wrightworth said

with a smile. "And then I want you to come again. And again," the man walked around me and flicked the flogger against my leg, my thighs, my lower back as he spoke. "And again. And once we're done? I still expect you to masturbate and come for me. How would you like that?"

I whimpered, not sure I could do what he wanted of me.

Mr. Wrightworth grabbed me by my hair and pulled my head back, between my arms. I stared up at him as he bent and bit my throat. With a twitch, I made a small sound.

Why is my body so hot around him?

Perhaps if he had his way with me, I wouldn't have reacted the way I did. Or perhaps it was the months and months of nothing.

His teeth dug into my skin until they caused real pain. When I tried to pull away, my hair was yanked, bringing me back towards him. Mr. Wrightworth held me there for a moment before he released my throat. He placed a kiss on the skin he had bitten, then released my hair.

Mr. Wrightworth struck my back with the same force he had used on my backside. The tails of the flogger bit into my skin, across my shoulders.

"Should I hit you here?" Mr. Wrightworth asked, tapping my sides gently.

"If Master wishes."

"No, the answer is no. That's where your kidneys are. I shouldn't strike you there. The velocity I like to hit you at might cause damage. Now here—" I cried out as the flogger struck my backside and thighs. "I can hit you. Spread your legs. Wider. Good, now here—" I flinched, but no strike fell. Mr. Wrightworth chuckled behind me, then flicked the flogger between my legs gently.

He moved around me and flicked again.

I trembled and tugged at the manacles.

"What do you want, Darling?" he asked, flicking me between my legs again. "Tell me, or I will strike you hard. What do you want?"

I shook my head, "I don't want to answer."

"Ah, me, my cock," Mr. Wrightworth said. "You want me inside of you, is that it?"

"I'm not—"

Mr. Wrightworth grabbed me by the throat and pulled me as close as the chain would let me move, then he stepped towards me to bridge the gap between us. The man's lip curled up in a snarl, the sound of it made me struggle and try to pull away.

Anyone would have been afraid of the animalistic sounds Mr. Wrightworth made when he was angry.

"Right now you are my sub. You don't get to think. You answer. Do you want my cock inside of you?"

"Yes, Master," I said.

It didn't make me feel happy to say it. I knew where the two of us stood, I knew what our relationship was and would never ask that of him.

"Maybe if you're good to me and tell me the truth at all times, you can earn it."

I whimpered and met those hazel eyes. I couldn't tell if he was lying, but he had never lied to me before. My breath hitched in my throat as his hand tightened ever so slightly.

"I'm going to untie you and take you to the spanking bench," he said. "We didn't agree to the how before. Now I'm telling you the how. I will release you, and you will stand here, looking forward. When I am ready, I will come back to you and blindfold you. Then I will drag you there by your hair, understand?"

"Yes, Master."

I stood as he released me and then walked away. Not knowing what he was doing, I tried not to shift uncomfortably. I heard him approach and saw the blindfold coming down, so I closed my eyes. The blindfold was tied in place, and Mr. Wrightworth pressed tight against me.

"Green, yellow, or red?" he asked.

"Green," I said.

"That's what I thought, most are at yellow by now. Obviously, I'm not trying hard enough."

Mr. Wrightworth grabbed a fistful of hair and dragged me backward. I stumbled, almost falling as I fought to keep my feet under me. Mr. Wrightworth pulled me towards the spanking bench.

The motion of falling backward stuck with me, I felt as if I was falling as he continued to pull me. I was afraid that I would fall and my hair would come out in his hand. My hands wrapped around his wrist, trying to support myself as he dragged me back to my feet and slammed me into the spanking bench.

The air whooshed out of me. I struggled to breathe as Mr. Wrightworth physically moved my body onto the bench and strapped me in.

The spanking bench was a great deal like Nathaniel's ottomans and served the same purpose. My hands were tied to the front, I was stretched across the padded top and knelt on the padded step. There were also manacles by the step to bind my knees to the back so that my legs were spread and every bit of me was presented to Mr. Wrightworth.

"Oh," he said. "I almost forgot. Tell me. What do you think of this?"

Something pressed against me. I struggled against my bonds, not understanding what was going on. My underwear was on, so it couldn't have been one of his toys. There was nothing on Mr. Wrightworth's wall shaped like the almost rounded item that was touching me.

Not being able to see was annoying.

And then he turned it on.

I cried out and writhed as that oh so familiar vibration sprang to life. Mr. Wrightworth hadn't just purchased a vibrator. He found the same one that Nathaniel had used on me.

Each type of vibrator has a different sort of feel to it, and that particular toy was very distinct.

He held it against me as I shuddered and tried to get away.

Mr. Wrightworth struck my back with the crop while maintaining contact with the vibrator. The pain mixed with pleasure confused me. He moved the toy off and struck me again with the crop.

Then the toy returned.

He bent down, his voice and hot breath at my ear as the toy buzzed against me.

"Come for me, Darling."

He's been practising a great deal more than just kissing.

My whole body twinged in reaction. I almost obeyed,

crying out through gritted teeth when I couldn't.

"That's it, Darling, come for me," he whispered.

The blessed release a moment before orgasm is probably my favourite feeling. That plateau where the whole world melts away, and there's absolutely nothing that exists except that moment in time. Every bit of me is flooded by a tingle so intense that it almost feels cold.

Being tied to the spanking bench, with Mr. Wrightworth's relentless ministrations, was the first time I consciously recall being in that place.

And then I tumbled over that edge.

The vibrator stayed in place a moment more, then pulled away.

"Have to ask, not an expert," he grumbled.

"I came."

"Good, easier to tell with males, but I think I've got the physical response down now," he said, moving away. "That's twice. It usually pleases me if my subs come twice and then again as I do. That's not exactly possible, and I'm told women can come a great deal more often. Let's test that notion, shall we?"

Let me be clear. Mr. Wrightworth was not some orgasm whisperer. He tried, but that first session was my being under-stimulated and him stumbling about. He would learn, but much of his ability was how hard he worked.

In that session, he was very much relentless. The vibrator was used a great deal, to the point where my very being would throb for days afterward. It was a buzzing feeling that was both unpleasant and yet so wonderfully arousing.

I came three more times over the course of about two hours. He would make me come and then beat me mercilessly until I considered calling my safe word and ending the session.

Then he'd make me come again.

Oh, to be had in such a way.

In the end, Mr. Wrightworth was the one who ended the session.

"Into the bedroom," he said. "I bought you another toy. It's in the nightstand on the side you slept on last time. Use it to masturbate while I clean the room."

"I don't think I can."

"I don't care if you think you can't," he said. "You have until I'm done cleaning the room. If you don't do as I say, I will bring you back here and discipline you."

"Yes, Master," I said, lowering my eyes.

"Go," he growled.

I rushed to the door and tried to get it open.

It appeared stuck. I yanked several times, but it wouldn't move. Mr. Wrightworth sighed quietly and walked up behind me, reaching up to undo the bolt.

"Please tell me I've addled your brain with how often you've come," he grumbled.

"Yes," I said, turning towards Mr. Wrightworth.

The man leaned on the door, glowering down at me. The heat of him seemed to surround me. It made me want to climb into his lap and beg for sex and kisses.

"I didn't get to come at all."

"Can I help with that?" I asked, daring to glance up to meet those hazel eyes.

"No, just answer me this—"

"Nathaniel never made me come that many times," I said, shaking my head.

I had to lean on the door as Mr. Wrightworth bent closer. My legs threatened to go out from under me.

"He knows better," Mr. Wrightworth growled out. "He was probably just afraid of breaking you. I will not make that mistake. Nor will any other Dom who plays with you. So that doesn't make me feel better."

"I didn't think of him, not the entire time I was tied up."

Which was true. I recognized the vibrator as the one Nathaniel had used, but that was all it really was. Recognition. After that, all thought of Nathaniel was gone from my mind.

Mr. Wrightworth smiled and pulled away.

"Good," he said in *that* tone. He moved away, chuckling as he added, "You had best get to the bedroom. It doesn't take me long to clean up when I've not thoroughly enjoyed myself."

I left the playroom and rushed to the bedroom.

The new toy wasn't shaped like the other one. It was

larger and had ridges on the sides instead of the top of it. The head was more round. I gulped at the look of it but prepared for what I had been commanded to do.

Half an hour later Mr. Wrightworth walked into the bedroom, and I was no closer to it than when I started.

"You haven't come?" he asked.

"No," I snapped, annoyed and frustrated.

When I tried to move to get rid of the toy, Mr. Wrightworth flowed around the bed and pinned me down. Grabbing my shoulder, he made me roll onto my front and pressed me down into the sheet as he reached.

"Maybe you can't get there by yourself," he said, moving the toy in and out. "Or perhaps I wore you out, but you should come once more, just once more, Darling. It would please me if you came for me."

He's relentless.

I moaned and thrust back against the toy. It didn't matter what Mr. Wrightworth said. It was not difficult to fantasize about him when he was the one pinning me down and using the toy on me. At the very thought, every bit of me trembled. Yes, I wanted Mr. Wrightworth, I wanted him to have me, and I knew that this was the closest I could come to having Mr. Wrightworth.

"Come for me, Darling."

And I did.

Chapter Ten

I felt so much better the next day. Like a weight had lifted from my shoulders.

We didn't play every night, but Mr. Wrightworth did have me come over often enough that it was believable that we were in a real relationship. He would use the other times to teach me things like tying ties and proper eating manners when dining with rich folk. After learning the normal tie variation, Mr. Wrightworth showed me how to make a trinity knot and then had me do it for him on several occasions.

He liked to beat me for not getting the perfect knot.

About a week after we played, Mr. Wrightworth arrived at my apartment and handed me a sundress. I gawked at it, then looked up at him, eyes widening as he smiled.

"Yes," he said, "I've managed permission for you to go to church."

I squealed and rushed to the bathroom to change. In the new dress, I couldn't help but turn this way and that way to look at myself in the mirror.

"Hurry," Mr. Wrightworth called from outside.

I left the bathroom and did a little twirl. Mr. Wrightworth made a sound at the back of his throat and left the apartment.

"You could at least pretend I look good," I said as I followed him.

He didn't say anything until we were in the car.

"You will behave," Mr. Wrightworth purred out. "You will wear yellow, but no one will try anything. This time. Best keep you obedient to the contract, but I want you comfortable wearing yellow. If you behave, I will make you come in any way you wish."

"Oh..." I said, determined to behave.

We arrived at the church without incident.

Ezekiel was not surprised to see me, nor was anyone else. They were all very, very aware of who I was and that I was there with Mr. Wrightworth. He must have talked to the entire congregation at some point. No one touched me except Nicole, who patted me on the shoulder and smiled, then asked Mr. Wrightworth about his week away.

"What?" I asked, staring up at him.

"I told you about this," Mr. Wrightworth said.

"I thought it was a month away," I responded.

"Don't worry, I'll keep you company," Nicole said with a smile. "We'll talk about his penis size."

"Nicole, you need to talk to her about something besides men and sex," Mr. Wrightworth said sternly. "She needs to have a normal relationship with another woman."

"Sometimes a normal relationship with another woman means talking about sex."

"Uh huh," Mr. Wrightworth said, not sounding like he believed her in the least.

"Speaking of sex, there's a rumour going around that you've jumped the line," Nicole said. "You know how many women are beating down my door, hoping to get your number?"

"I haven't jumped the line, Darling, have I jumped the line?"

"What's that even mean?" I asked.

"Is he still gay?" Nicole asked me.

"I don't know," I said with a shrug. "We don't have sex if that's what you mean. He doesn't play with my boobs or anything like that. The only times he touches me is to teach me not to flinch away from a man's touch."

"Uh huh," Nicole said in the same tone Mr. Wrightworth had just used, then turned to Mr. Wrightworth. "I'll let them know that you haven't jumped the line."

"Thank you," he said quickly.

"That it's just Darling that does that to you."

Mr. Wrightworth went stiff. He stared after Nicole as the nurse flounced, yes, flounced, off. She gave her hips a little waggle, creating that back and forth motion of the swing of her hips.

She would later teach me to walk like that. Let me just say, it is dangerous to do that in front of a sadist. It's baiting him, and he *will* take the bait.

Mr. Wrightworth almost walked forward, but then stiffened in place as Mayfair approached.

Her face was too smooth again, having just had some peel or lift or something. Her violet eyes were the only things that held emotion. I didn't like what I saw in those eyes, though I couldn't be certain if it was rage or haughtiness because no other part of her face moved.

She was beyond a porcelain doll. Mayfair had so much work done that she was starting to look like a blow-up doll instead. Except one with a nice mouth instead of one of those awkward open ones.

"Mr. Wrightworth, what's this? Taking Nathaniel's sloppy seconds, shouldn't that be the other way around?"

"Mayfair, where's Michie?"

"I released him, it got boring. I have a new sub now, but he's not fully trained yet, so I didn't bring him."

"That's a shame, I was going to ask if I could borrow Michie," Mr. Wrightworth said. "Darling lacks certain parts, and I know Michie sometimes enjoys being lent out."

"Perhaps you can borrow my new sub. I think he's your type."

"Maybe, but I should meet him first," Mr. Wrightworth said. "We should find our seats, Darling?"

I attacked Mayfair.

It had been her images sent to Nathaniel's father, her texts that had condemned us. She betrayed the trust that the community relied so much upon. She had outed us to Nathaniel's father.

And I beat that bitch just like she deserved.

From the outside perspective, it looked just as weird as it sounded. One moment I was standing at Mr. Wrightworth's side, determined to behave. The next my face contorted as some sort of insanity came over me. My hands came up in a type of strangling motion, and I lunged for her.

I took Mayfair to the granite floor, and I beat her

mercilessly.

When Mr. Wrightworth tried to drag me off of her, I dug my nails in deep and got away. The work I had done over the previous three months had built up muscle that Mayfair didn't have. Mr. Wrightworth hadn't expected me to pull away. He hadn't tested my strength before.

I lunged forward again and bit down on Mayfair's jaw.

Only to spit her out a moment later because she tasted like chemicals.

My tongue burned as Mr. Wrightworth got a proper grip and dragged me off. His hand wrapped around my throat as he commanded me three times to let her go. The only reason I eventually did was because my vision was narrowing down too quickly.

My hands released without any conscious thought from me.

I was dragged, quite against my will, into a side room.

"Thank you, Ezekiel."

"I thought you said she was stable," the greeter snapped out.

"I will get to the bottom of this. I swear she was," Mr. Wrightworth said as the door closed.

I struggled to get in a breath as I sat up. The man shoved me back down, knocking the air out of me.

"No. You stay."

There was some movement behind me, and Mr. Wrightworth bent over me, his tie coming down in front of me. I had just enough time to protest before he wrapped it around my throat and tightened. I could still breathe, but it was difficult. The edges of my vision darkened as Mr. Wrightworth tightened the tie. He straightened slightly, loosing his grasp on my throat just enough for me to get in a breath.

I heard the sound of his belt sliding off.

And then he tightened his grip again, cutting off the air a moment before he struck me with the belt. With the tie around my throat, I couldn't cry out, because there wasn't enough air to do so.

The belt bit into my skin, and it hurt without the benefit of pleasure. He was hitting me too hard for it ever to be enjoyable. Struggling for breath didn't help, and without breath, I couldn't withdraw consent.

The only time Mr. Wrightworth didn't exactly support consent was when he was disciplining someone. If I could have gotten in the breath, there isn't a shadow of doubt in my mind that I would have been released.

Mr. Wrightworth struck me five times with the belt, then loosened the tie to allow me to breathe. I was just catching my breath, my vision beginning to clear, when the tie tightened, and the belt rained down once more.

This repeated four more times.

And then the tie came loose.

Mr. Wrightworth grabbed a fistful of hair and yanked me up by it. There was a special sort of rage in his features, an ice to his hazel eyes that I hadn't seen in months.

"Why did you attack her?" he demanded.

My chest heaved as I gasped for breath. He gave me a shake and snarled.

"Why?" he shouted.

"She told him," I managed to get out.

Mr. Wrightworth went perfectly still.

He leaned in as if he hadn't heard me correctly.

"What did you just say?"

"She told Nathaniel's father."

The hand in my hair released and I fell to the floor with a squeak. When my backside hit the cold granite, I cried out, even though the act of crying out hurt.

"Are you certain?" he asked, crouching down by me.

His suit was rumpled, purple tie still wrapped around his hand. I glanced at the tie, then back up at Mr. Wrightworth.

I was afraid that he wouldn't believe me, and that he would use the tie and belt again to hurt me more.

"She sent him pictures," I said.

"Pictures?" Mr. Wrightworth asked.

"On his phone," I hesitated when Mr. Wrightworth smiled. "It had him and me and that pair in the background having sex on the stage."

"Oberon and Jake," Mr. Wrightworth purred out. "Stay."

The man left the room. I was stuck on the floor, in agony, wondering why in the hell he hadn't just asked before he hit me. My backside was in that kind of special pain that made breathing difficult. It seemed my lungs didn't want to work properly, and their dysfunction had nothing to do with the fact that Mr. Wrightworth had choked me as he beat me.

Mr. Wrightworth returned a moment later with Nicole and Oberon. The other man looked pissed. Nicole almost smiled at me.

"Do we get to play?" Nicole asked.

"No," Mr. Wrightworth said once the door closed. "It seems this little episode was because Elaina sent Albert an image, it's on his cellphone."

"Just because there's an image on a phone that's in evidence doesn't mean I'll fetch it for you," Oberon said sternly, crossing his arms.

"You and Jake are having sex in the background," I said, rubbing at my neck.

My voice sounded thick and gravelly. The pain in my throat was slowly coming to me, making existence all the worse because it wasn't just the one pain any longer, it was both sides that hurt.

"I'm not suggesting you delete it," Mr. Wrightworth said. "I want proof. If Darling is lying, you can have her to use as you please." I wasn't lying, but that didn't mean that the fear didn't drive a whimper out of me. "And no, she's not been trained yet. It's been months. She's almost fully recovered. It'd almost be like fucking a virgin."

"And if what she said is true?" Nicole asked.

"I'm going to peg that bitch in the face, but it supports the statements so far. It could speed up the process. We can't do anything until everything falls into place. I want them both in jail."

"You leave tomorrow," Nicole said quietly. "Are you going to be safe?"

"Safe as I ever am," Mr. Wrightworth said. "You need to look after her. Oberon, please pull some strings. If it is your face on there, you know what that could do to your reputation and life. I could have gone to Raul. He could get it and send me a copy and then destroy it. But you and I have a history. I'm giving the opportunity to you, to bring that bitch down a peg or two."

"I'll do it, but we need a founder's meeting," Oberon said. "Bring in Nicole to represent the Dommes. She can take Nathaniel's seat."

"Still not attending?" Nicole asked.

Oberon made a small sound, then motioned down to me.

"All right," Nicole said. "I'll take his vote, but she'll be asking about why there's a meeting without Nathaniel. She's really fucking interested in everything to do with Nathaniel's duties to the community. Tried to pawn off her new sub to me, and she hasn't even brought him to church yet."

"Tried the same with me," Mr. Wrightworth muttered with a frown.

"Mr. Wrightworth," Oberon growled.

"What?" the man snapped back.

Oberon made another small sound and motioned to me once more.

"She was disciplined," Mr. Wrightworth said.

"For an entirely natural reaction," Nicole said.

"She embarrassed me. We still have to go out there and see the rest of the congregation. They need to see her in pain."

"Fine, be a dick," Nicole grumbled.

"Just because you're empathetic, doesn't mean I have to be."

"I think you're just pissed because you're leaving tomorrow and don't get to watch her cringe as you fuck her," Oberon muttered. "If you'd like, Nicole could use that strap on she loves so much and tape the entire thing."

"No one else gets to play with her," Mr. Wrightworth said. "She's still following the contract, it works in favour if something goes wrong. Then she'll get the payout and maybe we can buy her a little cottage on your lake, Oberon. Then you can talk about other people playing with her."

"Oh, a neighbour," Oberon said with a smile. "All right, I won't suggest playing with her again. Can you at least make her wear a vibrating plug and—why are you sniffing at the air, Nicole?"

"I think she's bleeding."

"I'll get your kit," Oberon said, then left.

Mr. Wrightworth reached down and dragged me to my

feet. He pushed me against the same surface he had thrust me against while he struck me. He lifted my skirt and made an annoyed sound before he pulled my underwear down carefully.

I peered around the room as the two of them talked quietly about the damage done.

Several of the rooms in the church had been made up to be discipline rooms. That was just such a room. There were items hanging on the walls that one might find in a regular church, but there were also wardrobes, filled with play items, which were locked.

Mr. Wrightworth and every founding member had access to those wardrobes. He could have tied me up and done whatever he wanted to me, but he had chosen his tie and belt.

I realized the discipline had been personal, that he had truly been angry. If he had just been annoyed, he might have stopped and considered the toys.

"She'll have to wear a scarf until that marking is gone," Nicole muttered, then sighed loudly. "You know better than to do that. She doesn't wear that sort of thing generally, it'll be suspicious."

"I've arranged for her to have the next week off. I don't want her to run into any trouble while I'm away. Just ice cream and treats and staying in her room."

"How did you get that past them?" Nicole asked as Oberon returned.

"They want to wrap up the review, and I may have accidentally let slip that she's still obsessing about him, that she might stress out too much about it winding up and end up hurting herself unless I'm there to watch her. They're paranoid and don't want to risk it."

"Oh, so that weighed in on your decision," Nicole said pointedly.

Mr. Wrightworth hesitated, then said, "Yes, yes it did."

"Sure it did," Oberon said, setting Nicole's bag by my head. "You only beat someone bloody when they really piss you off."

"I'm just going to apply an antibiotic cream and then put a loose bandage. You did a number, so..." Nicole sighed. "I can't exactly place a bandage on damaged flesh, so, sorry

Darling, but you're going to end up wearing a giant patch to keep blood off your dress."

"Perhaps she will remember this the next time something comes up," Mr. Wrightworth said. "Instead of going mad, she would, instead, tell me about the problem in private."

"None of you want to talk about it!" I snapped. "No one wants to talk about what happened. No one has asked me how I got there. Though I would have thought you'd have known, since everything in Nathaniel's estate was recorded."

"We didn't subpoena Nathaniel's records," Mr. Wrightworth said.

"Why in the fuck not?" I shouted, or at least tried to. Nicole applied the cream as I spoke and I ended up squeaking off into nothing.

"What good would that do us? Nathaniel has a contract that allows his father to take anything that belongs to him, so we know how you came to be with his father. That's not the problem, and we need to prove that the contract was never meant to result in what happened."

"You *told me* you were the only one who could play with me. He *said* that this was never to happen. His father even gave him the option of the other one or me, and he chose the other one, but his father took me."

"He what?" Oberon demanded.

"And it was all recorded," I said.

"There, ready to go," Nicole said, pulling my underwear up.

I stood and straightened my skirt as Mr. Wrightworth scowled at me.

"I signed a contract with him that you two discussed, which determined what could and could not be done. Numerous items of which his father did, despite you two saying it wasn't allowed. He said that if something were to happen, I could play with you and only you. Not even with Nicole. It's all there, and you just ignore it because, what, you're afraid you're going to be outed?"

Mr. Wrightworth was quiet as Nicole giggled.

Oberon made a face and turned away.

"No, I didn't subpoena his records because I didn't think we could find anything there that we couldn't find elsewhere.

It's bad enough that all of Albert's videos are being viewed by the court, but parading out your most intimate details with Nathaniel? For the whole world to see? That isn't the sort of thing that I think you deserve."

"But it will settle it once and for all."

"I have it settled."

"It will make certain," Nicole said quietly to the air between us. "I know you like the challenge, Mr. Wrightworth, but there's still a chance at this point."

"This isn't a game, it's my life. Do you think I want to go back to that man? To live through that again?" I asked Mr. Wrightworth. "Just get the tapes. I don't care any longer, and I don't care if my family sees what went on in Nathaniel's estate. Why would I? They don't want me anyway, so it doesn't matter what they think of me. I haven't got any friends. No one is going to care really."

"You think I want that?" Mr. Wrightworth demanded.

"I don't know, with how you're behaving it's hard to tell," I snapped back.

"I don't want anyone within his grasp, I want the man in jail, where he can't hurt anyone else."

"Then subpoena the damned tapes!"

Chapter Eleven

After Nathaniel's records had been taken, the review ended within three days. Which meant that by Wednesday I was called in to be told that Nathaniel wasn't at fault, he hadn't violated the contract, but that I wasn't allowed to leave the Program building until after the civil suit was completed. Mr. Wrightworth wasn't present for the final review, which they apologized for, but they wanted to begin the paperwork necessary to file for back pay and get me on the payroll.

Until the civil suit was settled, I would be treated as a worker. Only after the suit would I be able to ask about the contract and what was going on about it.

Fucking morons.

It also didn't make sense to me that they still wouldn't tell me anything. I supposed it had to do with the same reason that Mr. Wrightworth had stated before, that they were afraid Nathaniel's father would use it against me, to get me back.

That didn't mean I had to be okay with it, though.

I went to my room, grabbed my stuffed animal and I cried out my frustration. Throughout the months, I had always imagined that at the end of the review, Nathaniel would simply be there to sweep me up and take me back to his estate.

I was wrong.

There was a sudden knock on my door. With a sniffle, I set the stuffy to the side and went to open the door. Nicole stared at me with two bottles of wine in her hands, and a bag hanging off her arm.

"Oh yeah," she said, pushing her way into my apartment. "They were right. You need girl time. Someone will be by shortly with ice for the wine, and we'll put on a good movie. I've got chocolate in the bag."

"What are you doing here?" I asked, sniffling again as I followed her back to my bed.

"Movie, uh, blockbuster, let's try one of those fantasy movies you three like so much," Nicole said as she sat on the edge of my bed and slid the bag off her arm.

"Nicole," I said.

"The controllers are having a panic because you came home and started crying, so they contacted me," Nicole said as she opened a bottle of wine. "So I have babysitting duty."

"I don't need a babysitter!"

There was another knock on the door. I yanked open the door and glowered at the woman on the other side.

"Give her the ice, Mary."

"Can I dump it on her?" Mary snapped back.

"No, give it to her, then go and do like I told you to," Nicole said in a steady tone.

Mary handed me the bucket of ice and marched away, apparently seething with anger. I closed the door, then stiffened.

Mary was the last grief councilor.

I returned to Nicole with the ice. She exchanged the bucket for a glass of white wine and smiled sweetly at me. I sat and sipped the wine, grimacing.

"I know, it's better cold."

"Why is she upset?" I asked.

"I've begun the process of releasing her," Nicole said, placing the opened bottle of wine in the bucket of ice. "She lacks a certain something. I'm surprised she kept my interest this long. Being here tonight is an excuse not to spend it with her."

"Why not just break up with her?" I asked, having another sip of wine.

"Because, I want her to do it herself, to give her some independence," Nicole said. "If I break up with her, it'll just be like Mr. Wrightworth and N-anybody he's ever had as a sub. Myself included."

"You dragged out the 'n,'" I snapped.

"How much wine is it going to take to keep you from asking about that again?"

"Probably both bottles."

It took both bottles.

It also took viewing the tapes years later for me to remember. At the time, I'm pretty confident I was just wondering why Nicole was referring to herself in the third person.

We watched the movie, I drank. *A lot*. And Nicole tucked me into bed after both bottles of wine were emptied. We talked the entire time, though I have absolutely no recollection as to what and I didn't watch the whole night, it broke down pretty quickly.

It took me two days to recover, most of which I spent by myself, watching old movies. Nicole visited with food three times a day. It wasn't until Saturday night that I felt normal again. Sunday I spent the day wandering the building. Monday morning I got up and tried to go to work, only to have the elevator open to Mr. Wrightworth's floor.

Awkwardly I walked to Mr. Wrightworth's door and raised my hand to knock.

The door opened, and Mr. Wrightworth seemed to stare through me.

"You aren't the food I ordered," he said, his voice sounding hoarse.

He looked haggard, ill even. All but the kitchen light inside his apartment were out, but the light from the hallway made him look far too pale.

I had heard enough conversation in the Program building to know that a person wasn't supposed to return from time off looking worse than when they left. I still wasn't allowed to ask questions, however. All I could do was explain what had happened and hope he would agree to sit down. Or at the very least let me call a doctor.

"I got on the elevator, and it brought me here," I said, motioning towards the elevator.

The man sighed, closing his eyes with a shake of his head before he stepped to the side and motioned me into the apartment. I stepped in, and he closed the door, only for there to be a knock a moment later. Again, he opened the door, took the container from the person on the other side and then slammed the door on their face.

"What do you want, Isabella?" Mr. Wrightworth asked, sounding irritable.

He shuffled to the kitchen and dropped the container on the counter. I watched as he snapped open a drawer and tugged too hard. The whole thing tumbled to the floor, and Mr. Wrightworth just stared at it like he was confused as to what had happened. After far too long, he bent and picked up a fork from the items scattered across his kitchen floor and opened the container to eat.

I moved into the kitchen and reached for the drawer.

"Leave it," he said through a mouthful of food.

I shifted backward, looking him up and down critically. Mr. Wrighworth was wearing a sweatshirt and pants, which covered him wrist to neck to ankle. His feet were bare, though.

Besides when he was wearing a suit, I had never seen Mr. Wrightworth's arms covered. In his apartment that had never happened. He seemed to prefer the t-shirts or to be shirtless while in the comfort of his home.

I stood awkwardly as the man ate most of the food, then simply left the kitchen.

The food was left on the counter, open. Which was not something many poor folks would do while in their right minds. We were very much a waste not, want not kind of people. Food and consumables were to be seen to before we fell asleep, collapsed or died.

My mother had said that to my brothers and me. If she had ever come in to our dead bodies and wasted food on the counter, she'd kill us again.

I glanced deeper into the apartment and listened as the bathroom door closed. Then I went about putting away the food and cleaning up the drawer of utensils. Mr. Wrightworth's entire apartment was immaculate, so I didn't think twice about putting all the items back into the drawer, even though I probably should have put them in the dishwasher.

Almost an hour later I realized that Mr. Wrighworth probably wasn't coming back.

Gritting my teeth and trying to steel my resolve, I went to the bathroom door and knocked. There was no answer to my knock. I tried the handle, only to find it locked. Kneeling, I peered at the knob and smiled.

Mr. Wrightworth might have been living like a rich person, but his bathroom door still had that little hole on the one side, to pick the lock. It took some searching, but I found a toothpick and stabbed the hole until I felt the pressure of the lock mechanism. I turned the knob at the same time and walked into the bathroom.

Where I found Mr. Wrightworth passed out on the floor. I rushed to his side and pushed his shoulder. He didn't seem to react at all. I found his pulse, but it wasn't right.

"What do I do, what do I do?" I repeated, tapping my forehead with my knuckles. "Recovery position."

Except I had difficulty recalling how that position went. I did eventually remember. I turned Mr. Wrightworth onto his side. Once he was on his side, he groaned and slipped the rest of the way on his own, as if that position was a particularly comfortable one that he slept in.

Not certain he'd be all right, but believing he'd at least survive if he did happen to vomit or whatever else might happen, I left the bathroom and looked around. I had no idea where Mr. Wrightworth's phone was, let alone how to unlock it or who to call. While I could have stuck my head out the door and shouted, somehow that seemed like a bad idea.

Like the kind of idea someone who was in the community would get beat for even considering.

Nicole was a nurse. She had said that if ever I needed treatment from accidental damage during play, she was the one they would call.

I left the apartment, headed for the elevator.

"Nicole," I said, a little louder than I meant to because I had never requested a particular place before. "Nicole, Nicole, Nicole."

I kept repeating the name as the elevator moved. When the doors opened, I found myself in Medical. I stepped out and went immediately to the desk, asking for Nicole. The woman behind the desk gave me an annoyed look and paged Nicole. Then she went about filing her nails as I paced.

Nicole appeared and blinked at me, then frowned ever so slightly.

"What's going on?" she asked.

I finally stopped pacing, aware that I couldn't just tell her what I had seen.

"Timmy fell down the well?" I asked, hoping Nicole would come close enough to ask what had happened.

The nurse responded by blinking at me several times. "Right. Let me grab my bag, just in case Timmy needs help."

She left and returned minutes later. She dragged me into the elevator and made a small, annoyed sound when the elevator opened on Mr. Wrightworth's floor. Then she pulled me to his door and into his apartment.

"What in the fuck did you do?" she snapped under her breath.

"Nothing, I didn't do anything," I hissed back. "I got on the elevator to go to work, and it brought me here. It's not my fault. I don't control the elevator because no one's even told me what floor I work on!"

Nicole pressed a hand against her forehead, growled through gritted teeth, then dropped her hand. The woman took a moment to shake her head before she turned those startlingly blue eyes to me.

"Where?" she asked.

I took her into the bathroom. She went immediately to Mr. Wrightworth's side. Nicole tapped his cheek, then found his pulse.

"Okay, it was smart to get me," she said. "He's clammy and pale. If he asks, you didn't find him, I did."

"What happened?" I asked.

"Oh, just a problem," Nicole said, opening her kit. "I'm going to give him something and prescribe antibiotics. How was he behaving before he passed out?"

"Pulled a drawer out and dropped it on the floor, left food on the counter and snapped at me," I said.

"Good, probably won't remember," Nicole said, jabbing Mr. Wrightworth with the needle. "This never happened."

"I thought it was closed in here, that the controllers didn't have access," I said quickly.

"He gives them access when he's not here, to make certain no one breaks in," Nicole said. "He wasn't supposed to be back until noon, which means he arrived back early, and they saw. They should have called me, not contacted you."

"Are you even allowed to prescribe antibiotics?" I asked. "I thought only doctors could."

"I'm in the middle of doing the schooling to be a doctor," she said. "Do all the work anyhow, might as well get paid for it. We're going to leave him here, but only because we can't lift him. You'll have to skip work and stay here. I'll call in and let them know he's taken sick. It usually only takes him a week or so to recover, he's a lot sturdier than most."

"But he's..." I said.

"He'll be fine."

"But—"

"For Christ's Sake, Darling, he beat you nearly senseless and then left you in pain when it was revealed that you weren't at fault," Nicole said. "A day on a cold floor isn't going to..." the woman trailed off and sighed. "If you want to tuck him in and get him a blanket, I'll understand."

I went to the bedroom and took a pillow and blanket from the bed.

On the way back to the door I spotted his rumpled clothing. Glancing through the open door to make sure Nicole wasn't headed my way, I knelt and picked up the shirt. There were spots of blood all down the back. Dropping the shirt, I stood and left the bedroom.

I had to take a moment just outside the door of the bathroom to compose myself.

Then I walked back into the bathroom. Nicole took the pillow from me and placed it under Mr. Wrightworth's head. She draped the blanket over the man's still form. Nicole stood and took me by the arm, pulling me out of the bathroom and back into the bedroom.

"You aren't supposed to snoop!" she snarled, jabbing a finger at me.

"I didn't snoop."

"You saw the blood, it's all over your face. They taught

me all I know. You can't pull one over on me, missy. Don't snoop. He practically killed the last one to start snooping."

"What happened?" I demanded, deciding to give up the premise of having done nothing wrong. "Why is he bleeding? Does this have something to do with him never being a sub to anyone else?"

"None of your business, because he's hurt, and..." Nicole hesitated and frowned. "Maybe. They shouldn't have told you about this or showed it to you. If they weren't in trouble before, they sure as hell are now. Unless they wanted to be in trouble. It has been a while since he visited them."

"What, Mr. Wrightworth visits the controllers? Couldn't they just ask for a visit?" I asked.

"Not visit. *Visit*, they're a triad."

"A what?" I asked.

"A triad," Nicole said slowly as if that would explain it. "Three people in a relationship. They control the entire building in exchange for absolute privacy and access to certain things, your fuck toy being one of those things."

"So the controllers are all male," I muttered.

"And see the same thing in you that Nathaniel and Mr. Wrightworth see, apparently. They sort of act as substitute subs for him. When they fuck up, he fucks them. Or if he has to write them up. Though he literally just wrote them up the last time they did something.

"Great, that's a needy you and a cranky triad messing up everything. When they want attention, things go to the shit pile."

My mind was reeling as I tried to wrap my head around the whole idea. Nicole stiffened and looked at the bedroom door. I turned at her look and skittered out of the way as Mr. Wrightworth shuffled past us, blanket in one hand, pillow clutched in the other. The man collapsed face first onto the bed and groaned, ever so slowly dragging the rest of his body up into the bed.

Nicole motioned to me, then out the door.

"Nikki," Mr. Wrightworth groaned, lifting his head. "Nikki, what'd I tell you last time?"

"If you caught me in here again, you'd beat me black and blue, no matter what Nathaniel said."

"Maybe I should beat him instead," Mr. Wrightworth managed to growl, almost sounding like his usual self.

"I'm sorry, Master," she said. "I'll be sure to present myself when you feel better. I'll book the time off. Will three days be enough."

"Four," he grumbled, dropping his head to the pillow. "I've been fantasizing about something I want to try with you."

"Yes, Master," Nicole said.

She waited a moment longer, watching Mr. Wrightworth pointedly. Then she rushed towards me, grabbed hold of me and yanked me out of the bedroom.

Ever so carefully, she closed the bedroom door, then shoved me towards the living room.

"Good God, I hope he doesn't remember that," she said quickly, cringing as she shook her hands. "Has a fantasy? Girl, what have you been doing to him?"

"Just what he asked," I protested. "You've walked in on him before?"

"Yes, I did. He beat me so bad I had to take six weeks off. Which is why he can't know you were here. Me being here is one thing, I already know, I've already seen. You can't be involved in this in the least."

"Then shouldn't I get myself to work so he doesn't question why I took more time off?"

Nicole thought about it for a moment, then swore.

"You're right, damn it. But I don't want to be the only person here while he recovers. All right. Fine, go to work, come over after work, we'll watch movies, and you can keep me company."

"Nikki!" Mr. Wrightworth shouted from his bedroom.

The nurse sighed. "Never mind, you have to go. He resumes control at noon, and they'll erase the past week, but if you're here when he calls out, he'll know you know. He's not stupid. He'll put it all together."

"Nikki!" Mr. Wrightworth shouted, louder this time.

There was a thump and Nicole swore. "Get out, he's up and moving but like a bad drunk."

"But what about you?" I hissed back.

"He's no threat to me," Nicole said quickly. "Get out,

now."

"Stay safe, Nicole."

I'm only a little ashamed to say that I fled from the apartment, and that I didn't try to talk her out of it. I left Nicole to it and rushed away to my job, to the safe choice because I couldn't face my Master not being perfect all the time.

I couldn't stand the idea of him being in pain and acting inappropriately.

I probably should have asked what would happen if Mr. Wrightworth decided to watch the video of the hallway outside of his apartment.

Chapter Twelve

I went to the archives and glumly sat around for twenty minutes or so before I recalled that I was being paid for my time. So I got up and started searching for a new contract to audit. No one told me which contracts to audit.

The first two contracts I reviewed had been completed within the previous year and had been for a gardener and a maid. All involved had been quite pleased with the result and the rich person had offered a second contract to the maid.

For the third contract I wanted it to at least appear like the audits were random, so I went searching for a contract that hadn't been completed in the past year.

It was Kathy, of all people, who helped me find what I wanted. After listening to her prattle on for an hour—about how it wasn't fair that Mr. Wrightworth got two weeks off every six months and no one was ever interested in giving her time off—she pointed to the back corner of the archives and said that anything pre-government grant would be found in the cardboard boxes.

I went off immediately, chose a box by reciting the "Eenie Meeeni" children's rhyme. They have it all on camera as I lifted the lid off of the box and, in a very professional manner, closed my eyes, stuck out my tongue, and waved my hand over the box before I slapped it down and selected a random contract.

The box I had selected was marked on the side for storage in an off-site warehouse. Many of the boxes in the archives were marked in such a way. It was my understanding that the Program had never done such a purge before. Once it was complete, all records from the first five years of the Program would be in storage and only available through the database.

Before the government grant that helped the Program get off the ground, rich folks were using contracts. There was simply no Program to be the watchdogs and keep an eye on everything, to make certain it was fair. What resulted was borderline slavery. Mr. Wrightworth had spent years fighting for the rights of those poor folk to free them from some of the weirdest contracts one could imagine.

The contracts had been entered into the electronic database. Any of these contracts could be chosen from the online archives and read on the computer, but I found that I didn't pay attention when it was an electronic copy. I always ended up with the hard copy.

And there always had to be a hard copy for contracts.

Reading hard copies made it more difficult for me to find terminology I didn't understand. I would have to bring up the search engine and type in the word. The archives had a built-in dictionary, so all one had to do was right-click on a word and up would pop its meaning and even some helpful law terms.

That wasn't the case if I used the search engine instead of the electronic archives.

The contract I found was old, almost pre-Program altogether. Finally, I thought, I could see the real life repercussions and long-term effects of a contract on both the rich person and poor person.

I might have only been there as an interim solution, but I took my job seriously.

All contracts were assumed to use the same terminology. For the most part, they did, though the streamlining of the legal contract terms didn't start up until the Program hit its stride. As the foundation was being set up and coming together, the contracts got stranger instead of more simple. Rich folk trying to hide what they were using poor folk for, from the group meant to protect poor people.

Contractor meant the rich person offering the contract. Contractee was the poor person. Sum typically was used in reference to how much the poor person would be paid and the term was laid out in the first few paragraphs of legal jargon. Then there were usually pages of addendum and additions, some few contracts had revisions to them, but these were often added when it was discovered that the contractee was allergic to something or had a medical condition suddenly pop up.

In the really old contracts, no one was listed by name until the signature page. I suppose that was because the contract was written up and then a poor person was found for it, without ever altering the contract.

Throughout the contract, on the hard copies, one might find initials in the margins, and I found them this time. Here was an N.E. There was a shaky 'X.' The X's were usually a poor person marking off that they had seen and understood the terminology. Typically that meant that the contract had been read to them, not that they had read it themselves. It was Mr. Wrightworth's idea, to protect a poor person.

Once everything started to be recorded, there was no need for the initials because everyone could see themselves agreeing to the terms.

Over the course of that next week, I threw myself into my work and read the contract, struggling to understand what I was reading because it was the weirdest one yet.

It also distracted me from the pins and needles sensation I had in my backside, though it was almost healed, and the pressure building under my skin.

The contract would run the course of eight years. During that time the contractor was permitted to take possession of anything of either of the contractees—yes, there were two contractees—as long as the law allowed. As in, as long as that possession was not a wife, or under the protection of a particular contractee.

That there were two poor folks who signed the contract wasn't all that surprising, rich folk did it all the time.

The instance that comes to mind is when they want live pornography, they'll contract two people who they want to watch having sex to do just that. Pays better than pornography, and no one back in the slums ever had to know what had been done.

A lot of contracts have the stipulation that the rich person could take possession of anything the poor person had on them upon entering the estate. Most contracts had a protective clause that kept the poor person from inadvertently losing an organ, or being used in any manner the rich person saw fit. I had to wonder, reading that contract, if it was the one that had caused that particular terminology to be added to nearly every contract.

The only ways for the contract to be complete was for the time to run out. If one or more parties ended up in jail or the hospital, the contract would not be put on hold. If one or more parties caused another party to end up in the hospital, or attempted to put someone in jail, they forfeited their lives. The exceptions being: if one or more parties placed the third in the hospital in order to make certain he survived, or if one party ended up having to prosecute another party in his day-to-day job.

There was one clause written in, initialled by the rich person. It stated that the marrying of the second contractee to a person of the contractor's choice and producing a legitimate heir would end the contract and reward the secondary contractee full control of all assets, including the first contractee.

Which, if I understood it correctly, meant that the contractor would be removed from the contract and the contractees would ride out the terms of the contract together.

The second contractee would be permitted to live as he pleased.

The first had six pages of rules to follow.

Always be clean and kept, fully shaven. No tattoos or piercings of any kind, no drugs, no alcohol, no relationship lasting more than six months besides that with the second contractee. There was even a list of food items that were permitted and the first contractee had a list of things he had to learn including sewing, cooking, mathematics, laundry, pole dancing, stripping, and many other things.

At this point I assumed the first contractee was a woman. Because... a man pole dancing? They're a little big to be trying something silly like that! It was really confusing for me to go back over the previous pages and see the male pronoun used for everybody. I had no idea if it was a legal thing, or if all of the people involved were actually male.

For a time to be determined based on behaviour, the first contractee would report to the contractor for no less than one hour and no more than one week. The contractee would then...

And the list of things that was expected of the contractee was absolutely insane. Sleep control, couldn't go to the bathroom without permission. Could only eat after the contractor had had a full meal and the contractee had cleaned up. There was a line at the end of the list that stated, literally said, "and to be used as the contractor sees fit."

My head snapped up at that line.

It was late, it was Thursday, and I had basically lost another day to reading the contract.

I set it aside and went to check on Mr. Wrightworth. Nicole denied me entry at the door, but I heard him inside. He called her by her sub name and she responded with his title as she closed the door. For a brief moment I was filled with a jealous rage. I actually thought Nicole was keeping Mr. Wrightworth from me so that she could have him all to herself. I almost knocked and demanded answers, but I couldn't bring myself to do it.

I went back to my apartment and watched videos of kittens and pandas. I read a bit of a book I had picked up somewhere, but couldn't really get into it because my head as swimming with all sorts of information.

The next day I went back to work as if I wasn't bothered at all.

The first contractee would serve the second contractee for a term of two years. There would be a six-month waiting period. Then the second contractee would serve the first contractee in terms set forward by the contractor at the time of the start of the second period. The second period would also be two years in length. At the end of the second period both were to go their separate ways and could not be linked in public but for the church the two of them attended. They could not attend together, they were not allowed to be seen together outside of church but for business functions.

"At no point is the second contractee permitted to take a submissive without the permission of the contract holder," I had read the line four times, then had to read it out loud for it to actually sink in.

Someone in the community signed the contract.

I wondered who it was, if I would be able to pick them out based on behaviour alone. Nearly everyone was clean and well kept. There were a few who were a little more ruffled than most. I immediately took them off the list. I couldn't tell just from the initials because nearly everyone went by different names in the community, to protect them from outsiders.

The contractor held the rights to three other contracts, which the contractees would make every attempt to fulfil. Not fulfilling a contract, or removing a legitimate body for the contract would result in termination of the contract. The voiding of the contract would lead to the forfeiture of the lives of the contractees.

If one of the contractees were found in breach of a minor line item of the contract, their entire sexual history would be broadcast to all friends and family.

Someone in the community was being held hostage by the contractor. If the entire sexual history of a member of the community were leaked to the public, it would out so many others. We would be forced into the public eye, and it would be the sort of chaos that the government wouldn't appreciate, the kind of fiasco Nathaniel had said they had promised not to cause.

It would mean the end of the community.

Through all of Friday, I waded through the jargon of the wrap-up. The ending of the contract and all of the clauses and subclauses that went through the factoids like a female didn't count as an heir. And everyone had to shave their pubes.

Okay, even for a contract, that's weirdly specific.

The amount that would trade hands was large enough that I had to count the zeros six times before I believed it. It was an obscene sum of money. I didn't think that any rich person had that much money.

I got to the signatory page and stared at it, frowning at the names.

Nathaniel Edwards.

N. E. the initials throughout the contract hadn't been that of the rich person who had signed the contract. Nathaniel had been the secondary contractee. Under his name, even, was the footnote that Nathaniel could be placed into the contract and held to it because there was a poor person involved.

If the first contractee hadn't signed the contract, Nathaniel wouldn't have been roped in.

The contractor?

Albert Edwards, Nathaniel's father. It made all the more sense suddenly. Nathaniel's father had given him the choice of giving me over or replacing me with the first contractee.

He had chosen the other person. Albert had a right to take whatever of Nathaniel's he wanted.

I was bound to Nathaniel by law, through the contract. Albert couldn't use me outside of the contract, which made the blank contract a double edged sword. One that would have protected me.

If only Mayfair hadn't outed us to him, I would have been safe.

Instead, she had sent Nathaniel's father pictures of us. She had made everything happen.

Did she know what she was doing?

Of course, she had. She was one of Albert's choices for a proper wife for Nathaniel.

My hands shook as I tried to remain calm. I just stared at the page. Mayfair had to of known what Albert would do to me, to us, if he caught Nathaniel. She had no remorse for what she had done.

I broke down into tears.

I did that a lot back then.

When the tears stopped coming, I sniffled and wiped my eyes. I stared at the name of the poor person, then shook my head and frowned. The name seemed utterly unfamiliar. No one Nathaniel had introduced me to had a name even close to that.

I rubbed at my eyes again. With a groan, I sat back in the chair and sighed out. The contract hadn't been fulfilled, which meant I couldn't just call them up and interview them over the phone. Not that I wanted to, or I might have, just a little bit.

I'm a sucker for punishment.

I sat in silence for a long time, debating with myself what I should do.

Find out if the poor person was still alive. If there was something they knew that could be used against Nathaniel's father. Who they were, what they were doing, why Nathaniel had been willing to throw them under to the dogs instead of me.

Him, I corrected myself. The poor person was male. I was just stuck thinking about that pole dancing mention, and it was impossible to picture a man on a pole.

I would learn years later that men can pole dance. And it can be kind of hot.

Attached to the back of the contract were a few additions. Clauses that allowed for a change of timing for the visits. An addition of days, an addition of days.

An addition of an entire visit for sipping soup the wrong way during a public dinner.

What?

A substitution, where Nathaniel took the second contractee's place. The reason wasn't given, but there was an additional clause saying all women he chose as a bed partner had to be reviewed by his father before Nathaniel could take the woman into the public eye.

What had they said?

That Albert had caught Nathaniel once before. Nathaniel was the one who suffered, was what they had said. The sub had been sent home. Mr. Wrightworth and Nathaniel hadn't thought Albert would take me. They had thought Nathaniel would be the one who was taken, that he would suffer the consequences.

The clause had been added a year and a half previous. I wondered who the sub was. Nicole? She had played with Nathaniel, had served as a sub. That was what they had said. She had never mentioned being that sub, though. The way they talked, Nicole had only served to see what it was like for a sub.

Clause after clause.

It wasn't unexpected, what with the contract having run for just over seven years.

At the very end of the contract, I found the contact page. Very little had changed over the course of the years. Albert's place of residence had changed fifteen times. His number had stayed the same up until six months beforehand.

I was a little-surprised someone had gotten into the contract to update it, but somewhere in the archives there was supposed to be an archivist to update everything. I just had never seen the man before.

Nathaniel's address and number had remained the same over the years.

The poor person's address had changed seven times over the course of six years, finally staying the same over the year and a half previous.

His number had remained the same throughout.

Of course, I recognized it.

Would I include the details of a random contract in my book?

It was impossible to forget. He had made me memorize it and had me recite it bac*k to him several times.*

Mr. Wrightworth.

Nathaniel was going to throw Mr. Wrightworth to his father, fully knowing what would have happened to Mr. Wrightworth. That was why Nathaniel had made the choice that he had. Mr. Wrightworth was a sadist. He would be able to stand up against the torture a great deal better than I had.

Only because he's been doing it every six months for the past seven years.

"Izzy," Kathy said from the archive door.

I tried not to swear at the woman's sudden appearance. She was the only person in the entire Program building who called me Izzy. Everyone else called me by my legal name no matter how many times I corrected them. I hadn't even told Kathy to call me Izzy. She just overheard me saying it to someone else.

"Yes, Kathy?" I asked, closing the contract to turn to her.

"Mr. Wrightworth is up, thought you'd want to know."

And then she left.

No story, no gossip. She didn't blather on for an hour and a half. She just said what she came to say, then left.

I stood and went to the archive door, catching my

reflection in the glossy glass. Shocked at the rumpled look, I left the archive and locked the door behind me. I rushed to my apartment and showered, cleaning myself up before I fled my apartment once more and headed to Mr. Wrightworth's apartment.

He opened the door in a suit, and I almost started bawling my eyes out then and there. Except when I arrived early, Mr. Wrightworth had only ever been in a t-shirt and pyjama bottoms or sweats.

Mr. Wrightworth stood to the side slightly, letting me into the apartment. He walked back into his living room without offering me food or drink. It was earlier in the day than I usually visited. He was a creature of habit, I knew that and assumed that was why he didn't offer me food or drink.

I followed him into the living room and watched him sit on his couch, watching a video on the television. Shaking all over, I stared at him, and all I could think of was his name. His actual name. It was there at the forefront of everything. Mr. Wrightworth glanced at me, hazel eyes holding some emotion that I couldn't identify.

I dropped to my knees and put my forehead to the floor.

"What's this?" he purred out, not moving from the couch.

"I found your contract, entirely accidentally, I swear," I said quickly, keeping my face on the floor.

"And?" Mr. Wrightworth asked, standing and coming towards me. His perfectly polished shoes stopped inches from my face.

"I know your real name."

Never use his real name.

It resounded even then.

Calling him Mr. Wrightworth wasn't just to give him a name, it was how he identified himself, it was showing him the respect a master deserved. He took it very seriously, as did most of the community. Those who did not take it seriously learned quickly enough why Mr. Wrightworth was called a sadist.

"And?" Mr. Wrightworth asked. "Do you plan on using it?"

"No, Master," I said, shaking my head.

"Do you plan on telling anyone else what my name is?"

he purred out.

There was just such a happy cat quality about his voice. Like a cat who had a mouse by the tail. The sound of his voice made me want to lower my backside, but I was afraid that it would give away my fear and he would use it against me.

"No, Master," I said again.

"Good," Mr. Wrightworth said in that tone.

It sent a shudder through me. I dared to glance up as Mr. Wrightworth reached for that tie of his. He had taught me how to tie it for him. I watched as he pulled it loose, then untied it. He wrapped it around his hand, then dropped the hand to his side as the other hand slid into his pocket.

"It's so good of you to tell me about this. Perhaps I should reward you. Is there anything else you wish to say to me?" he asked.

"No," I said.

"No?" he asked.

I could hear the smile in his voice.

I looked up at him. That Cheshire cat smile appeared as Mr. Wrightworth watched me. He turned his face towards the television screen. I followed his look, to what was playing on the screen.

Me leaving his apartment on Monday.

Mr. Wrightworth chuckled as a cold washed over me.

"They dumped the files for inside the apartment. I had to beat it out of them. Marvellous stress reliever. Nicole, now, she denied you ever being here, but that seemed a little odd to me. Why would my little Darling not come and check on me? Why wouldn't you beat on my door until I answered? I was gone for a week, and you didn't even get an explanation as to how long I would be out. So how is it that you didn't take an axe to my door?

"And there it is."

Mr. Wrightworth crouched, his hands coming before him. The tie dangled in front of my face, swaying ever so slightly back and forth.

"You entered my apartment. You were inside for over an hour before you left to get Nicole. And then the pair of you were in my apartment together for some time before she escorted you out. You snooped, then you got Nicole. You pried into my life while I was weak and out."

"You weren't out," I said.

"No, you're right, I answered the door, didn't I? But I was not present for that conversation. And you thought you could burst in here claiming to know my name and everything would be forgotten? Please, as if you could have found my contract."

I sat up, a little annoyed that Mr. Wrightworth didn't believe me. Screw the recording and everything else he was saying. He had just called me a liar. I had been called a lot of things over my lifetime, and I let people get away with those names. Liar had never been a title that I allowed anyone to cast upon me.

Gritting my teeth, I glowered up at him as he smiled slowly.

Fuck it.

I said his name.

Mr. Wrightworth's eyes went wide, but only for a moment. He reached down ever so slowly and wrapped a hand around my throat. He dragged me to my feet, his hand squeezing until I couldn't get in a breath.

Totally worth it, never call me a liar.

"I'm going to whip you, you snide little bitch."

I huffed out a breath. If there was one thing I couldn't stand more than being called a liar, it was being called a bitch. Typically speaking I'd just walk away, but he had called me a liar, then had called me a bitch. My anger was a bristling fury.

I latched onto his wrist and dug my nails in, but he wasn't phased by it at all.

The man jerked me close, as if I weighed nothing at all.

"Just to be clear, this has nothing to do with you snooping, *or* using my name."

"Why?" I managed to get out.

"Discipline for not telling me right away about your visit, whipping because you're being a snide little bitch. You hold onto that bone. I want to beat it out of you, then I want you on your knees, begging me for forgiveness."

Chapter Thirteen

Mr. Wrightworth pulled me into the playroom by my hair and threw me into the middle of the floor. I stumbled, hit the floor and peered up at him, fury rolling through me. He closed the door and locked the bolt, then turned and glowered at me.

There's nothing quite like doing something wrong to give him a reason to beat you because you know he needs it.

I wasn't completely stupid. I knew that Mr. Wrightworth had spent the week with Nathaniel's father. I also knew what Albert like to do with those he 'entertained.'

Mr. Wrightworth had gone looking for a reason to discipline me. He had already been through the controllers and Nicole, all of which he had almost complete control over. They could probably weather the storm a little better than I could.

He had gone down the list, rather than simply call me and demand I explain myself.

I weighed my options. I could cringe and cry and beg forgiveness. I could submit and allow him to do what he wanted—and hope it worked. Or I could take his advice and hold onto the anger.

Trust Master.

I lunged for Mr. Wrightworth. He was startled by my attack, giving me the time to smash him into the door. We grappled. I ended up on the floor, writhing under him.

Totally just because I was trying to get away, I swear. It had nothing to do with the heat flowing off the man's body or the fact that for the briefest moment, I fantasized about him having his way with me.

He dragged me to my feet, and I tried to get away. I only put in enough effort to give the effect of struggling, choosing to conserve energy for the beating I knew I was earning myself.

When he seemed to pull me too quickly, I pegged him between the legs with my knee. He went down, and I moved towards the door, hopping up and down to try to reach the bolt.

Again, not stupid.

I could have dragged over the stool by the door to reach the bolt. There was plenty of time for me to escape, had I been actually afraid.

From behind me, I heard a growl. I bolted from the door moments before Mr. Wrightworth slammed into it full force. He was off the door in an instant. Another growl escaped through his clenched teeth as he reached for me. I stumbled backward, over the caddy he kept by the door for used toys.

That was stupid.

That wasn't planned. It was an honest mistake. I hit the floor, and Mr. Wrightworth was on me in a moment. He grabbed a fist full of hair and dragged me back to my feet.

A squeak stumbled out of my mouth as I was yanked to the side and into the middle of the room. Mr. Wrightworth held me by the hair as he reached for the manacles. The problem with being such a small woman was that my wrists were tiny as could be. He held both my wrists as he brought the manacles down.

Using those manacles, Mr. Wrightworth bound me by my wrists. First one, then the other. I tugged ineffectually at the manacles, aware that they were tighter than they had been any other time we had played.

"I'm going to hurt you now," Mr. Wrightworth said, walking to the wall with the items hanging on it. His hands flowed over the toys as he turned and watched me. Without looking, his hand settled on the whip. "I think I'll stick to the whip. Ten lashes should do it."

He pulled the whip off the wall and flicked it, cracking the air with the tip.

I flinched at the sound.

Mr. Wrightworth approached me, moving the whip back and forth.

"Ten lashes," he said, stopping in front of me. "You will count each, and thank me for them."

When I didn't respond, Mr. Wrightworth used the whip's handle to lift my chin. "Yes, Master."

"I will try not to break the skin," Mr. Wrightworth said. "If your skin does break—as it is such soft, delicate skin—I will not stop. Understand?"

"Yes, Master," I said, unable to keep the tremble from my voice.

Mr. Wrightworth walked around me. I heard the whistle of the whip and flinched at the crack, but it hadn't struck me. The whip had snapped over my shoulder. I could feel the rush of air against my flesh as it drew away as suddenly as it had appeared.

My heart thrummed in my chest, which heaved as I tried to get air into my lungs. In those moments as I struggled with my breathing, the whip fell once more. This time, its aim was true.

The first strike hurt so good. And then the pain bloomed, and I cried out through gritted teeth.

My very breath had an edge of sound to it. It took several breaths before I managed to get control of my body again. I was hanging by my wrists, knees dangling above the floor as I swayed slightly to and fro. Fighting against the sudden weakness that seemed to come over my body, I stood, pulling myself up by the chain that I was bound to.

"One, thank you, Master," I said.

The second strike followed immediately after. Every bit of me trembled, my legs went out from under me again. All my weight was placed on my wrists, but only for a moment. Some part of me dragged myself back to my feet as my hands reached for the chain to hold on to for support.

That time I spread my feet, setting my weight against another strike. I couldn't keep going down with each lash of the whip, or I'd do serious damage to my wrists.

My world narrowed to the room. Everything else seemed to disappear. All that existed was:

"Two, thank you, Master."

My only existence was to count out the blows and accept them gratefully. I knew my role, but I wasn't certain my body would make it through.

The third strike made the cry sound more like a moan.

"Three, thank you, Master."

"That sounds like want, Darling. Are you enjoying this?"

"No, Master."

What is wrong with me?

I wanted him to hit me again. It was like he was stripping away everything I had done wrong, washing me clean with the pain. Reading that contract? No longer weighed on my conscience because he had taken it from me and I had given it up gratefully.

And so I thanked him for each strike.

"Four, thank you, Master."

I didn't think I'd make it. My body would betray me when I needed it to carry me through. The pain was that of a thousand hot needles under my skin. Separating from the pain seemed simple, though it only came in momentary flashes.

I felt the pain only so long as I didn't shift my entire and absolute focus away from it.

Whenever I achieved that place, the next strike would fall.

"Five, thank you, Master."

Five was the balancing point. After that, it was all downhill, surely. The middle of ten. I could make it. Anyone could make it through ten lashes.

"Six, thank you, Master."

He was going to make me stand through all ten lashes, I realized as the pain of the sixth bloomed, and I gritted my teeth. The sound that made it through my teeth was almost a high pitched squeal. Suddenly the pain was too much again. It began to fade as the world seemed to become foggy and distant.

"You are not permitted to scream," Mr. Wrightworth barked out.

His words were quickly followed by the crack of the whip over my head. Surely if the neighbours could hear my sounds of distress, they would have heard the crack of the whip. The lash fell again, but I kept from making a vocal sound so much as a gasp outward.

"Seven, thank you, Master."

Once more I was certain I'd make it through. There were only a few strikes left, I was almost to the end. My whole back was afire. There didn't seem to be a place that the whip had not already struck.

My hands, still wrapped around the chain, trembled. My grip was slipping, my legs shook in their attempt to keep me upright and keep my weight off of my wrists.

"Eight! Thank you, Master."

I almost yelped at the strike, but instead all but shouted the count. With gritted teeth, I hissed out a pained sound. I didn't want the last two strikes. I wanted to say no, to withdraw consent. It wasn't what he needed, though.

He needed this. That was what I told myself then.

That was true, in a way. But looking back, even knowing all I do about the community now, it seems crazy that I would just keep going when my limits were being pushed.

"Nine," I cried out, my head falling forward. Tears were flowing freely. They made my voice sound thick as I said, "Thank you, Master."

My body would betray me, I was certain of it. Every fibre of my being trembled with the effort to stay upright.

I should have told him to stop.

Mr. Wrightworth would drop a scene the second he heard the safe word. Whether in discipline—as I would find in later years—or play. So long as he actually heard the entire word. I could have ended it whenever I wanted to, whenever the pain became too much, but I so wanted to please him.

It's a very, very dangerous mindset, one that abusers take advantage of to get their way. Our urge to please drives most of our interactions in daily life and for a sub, the urge is turned into a need. I needed to please him like I needed to breathe, at least that's the way I felt in those final moments.

"Ten, thank you, Master."

Relief swept through me. Somehow I had made it through. The tears flowed freely as Mr. Wrightworth walked around me. He used the handle of the whip to raise my head, so that I looked at him.

Meeting those hazel eyes, I saw the mixture of amusement and pride as he studied me.

"That's so very *good,*" Mr. Wrightworth hesitated, a small smile dancing on his lips as I struggled to recall what 'good' meant in a play session, "of you, to take your beating like that."

As he spoke, he moved over closer, the whip's handle pressed firmly under my chin. At the end of his sentence, we were a mere inch from one another. His face seemed to swim in front of mine. I couldn't get my eyes to focus on something quite that close to me.

Mr. Wrightworth kissed me then.

It was a possessive, hard thing that stripped away the rest of my resolve as his tongue thrust into my mouth. His free hand wrapped around the back of my neck, holding me steady as the kiss deepened. Mr. Wrightworth's body was always a force to be reckoned with. His tongue was no exception.

Wonder if I can talk him into using that thing in other places.

When he pulled away, I whimpered and tried to follow him. The man chuckled dryly as he returned to the wall and hung the whip back up where it belonged.

"No blood, either. Your skin isn't as delicate as I thought. But you still have to kneel and beg my forgiveness."

He returned to me, a hand sliding over my shoulder and up my neck, tangling in my hair. My head was pulled back, almost yanked, as those hazel eyes narrowed ever so slightly.

"Where is your anger now?" he asked.

"Gone, Master," I responded, my voice weak and shaky.

"Good, I don't want to have to chase you. Don't run."

"No, Master," I said. Then, when it occurred to me how that sounded, I added, "I won't run, Master."

"Good girl," Mr. Wrightworth grimaced and looked away. As I watched, it seemed a hundred things went through his mind. Whatever it was, he muttered under his breath, "That'll have to do for now."

He released my manacles, and I dropped to the floor like a rock. My legs hadn't been hurt at all, but they just didn't seem to want to work. There was a roiling in the pit of my stomach. My body was revolting against the pain I had endured, yet the pain seemed distant. The whole world appeared to be in a pleasant sort of cloud.

Nothing existed except him and me, in that room.

"Now beg my forgiveness."

I shifted to my knees. Uncertain if I was supposed to look down or up, I peered up at Mr. Wrightworth. One of his eyebrows quirked up, as if questioning whether I'd actually be able to go through with it.

"Please forgive my rudeness, Master," I said, our eyes locked.

A flush of red came over Mr. Wrightworth's face.

I should know better than to kneel in front of a man and meet his eyes!

"I might..." he said, reaching for his pants.

He looked rumpled, but just a little bit. Mr. Wrightworth hadn't even bothered stripping off his suit jacket to whip me. His pants opened and out sprung his eager manhood.

Oh, sweet Mother Mary and Joseph. No wonder Nathaniel thinks he's small.

I gaped at it. I couldn't help it. Mr. Wrightworth wasn't just larger than average. He was a creature of myth. I also didn't understand where he wanted that thing to go, because I wasn't wearing a plug—and the plugs I had worn were nowhere near large enough to prepare me for that—and I couldn't just unhinge my jaw like a snake, damn it.

It wasn't just long either, oh no. It was the type of penis that one simply cannot put words to when they first see it. The magnificent silken heat was mere inches from my face. I was tempted, so very tempted, to reach out and touch it. A man like that didn't have to try to find sexual partners, they simply volunteered themselves and prayed they survived the ordeal.

"Open your mouth," Mr. Wrightworth said.

One of his hands slid down his front, wrapping around his aching member. I opened my mouth, I suppose I must have looked like a blowup doll, or at the very least slack-jawed. Mr. Wrightworth's other hand moved behind my head, drawing me forward. He held me just away from the tip. I saw it twitch and was almost smacked in the nose with it.

Yes, I do believe it was of a size to consider being struck in the nose as 'smacked,' that thing had no small force behind its strikes.

I dared to venture out my tongue, sliding it over the velveteen skin. As my tongue returned to my mouth, Mr. Wrightworth drew me closer. The head, and then several inches slid into my mouth. I made a strangled sound as he brought me ever closer. The startling feeling of something hitting the back of my throat was unpleasant, to say the least.

Oh, I wanted it. There was no doubt about that. Nathaniel might have only just begun his training, but the result had almost been the same. I was wet at the idea, until that moment I hadn't realized just how much I had wanted a cock in my mouth.

I tried my best to impress Mr. Wrightworth. He watched me as he attempted to edge me ever forward. Suddenly he withdrew. I raised up, almost following him as he pulled away. Mr. Wrightworth grabbed a fistful of hair and pulled my head back.

"I only pause to remind you to breathe," he said. Mr. Wrightworth seemed to hesitate, and then he made a mildly annoyed face. "When I pull out, breathe. Don't do it when I'm in deep. Otherwise you'll choke and gag. It'll be a mess and a savage way for this to go. Understand?"

"Yes, Master," I said, leaning forward ever so slightly.

I wanted it.

Blame Nathaniel, blame months of no true sex, blame nymphomania or whatever else you'd like to. You might even say that I wanted to please my Master. But I wanted him to shut up and let his most intimate part slide into my mouth. It should take a considerable amount of trust for a man to put such a part of himself inside of a woman's mouth. Do you know how easy it would be to bite him? Maybe even bite it off? It's the most sensitive part of him.

"So eager? Why..." Mr. Wrightworth trailed off, his lips curling upward. "Oh, he is a smart man. Come, Darling, please your Master."

He thrust into my eager mouth. I reached for the hardened piece of velveteen flesh. With my hand wrapped around him, Mr. Wrightworth continued to thrust. His hand, still tangled in my hair, held my head still. I couldn't back away. I did my best to breath out as he withdrew. It wasn't a great breath, but the next thrust allowed a little more of an intake of breath.

It was rough and fast. It was definitely a fucking, but I wanted it so much. It had been months since my last consensual sex act, and this was the closest I had come.

The wet heat I felt, the shuddering tremble that went down my back and then up again, the ache that started between my legs, all were signs of how much I wanted this.

I used my hand, moving it faster than he thrust.

In the middle of it, for some fucking reason, I stopped, as if the act of what we were doing was completely normal and boring. I considered what was going on, and I wondered if men liked having their balls touched. I reached out as I thought that and slid my hand into Mr. Wrightworth's pants.

The man gasped as I found my goal.

I had no clue what to do with them. I just stumbled through a grip and grope. After figuring out their position and size, I had the brilliant idea of treating them the way I liked my breasts to be handled.

Mr. Wrightworth moaned. His bottom lip trembled, I knew this because I peered up at him as his eyes slid closed. He continued, just a little faster.

Just a little deeper.

"I'm..." Mr. Wrightworth gasped. "I'm going to..."

Suddenly he withdrew. I leaned ever forward, eager to take him into my mouth.

As I did so, there was a spritz of something on my face.

Mr. Wrightworth swore.

And then I realized what had hit my face. My eyes had closed as I had been hit in my face. I tried very hard not to cringe at the feeling of something wet on my face.

He came on my face, who does that?

Lots of men, but Mr. Wrightworth had done it by accident.

The man shuddered and groaned as he pulled away. There seemed to be a twinge—I dared to peek out at him through one eye before closing it as he opened his—before he walked quickly towards the door. He returned a moment later.

"Hush," he said, something wet immediately against my face.

The wet went over every bit of my face, wiping away the remains of our scene.

"Open your eyes," Mr. Wrightworth said sternly.

I did as he commanded, obediently meeting Mr. Wrightworth's hazel eyes. There were a hundred things that must have gone through his head as he dropped the wet wipe into a little caddy with cleaning and first aid items in it.

And then he said, "I'm ending the scene."

"But—" I said, with a throbbing need between my legs.

"I should have called it—" Mr. Wrightworth frowned at me, his eyes narrowing as he considered me. "What's wrong?"

"Please, Master," I said.

Mr. Wrightworth was silent a long moment before something seemed to occur to him.

"Darling, deary, do you need something?" he asked as his hand slipped between my legs.

I gasped as his fingers found their target. It wasn't just found, his fingers moved in a clockwise motion, then moved counter clockwise. I knew I couldn't expect him to know how I would like to be touched. With a hesitant hand, I reached for Mr. Wrightworth's hand between my legs. He stiffened at my touch.

Our eyes met as I showed him what I liked. Then I shuddered and bit my bottom lip.

Why didn't he just make me do it myself?

"That's it, Darling," he said, edging closer. His other arm wrapped around me as his fingers worked deftly, voice dropping ever so slightly as his hot breath flowed over my ear. "Come for me."

Mr. Wrightworth's voice shook slightly. His tone caught between command and pleading. Every bit of me trembled at his words. I wanted to do as he commanded.

"Come for me," he growled.

That I respond to.

I cried out my release. Mr. Wrightworth held me as I spasmed. The incredible fog of orgasm washed over me. He held me a moment longer, then pulled away.

"Now I'm ending the scene," he said. "Probably should have stopped it when I first mentioned, but I couldn't resist making you mewl."

I dragged in several breaths, trying to steady myself before I spoke.

"Why?" I asked, wondering if I had messed up somehow.

"I went off script, shouldn't have done that," he grumbled. "I'm going to lift you now, and take you into the bedroom. You will let me."

I whined when he lifted me, my back hurting once more. He carried me into the bedroom and set me on the bed gently. Mr. Wrightworth left the room as I struggled to get my body to work the way I wanted. It wasn't necessarily that I was in pain, it was that everything wanted to fall asleep. The pain was causing a problem where I couldn't reach behind me to unzip the dress.

Mr. Wrightworth came back into the room with a bottle of water, half a sandwich on a plate, and a bottle of pills. He sat beside me.

"What are you doing?" he asked.

"Trying to unzip," I said.

He muttered a curse and set the items on the side table before he reached behind me and unzipped the dress. Mr. Wrightworth slid around me, his hands roving over my back.

"That's not good," he muttered. "I'll call Nicole in the morning, some of the swelling will hopefully have gone down. I forgot women have zippers on their clothing. Stand for me."

"Dunno if I can," I said.

Mr. Wrightworth moved around me and picked up the bottle, then the water. He took two pills out and opened the bottle. Under Mr. Wrightworth's watchful eyes I took both pills. When I tried to hand the bottle back, he pushed it gently towards my lips.

"Trust me. You need to hydrate."

I gulped the water. Having drunk almost half the bottle, I handed it back to Mr. Wrightworth. He set the bottle on the side table.

It was painfully difficult, but we got the dress off of me

without having to cut it off. With the dress in one hand, Mr. Wrightworth handed me the half sandwich and walked off. I ate single-mindedly, only looking up once I had finished.

Mr. Wrightworth stood before me, having showered while I ate.

He looked utterly exhausted.

"Did you drink water?" I asked, wiping my mouth with the back of my hand.

"Yes, and ate the other half of that sandwich," he replied quietly. "I also took a pill myself. Whipping you pulled some muscles in my back that weren't ready to be pulled like that."

"We should sleep," I said, looking to the bed I sat on.

He made a sound and walked around the bed. As he did so, I climbed under the blankets and laid on my belly. My back wouldn't have made sleeping any other way comfortable. Mr. Wrightworth slid into bed beside me. He pressed close to me, one of his legs hooking over mine.

"Sorry we can't spoon," I said with a groan as he set a hand gently on the middle of my back.

"That's my fault," Mr. Wrightworth murmured. "Don't worry about that, just focus on sleep."

I didn't have to focus on anything. The activities of the scene and then the pain killers did all the work of pushing me over the edge into a dreamless slumber.

Chapter Fourteen

When I woke the next morning, Mr. Wrightworth was in the kitchen making waffles.

Waffles.

I sniffed at the air and stopped beside him, watching the way he tensed at my presence.

Waffles always smell so delicious, and I hadn't had a proper waffle since Nathaniel's place. The cafeteria had something like a waffle, a frozen circle that was a great deal smaller than a real waffle. They toasted it as you watched. Those waffles weren't bad, but nothing compared to a real waffle the size of a dinner plate and slathered with real butter and whipped cream.

"I love waffles," I said.

"I figured you might," he said with a small smile that didn't reach his eyes. "Nicole will come over shortly."

"You're upset about something," I said, deciding just to get it out in the open.

"I am, yes," he responded, turning to the cupboard to pull out a plate. "I heard they concluded the review while I was away, which was fine. This morning I was informed that your contract was terminated."

"What?" I squeaked out, hand gripping the counter tight to keep upright.

A cold washed over me. Every bit of strength I had drained away as Mr. Wrightworth set the plate beside the waffle maker and finally turned to me.

"Your contract was terminated shortly after the review."

Black clawed the edges of my vision. All I could think of

was how I must have done wrong. Had Nathaniel heard about my playing with Mr. Wrightworth? Was that why he had terminated the contract? I struggled to take in a breath, but it seemed my lungs had forgotten how to work.

"Darling, what's—"

I fainted.

When I came to, there was something disgusting under my nose. I grimaced and pulled away, only to find myself on the floor. Mr. Wrightworth stood behind Nicole, looking mildly worried. There was a red colouring to one of his cheeks, across his cheekbone.

"Now," Nicole snapped, turning her head towards Mr. Wrightworth. "You want to try that again, properly this time?"

"The Program heads terminated your contract, not Nathaniel," Mr. Wrightworth said to me. "They did it because of our relationship. They believe that if you are still bound by contract to Nathaniel, but also seeing me, it sends a conflicting message. So the contract was terminated."

"And the civil suit?" Nicole asked pointedly as she helped me to my feet.

"Was thrown out of court," Mr. Wrightworth said, picking up two plates and setting one on his arm to take the third. "The judge said that while Nathaniel has a contract which allows his father to take his possessions, your contract states that you were under Nathaniel's protection, as all contracts do. Which meant that Nathaniel's father could not just take you, especially after he denied his father the ability to do so. No contractee can be taken by anyone else because of a previous contract."

"And?" Nicole demanded.

"It can wait, Nicole," he said sternly, walking out of the kitchen and into the dining room.

Nicole tugged me along with her as she followed him. "I think you lost that option when you made the poor girl faint."

Mr. Wrightworth growled as he set the plates on the table. Along with the plates, which had a waffle on each, there was a platter with diced potatoes and even bacon. There were two glasses in front of each plate along with a mug waiting. Two were empty, and the third had tea for me.

I sat at my place and gulped as my mouth watered.

"Fine," Mr. Wrightworth snapped, sitting across from me. I looked up at his hazel eyes, wondering how long this conversation would take. I really wanted to eat. My stomach protested loudly, which made him sigh. "You've read the contract, which means you know that I cannot press charges against Albert."

"You want me to," I said.

"I'm not even allowed to press charges on your behalf, which is what I would typically do," Mr. Wrightworth said.

"I'll press charges, fuck that, fuck him, let him rot in fucking jail!" I shouted, then put a hand over my mouth, surprised by my outburst.

Mr. Wrightworth considered me from across the table. "I want her head on a fucking platter."

"How?" I asked, understanding that he meant Mayfair.

"I don't know yet," he said, picking up his fork. "I'm sure it'll come to me."

We ate in silence, though I noticed that Nicole kept making eyes at both Mr. Wrightworth and me. There was an amused look on her face every time Mr. Wrightworth glanced up at me, as if she knew something we didn't know.

When Mr. Wrightworth set his fork down, so did Nicole. She hadn't finished her waffle, but she also didn't seem concerned by the wasted food.

"Are you a rich person, or a poor person?" I asked as Mr. Wrightworth cleared the table.

"Poor rich," Nicole said with a small smile as she picked up her mug. "It's not just the extremely rich and extremely poor. My grandparents lost their fortune. My brothers are living in a slum at the moment, having been stupid and incurred a debt they couldn't just repay with a job. Morons.

"So..." Nicole motioned at the table and frowned up at Mr. Wrightworth.

"You were a spoiled rich bitch," Mr. Wrightworth responded, taking my plate from me. "She is a well-mannered guest. I didn't even have to tell her to shut up, she just did."

"Damn, but she's a submissive, I'm not," Nicole said with a head shake.

"You're whatever I say that you are."

"I'm not playing today," Nicole growled out through gritted teeth. "That strip you took off me might be mildly infected."

"You're the one who wants to dabble in knife play," Mr. Wrightworth said, walking back into the kitchen.

"Fucking hurts," Nicole muttered under her breath. She stood and sighed, then raised her voice, "I'm going to take her to the bathroom and take a look at her back."

"All right," Mr. Wrighworth called from the kitchen.

Nicole made a motion, and I followed her into the bathroom. She closed the door, then locked it.

"You'll have to take your shirt off," she said, pulling a towel from the rack.

"I'm not wearing a bra," I protested.

"Trust me, I know," she said, holding the towel out to me. "What happened last night? You sound hoarse."

"I... I may have poked the sadist," I said, pulling my shirt off as I spoke. I used the towel to cover myself as Nicole gaped at me. "He asked me to. Said I should keep hold of the anger because he wanted to beat it out of me."

"That's a warning, not a dare," she said, lowering her voice as she walked away from the door. "What did you do, Isabella?"

"Izzy," I corrected for the millionth time.

"What did you do?" Nicole repeated, walking around me.

"I fought him, didn't make it easy to do what he wanted," I said, looking over my shoulder at Nicole as she stared at my back.

"And yet you have not been flayed," she said, an annoyed edge to her voice. "Others have poked the sadists before. Do you know what happened to those people? Of course not.

"They tag team anyone who fucks with them. If they get you alone in a room with just them, be afraid, very afraid."

"He asked for it," I sighed out, then whimpered when Nicole touched my back. "He wasn't angry with me."

"Did it end in you coming?" Nicole asked.

"Yes," I said.

The woman swore. "What the fuck are you two doing?"

"What is your problem, Nicole?" I demanded, turning to

glare at her. "Why do you have a problem with everything I do? With everything he does? If he wants to face fuck me and I consent to it, it's none of your damned business, okay?"

"He face—" Nicole stopped suddenly and raised a hand as if to stop me. She shook her head and frowned. "He did not face fuck you."

"Why do you think I'm hoarse? From screaming? Don't you think the neighbours would have heard that?"

"Oh my God, he face fucked you."

"Why is that a problem?"

"Mr. Wrightworth is gay, and he's performing sexual acts with you," Nicole said, jabbing a finger at me. "I don't get it. What is so special about you, that the two of them are head over heels over you. It's ridiculous. There are men and women throwing themselves at the feet of the sadists, many of whom are real masochists, yet it's you they're chewing on."

"Are you jealous?"

"No, I'm not—fuck," Nicole muttered, then crossed her arms. "Maybe, a little bit. Of converting Mr. Wrightworth. If you turn him? I'm jumping on that man and never letting go."

"I don't think he's changing sides," I said.

"No, like he said, it's probably just you," she grumbled. She was quiet a moment. Then her face fell, she looked utterly devastated. "He did something different. Did he tell you it was going to happen beforehand?"

"Well, he said I'd end up kneeling and begging for forgiveness," I said.

"If it were planned, he would tell you very specifically that it was happening," Nicole said. "Which meant that he went off script."

"That's what he said. What is going off script?" I asked.

Nicole drew in a long, slow breath, then let it out. "He didn't plan to do what he did, which means that the breakfast and calling me over to check on you isn't part of your aftercare. It's a part of *his* aftercare."

"What?" I asked.

"Doms can drop just like subs can, except it's a little different. He's probably pacing outside the door right now, thinking he went too far with you. That he crossed a line."

"But he was the one who ended the scene."

"That's him calling yellow," Nicole said, paling slightly. "Okay, okay, we can do this."

I watched as the woman chewed on the edge of her nail and frowned. She seemed caught in thought as she looked around the bathroom. Her blue eyes moved down me. I got the feeling, watching Nicole, that Mr. Wrightworth either didn't usually drop, or there was someone else he typically called if he did.

Nathaniel, maybe? I dimly recalled a comment in the church during my first visit. Of Nathaniel saying Mr. Wrightworth was his first call, if he dropped. That could very easily go both ways.

"All right, let's do this," she said, motioning up and down me. "You need to shower. It'll help with the back a little bit. Then, after you've showered, you'll come out, and we'll all watch a movie together. No topics he wouldn't want to discuss. Like... Nathaniel or the contract. Unless he brings it up. You will cuddle up to him, make sure to thank him for last night at some point. So everyone knows it was play, and he didn't actually hurt you."

"It wasn't exactly painful."

Nicole frowned at me, looking down and up me again. "Maybe you are a masochist."

"A masochist who is sometimes a little," I muttered.

"Who called you a little?" Nicole asked.

"Mr. Wrightworth said I was behaving like a little before we started playing," I responded.

"We had just met a little on the other end of the spectrum..." Nicole muttered. "Let's try you in his lap, sleeping or pretending to sleep and see how that goes."

"How is that helpful?" I asked.

"Would you sleep in the lap of a man who had hurt you?" Nicole countered. "Because I wouldn't be anywhere near such a person. Later today we'll talk about massages, and I'll position you to give him one."

"I don't know how to."

"Perfect, I can teach you how and use him as the example," Nicole patted me on the shoulder as she spoke.

"Shower, I'll get you some clothing, then we'll see about him. Don't mention it, never mention it. If anything is alluded to, pretend the aftercare is for you. Doms don't like feeling vulnerable, especially around more than one person."

"Then why did he call you?" I asked. "Wouldn't he want to keep it private?"

"Mr. Wrightworth always calls me when he feels unstable. We watch a movie, do the whole friend thing. Shower, now."

I watched Nicole leave, then sighed. I turned my attention to the shower and gritted my teeth. The reason I hadn't gone immediately to shower in the morning was because of my back. I had been able to ignore the pain through breakfast because I had something else to focus on.

Alone in the bathroom, I could feel every ache and pain through my back and shoulders. The idea of being hit with hot water didn't make me feel any better.

With a grumble, I dropped the towel and headed for the shower. The hot water hurt, but also helped me relax. I washed for much longer than I needed to before I shut off the shower and stepped out. After drying, I found a set of clothing by the door in which I dressed.

I ventured out of the bathroom, afraid of what I'd find.

What I found was a great deal more disturbing than the kinky stuff that had been going through my head.

Mr. Wrightworth and Nicole were sitting in the living room debating what movie we should watch. There was popcorn sitting on the coffee table and a chocolate bar sitting beside it, ripped open with a bit missing.

I went to Mr. Wrightworth's side and wrapped myself over him as he stiffened. Ever so slowly his arm lowered over my shoulders and pulled me closer.

"Back hurts," I said. "But otherwise last night was..." I struggled for the word I wanted to use. It suddenly seemed so far away. "Feelings."

No, I hadn't had a complete meltdown. Sitting with Mr. Wrightworth, with popcorn in front of us, I was suddenly taken back to Nathaniel's entertainment room. The other time I struggled to get a word out.

"Feelings?" Mr. Wrightworth asked, setting the back of

his hand against my forehead.

I miss Nathaniel.

Who could be a smart alec at times, sarcastic and witty when I needed him to be, who wouldn't judge me for getting the wrong word out. Mr. Wrightworth didn't think it was adorable that I had said 'feelings' in place of the word I meant to use. I had no idea f he found anything adorable.

That kind of upset me.

"Good, I meant to say good," I responded, dropping my head to his shoulder. "Last night was good. I enjoyed it, at least." Mr. Wrightworth tensed under me, which only made me feel the need to defend myself. "I mean, not on a regular basis or anything, but it was weirdly good."

"She's probably dropping," Nicole said in a singsong voice as she stared at the television and jabbed a button on the remote.

Mr. Wrightworth's arms tightened around me, drawing me closer. "You don't need to defend why it felt good."

"It was supposed to be discipline," I protested.

"Sort of, weirdest scene I've ever played, more like," he grumbled in response. "Typically everything is negotiated beforehand. I don't go off script at all, except when you call your safe word."

"Well, thank you," I murmured, feeling the flush over my face as my throat ached slightly. It reminded me of what we had done. "It just had a different sort of quality to it than the scripted stuff."

We had been caught up in the moment. It was a dangerous way to be caught. Both sub and dom might go beyond their limits when in that place, but it's so much fun introducing a new thing every once in a while. Not everything can be written in stone, and, as much as I need to know what is going to happen, it can be boring to always play within the parameters negotiated before play.

"Ah, they have that movie you like," Nicole said loudly.

"That's amusing, considering they didn't have it yesterday," Mr. Wrightworth grumbled. "I think the controllers slipped something in."

"How hard did you beat them, that they think you need this movie?"

"Shut up and press play," Mr. Wrightworth growled.

Mr. Wrightworth's favourite movie was from before the collapse and then another twenty or thirty years. The dates on movies were often lost. The dates were more of a generalization created around the lives of the actors who participated in the movies.

Whenever Mr. Wrightworth was feeling unstable, he'd flick through all the movies available until he either found the movie or discovered it wasn't there and settled on something else.

He'd never use the search function.

Which drove everyone mad.

What likely happened that day was that Nicole had started the search and texted the controllers at the same time. They didn't just control the building. They could also launch imitations of the services that the building received. Mainly streaming services, which was about the only way anyone outside of the slums watched movies besides Nathaniel. The controllers had then loaded the movie to save us three hours of searching to settle on something else entirely.

That day I didn't get to watch the movie. I ended up falling asleep on Mr. Wrightworth. When the movie ended, he shifted me off of him, waking me momentarily.

I woke up entirely when a hand tightened on the back of my neck. Almost like picking up a cat by the scruff of the neck, Mr. Wrightworth lifted me, and I moved with him. It was the oddest sensation, made a little stranger when he deposited me back in his lap and wrapped his arms around me.

"I'd offer a massage, but I suspect that would be more painful than not," Mr. Wrightworth said.

"And I'd offer you one, but I don't know how so it'd probably just hurt," I grumbled in response.

"Oh, I can help with that," Nicole said, sounding far too interested. "Come on, you know whatever Dom she goes to will want that service at some point."

Mr. Wrightworth sighed. "You're right. Nearly everyone uses it at some point."

"For what?" I asked.

"Could be discipline," Mr. Wrightworth said. "Or even

have you give someone else a massage. If your Dom is a rich person, such so called services will insinuate sex without being sex. Your Dom will want to share you in a capacity that others will view as him being loose. Those who keep a sub close are usually muttered about by the rich folk. Whining and bitching about classless whores."

"So it's something I should learn," I said.

"Yes, it'll also help knowing pressure points," Mr. Wrightworth said with that Cheshire cat smile. "He makes a lewd comment and you just need to put the right pressure on the right part of the back. You can bring any man down."

"Or by their thumb," Nicole said, standing to move to the same couch as Mr. Wrightworth and me. "Men follow their thumbs, pretty well their entire balance can be controlled with the thumb alone."

The rest of the day was spent teaching me massage and relaxing. Nicole didn't stop adjusting what I was doing until Mr. Wrightworth moaned and shuddered under my touch. After the massage, Mr. Wrightworth went off to take a bath. Nicole told me to lay down, and I fell asleep again.

So tired.

Thank goodness it was a Saturday. There was nothing to pull us away and no one had any expectations of us. We rested, we relaxed, we ate.

And Sunday morning we got up and went to church.

That was a stupid idea.

Chapter Fifteen

On the way to church, I was told very simply, "Do nothing to Mayfair. At all."

Which made perfect sense given the incident when I attended church last.

I was resolute in my determination to obey. Mr. Wrightworth knew what had happened and why, though he hadn't done anything about it as far as I knew on the way there. Walking into the church, I kept my eyes downward, embarrassed that everyone had witnessed what had happened the last time I was around.

"Cellphone, Mr. Wrightworth," Ezekiel called as Mr. Wrightworth tried to walk off after receiving his wristband. The greeter stepped up beside me and looked down the sundress, then back up to my eyes. "And I have to ask because you' d be surprised where women can hide things. Do you have a cellphone on you, Darling?"

"No, sir, I don't," I murmured, with a shake of my head before I lowered my eyes once more.

"I'm a Daddy, not a Sir," Ezekiel grumbled.

"I think Darling meant it the way she'd call any man 'sir,'" Mr. Wrightworth said, returning to the table with his cellphone held out to Ezekiel. "I forgot."

The no cellphone rule was new. There were many reasons to ban cellphones in a place that actively participated in technically illegal activities. The police, the government, even the people in general, were willing to ignore us and live as we wished to live. So long as the video and photographic evidence was not leaked to the public at large.

I wondered, even hoped, that the new rule had come about because of Mayfair. I hoped that the Doms of the community were taking actions to correct a mistake.

"Sure you did. Like Mayfair wasn't looking for blood when we demanded her phone," Ezekiel said. "Her sub's not very well trained, makes faces behind her back. Almost full on laughed."

"Subs need to be respectful of their Doms, no matter how they came to be a sub," Mr. Wrightworth said to me before he turned his attention to Ezekiel. "Funny, I don't recall seeing a sub contract come through for her."

"Not a poor sub," Ezekiel whispered as he took a step backward.

The motion of stepping back was not usual for a Dom, let alone Ezekiel. Certainly, I had only seen the man a few times by then, but he was of the sort that you knew he didn't cede ground to just anyone. There was something about the way his other foot seemed to shift as if he were getting ready to bolt, which made me wonder what was going on.

Mr. Wrightworth's eyes narrowed to pinpricks. He glanced at me, then back to Ezekiel. The greeter seemed to cock his head in my direction, but barely so, causing Mr. Wrightworth to make a sound at the back of his throat and turn his full attention to me.

Obviously, they know each other well enough to talk without actually talking.

"Come, Darling," Mr. Wrightworth said, holding a hand out to me.

I slid around Ezekiel and went to Mr. Wrightworth, accepting his hand. He led me down the aisle of the church as I kept my eyes on the floor. I didn't want to meet anyone's eyes. I was afraid of them judging me. We came to a sudden stop. I glanced up once, meeting Mayfair's almost purple eyes before squeaking and trying to hide behind Mr. Wrightworth.

The man stiffened as I buried my face in the back of his suit jacket.

"Mayfair," Mr. Wrightworth purred out.

"Wrightworth," Mayfair responded arrogantly. "Is Darling going to apologize to me?"

"No," Mr. Wrightworth responded, a chuckle altering his tone. "She's not. Darling suffered from a break. I'm not going to risk her breaking again by making her confront the person who caused the break in the first place. The poor thing's trembling in fright already."

"She should. Do you know how much it cost me to get my face fixed after that incident?"

"Probably not as much as it cost you to get that permanently perplexed expression," Mr. Wrightworth said. "I heard you made a fuss about the new policy."

"I run a business, I can't just be separated from my cellphone," Mayfair snapped back.

"So do I, so does Nathaniel, and a great many of us here. Nathaniel has never used his phone at church, shuts it off before he attends. I have only ever used it to entertain a nervous sub. Church is for us, not for business. If you're so concerned about your business, you need not attend."

The response to a disgruntled Dom was so fluid that it hardly seemed practised, though it must have been. It was also worded in such a way that no one who wanted to continue attending meetings would be able to protest.

"But my sub would be stripped of me if I didn't attend with him in tow. Isn't that what you said to me about Michie?"

"It is because I would. As you well know, anyone who touches Michie answers to me, then to Nathaniel if anything is left of them."

"I believe you know my new sub. Would you two like to greet each other like the old friends that you are? Dear?"

Mr. Wrightworth seemed to lurch forward, making me squeak and step back as I almost followed him. I was still regaining my balance as everything else happened.

There was a loud crack. Then the rumpled sound of someone hitting the floor.

Mr. Wrightworth snarled as Mayfair peered up at him from the floor, blood flowing from a crack in her lip.

"Ow," she said, a hand touching her bottom lip gently. "What was that for?"

"I believe Mr. Wrightworth thinks you may have intended that I use his real name," Nathaniel purred out.

A cold washed over me.

Then the tingle of fear made everything feel weak. I felt the way I had that day on the plane, like everything else was moving and I was just trying to stay still and upright.

I lifted my head and met those icy green eyes as the man smiled ever so slightly.

The smile disappeared, and a mask came over Nathaniel's face as he bent to help Mayfair to her feet. I had to watch as Nathaniel smoothed out Mayfair's dress and offered her a handkerchief to hold to her split lip.

"No," Mayfair growled with an attempted frown. The woman's face wasn't moving the way it should have been. "I know the price of doing that. No, Mr. Wrightworth, I wouldn't do that to you. I wanted Nate here to greet you with the respect you deserve as a founding member."

He's her sub.

That was why, I thought. He had moved on and had become a sub to Mayfair, though I couldn't understand why. I had supposed that he wanted her because she was rich and pretty and had everything.

Whereas I was poor and stupid and couldn't pull off that dress no matter how much I starved myself.

I dared to glance up again. My eyes flowed over Nathaniel's tailored suit, to the perfectly rumpled hair and the shape of that face. He was perfectly shaved, as he always was, though there was a darkness along the left side of his jaw as if he were recovering from a bruise.

How well I knew what sort of damage a sub could suffer under the hands of a Dom. Mr. Wrightworth and Nathaniel had avoided my face. Most Doms did because bruising on the face was difficult to hide from the public eye. To see any bruise on Nathaniel was a shock.

To try to imagine Mayfair striking him hard enough to cause such damage? That was just absurd.

Around Nathaniel's throat was a black choker, which looked a little ridiculous on a man. I turned my eyes to Mayfair and over her dress. The fabric hardly made an impression on me. I skimmed over the look and colour of it.

What I did catch was the ring.

She wore the purple ring on her left hand. The one that

Nathaniel had worn around his neck when we had attended church. At the sight of the ring, I stiffened like a board, reaching for Mr. Wrightworth, eve though he was out of reach. I had to step forward so that I could touch him.

She was his Mistress before.

I poked Mr. Wrightworth in the back as he stepped back, peering around him to the ring.

Nathaniel wore the ring that last day, perhaps—I decided in those moments—that was why he had gone to Mayfair. Maybe he had only gone to her because he had felt out of place after I had been taken.

Mr. Wrightworth trembled ever so slightly and turned, pulling me to his side. I couldn't hide at his side. Feeling self-conscious, I gripped my left arm with my right hand and kept my eyes down. My eyes fell to about knee level on Nathaniel. The man had his hands in his pockets. As I tried so desperately to block out what was going on around me, a hand slid out of his pocket, and a finger jabbed upwards.

I looked up, my legs feeling weak again. Nathaniel's mouth opened just slightly, eyes sliding down me in a seemingly pointed manner, before he glanced at Mr. Wrightworth and suddenly down and away.

Nathaniel looked away just as Mayfair turned towards him.

It took a moment to realize that Mr. Wrightworth had said, "Your sub needs to learn to respect you. Put some fear into him."

"Perhaps I simply cannot strike him hard enough to drive the point home," Mayfair grumbled.

"Workout more," Mr. Wrightworth responded blandly.

"You still do discipline?" Mayfair asked.

To which both Nathaniel and I stiffened. Mr. Wrightworth made a sound that almost sounded like the purring of a cat.

"I haven't since taking on Darling, but... I can make an exception for Nate, I suppose."

"Trade you."

"*Trade* me?" Mr. Wrightworth demanded.

"One night with Nate, whatever you please. And I mean... whatever you please. With his consent to the one small thing," Mayfair hesitated as Mr. Wrightworth shuddered. I couldn't decide if she was claiming Mr. Wrightworth was small, or that it'd be no trouble to talk Nathaniel into it. "And I get one hour with Darling."

"Yes, but a night is almost half gone after sleep," Mr. Wrightworth said.

"Oh, Mr. Wrightworth. You forget that I know exactly what you like. Sleep deprivation isn't in his hard limits. If necessary, he can sleep when he returns to me. But I know that of all the people here, you can drive a fearful respect into anyone. By the time you return him to me, I'm sure you'll have driven home the fact that if he doesn't obey, he will spend more time with you and he won't like it."

"I'd beat it into his thick skull," Mr. Wrightworth said.

"No beating around the face or neck, he does have a corporation to run, and they'd ask questions if he showed up with one of your love taps," Mayfair said. "Do we have a deal?"

"Let me mull it over," Mr. Wrightworth murmured. "As you can tell, my preferences may have shifted somewhat."

"As if they'd shift that far, but it's a standing offer. Just let me know. I'd love to get my claws into her."

Mayfair walked off towards the front of the church as Mr. Wrightworth drew me to the back of the church, on the other side of the seats where she sat. We were literally on the other end of the church.

"He makes a terrible sub," Nicole said, thumping loudly into the seat beside me.

"Nate is a very good sub," Mr. Wrightworth purred out, a finger rubbing over his bottom lip.

He seemed suddenly distracted. Like he was caught in thought.

"Then... she makes a bad Dom?" Mary, Nicole's sub, offered up from the other side of Nicole.

I knew she was the grief councilor I had met when I had first entered the Program, but I still couldn't seem to place her face. I recognized her as the person who brought me free wine, but after drinking both bottles, the entire thing was hazy. It was as if we were strangers. We had only spent an hour or so together, something like six months previous.

"Well, yes," Mr. Wrightworth said, draping an arm

around me possessively. "But I suspect we'll see a much more submissive Nate over the rest of the meeting."

How could he have known that?

Ezekiel stepped up to the pulpit and raised his hands to draw everyone's attention.

"As you all no doubt know, we have now banned cellphones from inside the church," Ezekiel said. "It seems that a walk-in that we knew was here, had a cellphone and took several images which then fell into the hands of authorities. Photographs in the hands of the authorities would count as causing a raucous. It would work against everything we've done so far. These images have been retrieved and dismissed, thank God, but we are taking steps to prevent it from happening again.

"If you have a problem with the ruling of the founding members, you can kindly go fuck yourself, as per usual. The punishment for having a cellphone within the church will be four hours submission to Mr. Wrightworth and one other Dom of his choice."

The whole congregation began murmuring amongst themselves as Ezekiel paused to smile.

"That's right, ladies and gentlemen. If you are caught with a cellphone within these walls, you will be poking the sadists. At the moment the Dom of choice is Nicole, so gentlemen, I'd watch your backs. I hear she likes ball busting and titty twisting."

"I also love pegging," Nicole called out, which drew a few chuckles and yet made several people—myself included—shift uncomfortably.

"Refusal to submit does, of course, mean excommunication. You would be banned from the church and the community. Cellphones are not life or death. You do not need an outside connection while in the church. If it does happen to be life or death, then you need to let the founding members know. Only the founding members can make an exception.

"Just so all are aware, there is a rumour of a trial in the near future. It seems the victim of abuse has decided to go ahead and press charges, as is their absolute right and is not considered stirring up trouble. However, there are those present who have interacted with this person and their abuser, and those people may be approached by the authorities. You *must* cooperate and tell the truth at all turns.

"To do otherwise will result in excommunication.

"I'm not fucking around here. Our lives have spilled into the real world. Someone has been severely hurt, against their will and despite removing consent and using a safe word multiple times. If we could just kill the abuser and make an example of them, we would. However, we cannot. So we must allow the justice system to do as it can, which means full cooperation with the authorities.

"Details on the trial cannot be found until after all is said and done. Though I'm sure that if you are one of the people approached, you will know what is going on.

"Now, the live show has been canceled, so we are looking for some voyeuristic folk to show off a bit. If you'd like to do so, please find a founding member and let them know. We will vote during downtime. The orgy is back to the usual place this month. The renovations are finally done, and the cost has dropped but is at seventy per person instead of fifty due to the party sized jacuzzi that was added to the rooms. We are planning a...a...what was it called?"

Ezekiel pointed to someone in the front row and shook his head. The woman he pointed to stood and moved up the pulpit beside him.

"We're planning a munch," she said. "Recently the databases were opened to me, and I managed to access a website. Yes, it's the mythical site. We're combing through a lot of information. One thing we have learned is that everyone would have little meetings called munches. They'd be held in restaurants and pubs, in homes, in public areas that were understanding of the lifestyle. So we are looking for places to hold the munches, but the first one will be held here on Wednesday night.

"A munch is not like our Sunday meetings. It's very informal. There'd be no speakers, nothing. Maybe some classes going on, well, we're winging it at the moment. So the one on Wednesday is like an introduction for everyone at once, where we'll come together and just talk about a few of our fetishes and what we like. Coffee and cookies will be provided, and I'm hoping I can bring some of the information I've been reading through, from the archives."

Melly was her name, and she was our first contact in the archives. She worked with them for years before getting clearance to the blacklisted items. That Sunday as the beginning of us learning about the lifestyle we dabbled at. We learned a great deal, and thankfully the community was relatively new still.

Yes, it had been around for some ten years or so by that point, but it was still new enough to change and evolve.

I trembled all over as Melly went over who would be hosting the munch and what would be going on.

"He meant me," I whispered to Mr. Wrightworth.

"He did, yes," Mr. Wrightworth responded quietly. "Tomorrow morning you will file formal charges, but I think the community deserves as much warning as possible."

"What if they decided not to cooperate?" I asked.

"There was no chance of that," Nicole whispered quickly. "We've wanted him behind bars for years. Most of the trouble that's been laid on us was because of his actions."

I trembled again.

"Don't worry, sweetie," Nicole said, patting my shoulder. "I'll be watching the subs. You can hide behind me."

"Hide behind you?" I asked.

"Nate," Nicole said as if that explained it all.

I looked up to where he sat beside Mayfair. He was talking to her, facing the pulpit as he spoke. Mayfair laughed loudly in response, then turned to the person beside her and began relating whatever Nathaniel had told her.

Mr. Wrightworth leaned forward ever so slightly.

"I need to speak with Darling in private," he said, standing suddenly. "Darling?"

"Coming," I said, standing to follow him.

Mr. Wrightworth led me away from the pews and into one of the private rooms. He closed the door behind us and then leaned against it.

His hazel eyes roved over me. He sighed loudly.

For once, he seemed uncertain. He had asked to speak to me, not the other way around, which meant that he knew what he wanted to say, but still hesitated. Like he was afraid of what I might say.

"You aren't going to like this," he said.

"You want to do it," I said, motioning to the rest of the church. "Trade me for Nathaniel."

"Nate," Mr. Wrightworth said sternly. "An hour with you for a night with him. But I need you to agree to it. You can withdraw consent at any time, like any other thing."

"So that you can play with him," I snarled.

"Being petulant isn't going to help either of us," Mr. Wrightworth said.

"Why do you want to play with him?" I demanded.

"Why wouldn't I want to play with Nate?" Mr. Wrightworth countered, then the man stiffened and straightened.

He was off the door in a moment, his arms wrapping around me as he drew me close. I let out a hiss of pain, my back still hurt from the whipping only a few days before. He had even made certain that the dress I wore covered the entirety of my back and shoulders.

It was the most covering any dress had provided since before I had signed the contract for Nathaniel.

"It has nothing to do with you not being good enough and everything to do with figuring out why. Nathaniel couldn't stand Mayfair, and I don't think he'd willingly accept to be Nate around her. I need to do this to make certain he's okay."

I sighed and dropped my head to his chest. I felt like something was going on that I should have understood. That Mr. Wrightworth had come towards me because he had realized that I just didn't get it. It was one of those things that I knew should have been obvious, but I just couldn't figure it out.

From that point onward it kept running at the back of my mind. turning over as I tried to make the connection.

"I'll let Mayfair know that we'll do it, she'll probably arrange for Friday night. That's typically the play night for most of us since a majority of us work Monday to Friday. She'll also probably arrange to do it two separate days. Especially given the fact that I would push to be there waiting until she's done. We'll have to set limits, easy enough to do. The yes and no and hard limits."

He pulled away from me, tugging at his suit jacket to straighten himself out. He seemed suddenly distant like his mind was in another place. Mr. Wrightworth bit his bottom lip and smiled.

"Oh yes, that will work out quite well."

"You're going to play with him, aren't you?" I asked.

"If I don't play with him, she'll be suspicious," Mr. Wrightworth said. "Now, he will behave himself for the rest of the meeting, which means I need you to as well. Otherwise, it could bring attention to what I plan to do. When I'm done with him, he won't be able to stand. That'll give us a few days to get you ready for your hour with her."

"How do you know he'll behave?" I asked.

Mr. Wrightworth's smile grew. "Because Nate knows he doesn't get to play with me if he's disrespectful." The man reached out and caressed the side of my face. "And if you're not on your best behaviour, I will chain you up alongside him and beat you until you break. Understood?"

I shuddered at the implication. "Yes, Master."

"Good," Mr. Wrightworth purred out, in just that particular sort of way. A red came to the man's cheeks as he hesitated. "Of course, if you're good, you will be greatly rewarded. Especially given the way things have fallen out."

"Rewarded?" I asked, wondering what Mr. Wrightworth would count as a reward.

"Yes," he said, tugging at first one, then the other sleeve. "Yes, you behave, and you will be greatly rewarded."

I stepped carefully towards Mr. Wrightworth, wondering what exactly my reward would be. I looked him up and down, meeting his hazel eyes as his lips parted just slightly, revealing a toothy smile.

"If all goes well, I might even get something on Mayfair that will let me destroy her. It would have to be terrible, though, to take her down."

"But I still have to go back out there," I said.

"Yes," Mr. Wrightworth said. "You have to go back out there and not attack her. Or him. Or anyone else unless somebody provokes you. But not them. If they speak with you, you will be civil. You won't be rude to them."

"Why her?" I asked, making a disgusted face. "He knows

she's the one betrayed me."
"Yes, she is the one who betrayed you."
"So why?"
"You forget, Darling. Mayfair didn't just betray you. She also betrayed Nathaniel. So the question is very much 'why her?' Unless Nate has a plan that he hasn't shared with us. In which case, I will beat it out of him. Then beat him some more for mind fucking you. Some heads up would have been great.
"Met him for coffee three weeks ago, he doesn't fucking tell me he's decided to be a sub."
"You... met him for coffee."
"I couldn't exactly tell you during the civil suit and review."
"But you met him for coffee after you kissed me the first time."
"Yes."
"And *before* you kissed me again."
"Yes," Mr. Wrightworth said with a small frown. "Where exactly did you think I had learned that trick from?"
"You told him we were together?" I demanded.
"Of course, I wouldn't have proceeded without his blessing."
"No wonder he found someone else!"
"That's not why he's with her," Mr. Wrightworth responded, his hands sliding into his pockets. "Nathaniel knew what might happen. He also had no qualms about sharing with me before everything happened. He wouldn't have turned his back on you because his gay friend decided spanking you might be fun."
"Yeah, but why would he keep me around? He only knew me a couple of weeks. I'm the crazy one who's been latched onto the idea of being with him all this time. Obviously, he's moved on and wants nothing to do with me."
As I spoke, I teared up, my voice broke. I didn't even realize just how upset I was until I struggled to finish my last sentence.
"No tears, not today," Mr. Wrightworth said, coming towards me quickly. He drew me into his arms and kissed my forehead gently. "We don't know what is going on. You don't

get to cry over a maybe, only over the real thing, and for you, Darling, I'd be happy to beat it out of him."

"You're just looking for excuses to beat him," I said with a sniffle.

"Well, yes. It's not as much fun if I don't have a reason to do it."

Despite myself, I giggled.

Chapter Sixteen

When the subs went one way and the Doms the other, I was the obedient sub and went to the sub room. I sat at Nicole's feet, between her and the door, and Mary knelt at her feet on the other side. Nicole reached down and patted me on the head, a reassuring gesture as the other subs filtered into the room.

Nathaniel stopped in front of Nicole, who raised her nose slightly in defiance.

"Go play with the others," she said.

"Play?" Nathaniel asked.

I'm pretty certain they both used the word in two different ways. Nicole meant it like a child might play, Nathaniel seemed to be asking if the subs played while the Doms did work. He glanced at the others, then turned back to Nicole.

I swear he looked disappointed that the subs weren't stripping down and grabbing pillows for the pillow fight.

Doms are weird.

"Like a good sub," Nicole growled.

"I will, but the Doms talk about stuff, why are the subs sitting about on the floor with a thumb up their asses like they haven't got brains between their ears?" Nathaniel asked, then looked at Mary and me. "Here at your feet are two women with above average intelligence, yet they sit glassy-eyed and stupid."

"If the subs want to talk, they can talk. However, they don't bicker like the Doms do because they don't exactly step on one another's pride. You will not be speaking with the two at my feet. Go play with the others, Nate."

"I don't want to play with the others," he muttered, turning away from Nicole to look over the room. "Can I go sit in the corner and keep to myself?"

"No, I want to see you being an obedient sub," Nicole said, her hand running over the back of my head as Nathaniel turned back. The woman smiled as a scarlet rage came over Nathaniel's face. "It's not that difficult to play nicely."

"It is if I've disciplined half of them."

"Oh, poor baby," Nicole said in a babyish voice. "Are you a little now? Should I call your mommy?"

I wonder how much that comment will cost her if he ever becomes a Dom again.

Nathaniel frowned ever so slightly and wiped at his bottom lip. The man turned and walked towards the other subs, who scattered at his approach. None of the subs in attendance that day had been a part of the community when Nathaniel had been a sub last. They had only ever known him as a dom and were confused as to the change. I know that fact now, but at the time I watched the other subs scatter and wondered if Doms often came into the room and did something like snatch the first sub they got their hands onto.

Nicole chuckled quietly and leaned towards me.

"I'll pay for that," she murmured to me. "But he was a dick and said the same to me when I complained about the sub rooms."

"Why not see if he can pose?" Mary asked in a voice that almost sounded distant.

"You're so bad," Nicole said with a small gasp as she swatted the air over Mary's head. "Darling, it's been some time, and I know Mr. Wrightworth hasn't used posturing yet. Let's make sure you can still do the face down position."

"I did that for him," I said.

"Do it for me," Nicole said, almost sounding bored. "Face me. I want to make certain you're doing it properly."

Trying very hard not to sigh, I stood and walked in front of Nicole's chair. I didn't want to do posturing in front of all of the subs. I certainly didn't want to do it in front of Nathaniel. However, to be a good, obedient sub like I had to be, I had to obey the Dom in the room with the subs.

Under her watchful eye, I knelt and shifted into the face down position, which presented my backside upward. For a moment I struggled because something about the posture wasn't right.

Nicole knelt beside me and adjusted my body with her hands gently. The moment I was in the position, I knew, it felt so nice. She ran a hand over my back, then down one of my hips, around, up the other hip and back up my spine. The hand barely touched me and didn't quite cause pain, but everywhere it flowed over my back, there was a tingling sensation that wasn't quite either pain or pleasure.

"There are lots of different variations of this, where your master could tie your hands behind your hips, like so," Nicole guided my hands behind me and positioned them. "When I was a sub, my Dom bind me like this with a vibrator tied between my hands and placed just so. Then he beat me until I came. It was amazing amounts of fun."

"I'd rather not..." I grumbled to the floor.

"Nate," Nicole barked out suddenly. "Are you allowed to look at other women?"

"Mistress hasn't said as much," Nathaniel responded, his voice coming closer. "She might enjoy that position, though, I've never done it myself."

"Down on your knees, and I'll show you how to do the face down position," Nicole said, patting my back gently. "Stay there, let's see if it bothers your leg. You've been working out, right Darling?"

"Yes," I said.

"Yes Mistress Nicole," she responded. "In here I get a title. Out there, I'd just be Nicole."

"Yes, Mistress Nicole," I echoed back.

"Good," Nicole said in that tone of voice before she turned to Nathaniel and began to show him how to go into the face down position.

It looked ridiculous because he was still in his full suit. I was a little surprised he could manage it.

"What are you snickering at?" Nicole demanded suddenly, jabbing a finger at one of the other subs behind us.

"She moved," a sub said quickly.

"And?" Nicole asked, walking around behind me. "Oh,

oh dear," she reached gently and pulled my skirt back to where it belonged. "Normally I catch that before they do, sorry, Darling. How's your leg?"

"Fine, Mistress Nicole."

"Good to know. When you first visited me, that hurt after a few moments. Why don't you sit up? Don't want to push it too far."

I sat up, easing back as my hip did protest. It had been fine sitting forward, but I wasn't often in positions for long periods of time. Mr. Wrightworth had continued with the workout that Nathaniel had set up for me. My hip certainly didn't hurt as often as it used to.

Nicole winked at me as I stood, then looked down at Nathaniel.

"Mr. Wrightworth tends to prefer males. Most Dommes, females who dominate men, prefer a man to sit up. Nath—Nate, show Darling how you would sit for her if she were a domme."

Nathaniel sat up, but there was something arrogant about how he did it. The man seemed to stare past Nicole as he straightened and shifted his legs. His weight went onto his heels, knees apart with his hands on his legs, palms facing upward.

His face was blank, no mask in place, but no readable emotion.

"And there," Nicole said, pointing at Nathaniel's face, "there is the good sub. You see the readied expression. No anger, no hesitance. That is the face of a man who would be willing to do whatever you asked of him, just to please you."

But he'll never be mine.

A panic welled up inside my chest. I felt as if air wasn't getting into my lungs. I must have gone pale, because Nicole was there in a moment, leading me out of the room. The door closing behind us seemed far too loud.

"Why are you panicking?" she asked.

I dropped to my knees, to keep the floor from jumping up to meet me. I got in several breaths as the door opened.

"Get back inside," Nicole snapped.

"Is she all right?" Nathaniel asked.

"It's not your concern, get back inside!" Nicole all but

shouted.

The door closed quickly. Nicole knelt as a door across the church opened. A voice called out, asking what was going on. Nicole called back, but I didn't hear her answer. The whole world was narrowing down to pinpricks. I heard footsteps, then felt a hot hand against my back.

Mr. Wrightworth wrapped an arm around me, pulling me close as he pushed my face against his suit. The scent of the man brought me back. Tears spilled from my eyes as I pressed against him.

"It's okay, Darling, you're okay," he said, pity colouring his voice.

It had been so long since I had heard pity in Mr. Wrightworth's voice. His arms tightened around me. The throbbing pain from my still bruised back was what brought me back the most.

The panic, however, had taken everything out of me. I curled closer to Mr. Wrightworth but no longer tried to get away.

"What happened?" he asked Nicole raggedly.

"I just did what you told me to do, tested him to see if he'd behave. We were going through some positions. I mean, I've never seen him look like that before, but I don't know why seeing someone else look like that would make her react like that."

"Look like what?" Mr. Wrightworth demanded.

"Well, you know, the waiting sub face," Nicole said.

"He... he did that for you?" Mr. Wrightworth asked.

"Technically I told him to show her how he would sit if she were his domme," Nicole said. Mr. Wrightworth made a choking sound, to which Nicole responded with, "Right? Anyways, I have to get back in there. He's not that good."

"Good enough?" Mr. Wrightworth asked.

"He's breaking her rules, not yours, Mr. Wrightworth," Nicole said before she slipped back into the sub room.

Mr. Wrightworth was silent for a while before he lifted my face off his suit jacket.

"I'm going to hurt him, for making you cry."

"It's not his fault," I said. "I'm just stupid, and I don't even know why that happened."

"You melted down when you saw him go full submissive," Mr. Wrightworth said.

"I know, and it's stupid because he is a sub."

Mr. Wrightworth's hand slid from my chin to my throat, tightening until I whimpered out. He had my full attention, and he knew it as his hazel eyes narrowed just slightly.

"It took his master six months to make him submit like that," Mr. Wrightworth murmured, then shook his head. "And he just slipped into it."

"Once you know it—"

"Once you know, it's hard to deny," Mr. Wrightworth said sternly. "Nate hasn't submitted to her. He's obeying my rules, not hers and just then? In there? He submitted to you, not Nicole."

"No, he did what she said, to do your thing," I said, shaking my head.

Mr. Wrighworth sighed and pulled me to my feet.

"We'll just have to figure out if you want to be a domme, but that's still at least six months away before you're ready to pout and stomp your feet and be bratty. Domme is a year or more."

"I can be bratty," I grumbled.

"Not yet, you can't," Mr. Wrightworth muttered. "But if anything, Friday proved you still have that capability." The man paused to smile, then motioned with his head to the sub room. "Get back in there. And if you're feeling unstable, just stretch."

"Why?" I asked.

"It's chilly in here," he said, that Cheshire cat smile appearing.

"I don't get it," I said, shaking my head before I walked back into the sub room.

Nicole had her crop in hand and an annoyed look on her face as she turned towards the door. I blinked at her, and she motioned with the crop to the seat she usually took.

"Sit there," she demanded.

I rushed to the seat and sat. Over the next hour, Nicole lectured the room about being petty cunts—yes, that was the word she used to describe the mingled genders of the room—when someone else was feeling unstable. She ranted, raved a little bit, and delivered several whistling blows to anyone who shifted or adjusted their weight.

As her lecture ended, she allowed the subs to move. I stretched my arms upward, cracking my back as I did so. With my arms up in the air, I groaned and then opened my eyes slightly.

And found every man in the room staring at my chest.

Arms still up in the air, I frowned as Nicole turned around. The woman almost laughed, placing a hand over her mouth.

"Dismissed, get out," she said to the others. "I just can't stand to look at any of you."

The other subs, Nathaniel included, left the room. Only the other subs seemed to flee from Nathaniel as the man almost stalked them. Nicole motioned to Mary, who also fled the room.

"Uh, are ya cold, Izzy?" Nicole asked.

"No," I said, shaking my head.

"You're used to having them bound, so it's probably never come up before..." Nicole said as she approached me. "And you don't need a bra with how perky those things are. But your nipples stand out when you're cold."

Frowning, I looked down, then gasped and slapped my hands over my breasts. Horrified, I gaped at Nicole, who giggled and waved a hand at me.

"You'll see a great deal more here. They were gaping at you because of that whole sundress, girl next door look. And because some subs swear they get wet anytime a Dom is aroused, and that was definitely some hard Dom that walked out of this room."

"What's that even mean?" I asked.

"Oh, Darling, I always forget how silly you are, come on," Nicole said, offering me her arm.

I took her arm more out of habit than because I wanted to. Nicole led me out of the room and then across the church to Mr. Wrightworth's side. She handed me over to Mr. Wrightworth, then frowned slightly at him.

"They're called nipples," Nicole said.

"I know that," Mr. Wrightworth growled, eyes on my chest for a moment before he jerked towards Nicole and glowered at her.

The woman laughed, laughed like they were sharing a good joke, then she turned and walked away. Her hips swayed back and forth as she went as if daring the man to come after her.

To my surprise, Mr. Wrightworth seemed to lurch forward, then caught himself and straightened, tugging at his jacket as he looked me up and down.

"My shoe needs to be tied," he said. "Bend over and do it."

"Bend?" I asked. "As in at the waist?"

"Yes, bend at the waist and tie my shoe."

Weirdest request ever.

I bent at the waist and found his shoes were both tied. "Uh, both are—"

"Retie them," he said quickly.

"Oookay."

I untied, then retied first one, then the other shoe. After having tied the shoes, I straightened and looked up at Mr. Wrightworth to see if I had done a good job. I found the man staring off across the church.

I turned to see what he was looking towards.

Nathaniel's icy green eyes were on me, every line of him screaming a challenge. My body responded with a tremble, each muscle vibrating as I fought the instinct to run. As it was, I reached to Mr. Wrightworth for protection. He was the only Dom in the church who might have stopped Nathaniel from acting on his desires when he had that particular look on his face.

Did I want to run to him, or away from him?

I was caught up in Nathaniel's eyes until Mayfair stepped in the way, her bleach blond hair swaying like straw in the wind. She looked up at him, and Nathaniel turned to her woodenly, a mask coming over his face as he responded to something she said. I turned away when I saw her turning towards me.

My eyes shifted to Mr. Wrightworth.

"Go sit beside Nicole," he said.

I went off towards the back of the church, where we had been sitting before. It was easy to spot Nicole. The subs hadn't wanted to sit near her and so the pews were all but empty. All the other seats were stuffed full of people, leaving rows and rows empty.

Nicole smiled at me as I slid down the aisle and sat beside her.

"What's going on?" she asked quietly.

"I don't know," I said, shaking my head.

Mr. Wrightworth approached Mayfair and Nathaniel. He spoke to Mayfair, keeping his eyes firmly on the woman. With his hands in his pockets, Mr. Wrightworth nodded and even managed a smile. Finally, he and Mayfair shook hands, and he walked away without looking back. I kept my eyes on Mr. Wrightworth as he slid down the aisle and sat beside me. He draped an arm over my shoulders.

"Friday night," he said, keeping his eyes front. "Don't look that way, she's smiling at you in a fucked up sort of fashion. Do you need any more proof?"

"Proof of what?" I asked.

Mr. Wrightworth looked around me, to Nicole.

"Apparently it hasn't sunk in yet," Mr. Wrightworth said.

"Well, proof of how dense she is is really in the answer the question no one dares to ask," Nicole murmured. "Who was Nate's original master?"

"Mayfair," I said, catching myself as I tried to motion to the woman. "She's wearing the ring, and it fits her."

"Yes, she is," Mr. Wrightworth said. "And I'm going to break the bitch's fingers."

I looked at Mr. Wrightworth, then focused on his purple tie. Frowning, I turned and looked at Nicole, who shook her head in response.

"Oh, hell no," she said. "I'm not getting more involved in this."

"What do I need more proof of?" I asked quietly, trying not to speak above a whisper because I figured that whatever I needed evidence of, the rest of the congregation didn't need to know.

"She's wearing the ring?" Nicole asked Mr. Wrightworth over my head.

"Yes," Mr. Wrightworth said. "Wish I had a drink at least, to take the edge off."

"Poor dear," Nicole murmured. "Mary, give him your flask for a moment, would you?"

"Sure," Mary said, fumbling with her purse.

She withdrew a flask, which she passed to Nicole who handed it to Mr. Wrightworth.

"Why does she have a flask?" I asked Nicole.

"She's an alcoholic who can only drink when I tell her she can," Nicole responded blandly.

The two facts didn't quite link up in my mind. As it turned out, Mary's previous master had started a dreadful habit. It would take several years for her to recover, but she would.

Mr. Wrightworth brought the flask to his lips, then resealed it as he continued to look forward. He handed the flask to me, and I gave it to Nicole.

She arched an eyebrow at me.

"I don't want any," I said, then looked forward.

Ezekiel stepped up to the pulpit and cleared his throat gently. "As we all know, there is a member of the congregation that is still recovering from a trying time. It's been brought to our attention that several subs were saying inappropriate things when this person began to become unstable. For those who would like to know if your sub was one of those involved, please see Nicole after the meeting."

"You worked faster than usual," Mr. Wrightworth muttered.

"I only had to tell Ezekiel," Nicole whispered in response. "He was represented first and foremost in the event. I thought he'd like to know. Maybe the next time she wants to disrespect me, she'll think twice."

"You and her fight like cats and dogs."

"Bitch took my man."

"You aren't built to be a sub," Mr. Wrightworth said as if it was a conversation they had had too often.

"For that man, I would be a sub," Nicole growled out.

"For, like, a week," Mr. Wrightworth responded.

Nicole bit her bottom lip. "But what a week it would be."

Mr. Wrightworth was silent. Apparently, this was not part of the ritual, for Nicole shifted and frowned at him, then at me as if I had kept Mr. Wrightworth from talking.

"Darling will need to play at being a domme," Mr. Wrighworth said, keeping his eyes carefully forward. "It was also brought to my attention that she might enjoy playing with another woman."

"I wasn't playing with my boobs!" I protested louder than I meant to.

The entire church turned towards me, which made me sink lower in my seat. My face heated up as Nathaniel's eyes locked with mine, then Mayfair's. I wanted to melt into a puddle and ooze away.

Slowly, everyone turned back to face Ezekiel.

"That could be interesting," Nicole murmured. "But I think she'd rather top a man and be topped by a woman. Not this woman, though, she's not got that flavour of damaged that I like. You can keep her special kind of crazy to yourself."

"What special kind of crazy is that?" Mr. Wrightworth asked before he turned his full attention to Nicole.

"The kind that makes you and everyone else who plays with her lose their fucking minds and think that she's just the best sub ever. Because there are already two of you competing for her attention, I think three of us might be a bit too much for her tiny brain to handle. Let alone the community.

"You two are going to rip each other apart over a woman without any concern to the fact that she has a mind of her own and should use it to choose rather than have you spill blood."

"What do you mean the two of them would tear each other apart?" I asked. "Obviously I don't want Mayfair, so there's nothing to fight about."

"Oh, Darling," Nicole said, patting me gently on the shoulder. "There's no way in hell that Mayfair wants you because she wants you. She wants you because she wants to kill you but can't, so play is the nearest she'll ever come."

"Then who's the second Dom?" I asked.

"You were warned not to poke the sadists," Mary muttered.

I had no idea what Mary meant at the time. I was a little naive at that age.

Nicole, however, found it hilariously funny.

Chapter Seventeen

Monday morning at ten, I was sitting before the review board. They gaped at me as if they couldn't believe their ears when I made my demand. The only one who wasn't surprised was Mr. Wrightworth, though technically he had talked me into it.

"You do realize that, if you go through with this, you will have to stand as a witness during his trial?" one of them managed asked.

"I do, yes," I said. "What I don't understand is why charges weren't laid when I was taken from him. Clearly, I had been raped and tortured. Yet the Program did nothing to help me in that way. You allowed it to go untended for months on end. Evidence could have been lost or altered in the meantime. You may have enabled my assailant to go free."

"Did Mr. Wrightworth advise you to press charges against Albert Edwards?" another asked.

"Mr. Wrightworth told me that charges could not be laid unless I laid them against Mr. Edwards, but he in no way coerced me into pressing charges. I was assaulted, and you did nothing!"

"The civil suit meant that we couldn't press charges," Mr. Wrightworth said in a bored tone.

He hadn't told me that before. It would be years and years later that I would learn that the civil suit was started almost immediately because Albert hoped that the evidence would be destroyed. The laws are not what they are now. They did not always protect the victim of an assault.

"You don't get to talk to me like that," I snapped at him. "You knew this entire time that charges hadn't been laid, and you didn't tell me. When it finally did come up, you said that after the civil suit completed, the criminal charges could be laid. At no point did anyone tell me that I had to do it. You're fucking pathetic! This is the great Program?

"First you forget my orientation. Then I don't get told about my job, then you forget to invite me to myown review, and now you've neglected to mention that I'm the one who had to lay charges against my assailant. If I were attacked in the slums like that, the police wouldn't wait for me to say yes, they'd charge him. Yet here you are, just letting it all slide.

"Why haven't you been building a case? Why haven't you collected every scrap of evidence that you could? Why is it that the civil suit was thrown out last week yet none of you mentioned that I still had lay charges?

"How many of you has Albert paid off?"

There was an uncomfortable shifting down the whole table. The shifting made Mr. Wrightworth look livid.

The man's lips, which a moment before had been curling upward in that smile of his, were suddenly pressed into a thin line. All other expression seemed to be gone, and yet that irritability was still there. It very much looked like the expression of a man who was about to start planning the detailed and excruciating murders of his coworkers.

Suspecting that I had just struck a cord, I stood and clenched my hands into fists at my sides.

"I want to press charges against Albert Edwards. If there isn't a police officer here to take my statement, I'm going to sue you all!"

Everyone went deathly still.

"Yeah, that's right, I've been watching television, I know I can do that now," I spat out at them.

I left the review room, slamming the door behind me. Furious, I paced outside the door. When they left the room, I snarled at them all. Mr. Wrightworth left last and cocked an eyebrow at me.

"They probably aren't taking money from Albert, but likely are afraid of the man, as most sane people are," Mr.

Wrightworth said. "But your accusations also means that there will be a full audit. Which also means someone is going to find out how much I spend on sex toys and my tithing to the church."

"That's a problem?" I asked.

"My sexual preferences are not up for public consumption."

"Neither are mine, but I'm going to have to stand trial alongside Nathaniel's father," I said. "It's going to come out. It's all going to come out. And you are going to be more than just audited for what's happened. They'll ask how many others you've taken on, who you've slept with, the whole nine yards."

"What in the name of hell have the controllers been showing you?" Mr. Wrightworth asked.

"I got bored when you weren't available, okay? They kept me entertained."

"With what?" he asked.

"A few shows from just before the collapse that involved politicians and dirty cops," I said with a shrug.

"That's more than just a wee bit frightening," he responded with a sudden accent.

"Did you just—"

"Ah, Officers Randal and Janine," he said, looking past me with a broad smile. "Good of your captain to send you. Do you understand your purpose?"

I turned as the two police officers came to a stop. Not Program guards, they were dressed in full black uniforms. Both of them looked bulky because of the bullet proof vests they wore and all the equipment they carried with them wherever they went.

"We were checking on my sister during a break," the woman, Janine, said, then glanced at me. "We weren't told why you requested at least one female officer."

"This is Isabella Martin," Mr. Wrightworth said gently, reaching out to set a hand on my shoulder. "Concerning an event that I have a case number for in my office. Miss. Martin wishes to press criminal charges against Albert Edwards."

"Albert Edwards?" the man, Randal, asked, his eyebrows

almost meeting his hairline. "With all due respect, it'd be easier to kill the man than press charges against him. He's got more money than most rich folk, and a team of lawyers to back him."

"I want to press charges, not have people try to talk me out of it!" I snapped at Randal.

"Easy, Miss. Martin," Janine said, raising her hand to stop me from protesting more. "We would never suggest that you let an assailant go. Why don't we go to Mr. Wrightworth's office, bring up the case file, and go from there, okay?"

I went through hours of interviewing. Their main question was why I hadn't pressed charges earlier. The Program heads had nearly screwed me over. While I could not have taken Albert to court for criminal charges while he was attempting a civil suit to have my contract—and me—turned over to him, I could have made my wishes known.

Fucking men, they nearly let him walk!

Mr. Wrightworth saved me by admitting that the Program had obviously made a huge mistake. He threw the entire contract system under the bus, himself included.

In reality, I don't doubt that Mr. Wrightworth had always intended for me to press charges. I fully believe that he put off telling me that I had to press charges until he was certain that I was his. Yes, his actions had brought me out of my shell, it had saved me in so many ways,

but at its core, Mr. Wrightworth took me on to put an end to Albert Edwards.

I don't blame him, who could? He had waited years, patiently biding his time, for Albert to make a mistake. In me, he had made the mistake. Not because I survived, not because Mr. Wrightworth had it on record that Albert had broken the law, but because Albert had failed to break me.

He had come close. He had done terrible things, things that I still dream about, things that aligned with that fucked up first contract I had been offered. But at the end of it all, Albert had been unable to break me. If he had managed to do that, I would have been dead and disappeared like so many others.

After establishing the reason why I hadn't sought to press charges earlier, I was then questioned about everything. That was when it came out, just how much I remembered. I told them what I did remember, I was honest about the foggy parts. At the end of it all, I heard the most horrifying words I have ever heard:

"The building she was held in had working surveillance, it's all on record and was used during the civil suit," Mr. Wrightworth said. "As part of the review of the contract between Miss. Martin and Nathaniel Edwards, Albert Edwards' son and heir, I was required to watch the videos to determine if the contract was breached."

I shut down after that.

It's easier to function when you don't know that others witnessed your every folly. Coming to terms with the fact that Mr. Wrightworth saw everything was difficult. Despite hearing it then, once we left his office, I just sort of blocked it all out. Like it didn't happen.

The police officers questioned me for several hours then left with their reports. They filed their reports, everything went through the processes and then two detectives were sent out the next day.

They wanted pictures taken. Pictures had been taken before but now was different. What they wanted were pictures of the scars, the lasting damage of Albert's actions.

It was the first bump in the road.

Mr. Wrightworth and I had to explain our relationship, to which the detectives scoffed and left.

Yes, I was left because it was believed that because I was a sub because I enjoyed impact play, I had wanted Albert to do what he had done to me. They not only thought I deserved what I got, but that I liked it and now, months later, I was pressing charges like a lover scorned.

Mr. Wrightworth made a call, and the same two detectives came back, only with a third in tow. The lone detective listened to what the detectives said, then he listened to what I said.

Little did I know, the detective was one of Oberon's 'victims.' The man was seducing anyone he could at the capital, introducing them to the life, no matter how vanilla their interactions were within the community. He was trying to spread understanding as quickly as possible, then transferring those of certain positions to other cities where he knew the community existed.

The detective listened to us all and then requested the pictures. He asked Mr. Wrightworth to step out of the room and then began questioning me with the other two detectives.

My behaviour changed almost immediately.

I was nervous and fidgety. One of the first detectives asked me a question in such a tone that I started crying. The detective called Mr. Wrightworth back into the room, and the interview continued.

His concern wasn't whether I had enjoyed what Albert had done to me. He had separated us to try to find out if Mr. Wrightworth was taking advantage of a victim. Upon putting us back together, I became more stable. I trusted Mr. Wrightworth to protect me.

I trust my Master.

Unknown to me at that time, this detective would question everyone about us and subpoena Mr. Wrightworth's records. A thing that had never been done before. Mr. Wrightworth was quite upset when it happened, but he didn't explain what had upset him.

He didn't just investigate my claims against Albert.

He investigated Mr. Wrightworth and then Nathaniel.

He protected me, the victim. That's not something that someone from the community could say about themselves. Nicole defended victims. Mr. Wrightworth would do what he could to discipline members, but at the end of the day, a victim was still left to their own.

This man spent his time making certain that I wasn't being taken advantage of. He did it in a way that was out of sight of me, and it only came to light when he was testifying later on. He never asked for anything in return. He never joined the community, and we did not become good friends afterward.

But I watched his career and his life. A man like that doesn't come along every day. I wasn't the only one he helped, but I was probably the first.

Pictures were taken. I had to do a special session with a court-appointed therapist, to gauge whether or not I'd be able to take the stand.

Charges, they said, would be laid. Warrants and the like had to be found. It might be another week before Albert was taken into custody. He would stand at a bail hearing almost immediately—most rich folks do—and then be released.

Except. One of the first warrants issued was one to search the grounds of the estate he took me to.

Oops.

They say karma's a bitch.

On Wednesday I was taken from the Program building, with Mr. Wrightworth in tow, and down to the building thing. It was the place where the prosecution worked out of or something. I don't know. I wasn't paying that close of attention because I was all but keening in the backseat of the town car that picked us up. Mr. Wrightworth looked uncomfortable and drew me into his arms the moment we stepped out of the car.

It was nothing like the other times I had been upset. Sure, I think he enjoyed himself, he enjoyed seeing me upset. But there was a limit to even his tolerance. I had gone from strong woman submitting to his whim to a broken toy that was about to collapse at any moment.

He had to pull me into the room because I had set my feet and didn't want to go.

Mr. Wrightworth sat me down as the prosecutors stared at me. They questioned my stability, and Mr. Wrightworth delivered a blistering lecture. His tone of voice was very much the strong Master. My confidence returned because he stood up for me.

I apologized and asked them what they needed.

And then I had to reiterate everything I had said to everyone else. They asked all the difficult questions, but it all boiled down to:

"Did you enjoy what Albert Edwards did to you?"

"No."

"Are you confident that is your answer? Given your lifestyle—"

"Based on your face, you're a fucking idiot."

"Darling!" Mr. Wrightworth barked out quickly.

I lowered my head and gritted my teeth, struggling with my emotions.

Finally, I looked up at the prosecutor, who sighed.

"They're going to ask this question. We aren't allowed to tell you what exactly to say, but we strongly suggest that you don't respond with sarcasm or hostility. I would recommend allowing them to finish what they are asking. It shows respect."

"But it also shows submission," Mr. Wrightworth said. "The point of this all is that Isabella doesn't just submit to anyone. She didn't agree to submit to Albert. That edge to her is what kept her alive, what got her out."

I sat through their little debate, turning it over in my head.

"My chosen lifestyle is one which results in physical pain at times," I said, interrupting their debate without warning. "But it is also about consent and submission. I have only ever agreed to submit to two men. Nathaniel Edwards, my original contract holder, and Mr. Wrightworth, someone who Nathaniel told me I could trust and should submit to if something were to happen. I never submitted to Albert Edwards. I definitely did not consent. The important part of my lifestyle is being safe and giving consent. I think the medical reports will tell you that it was not safe, and I am telling you that there was no consent given."

The prosecutors gawked at me for a very long time before one of them jabbed the other one.

"Good," he said quickly. "That's a good start."

And their questions continued. They hounded me the way they expected the defense lawyers would, to prepare me as best they could.

It helped, in some ways. In others, it just made things worse.

Their job, they said, was to get me through the trial.

In reality, their job was to put on a good show for the citizens. Whether win or lose—because against Albert Edwards they fully expected to lose—they had to make it appear as if they stood for the victims no matter the Goliath they stood against.

They didn't talk about the videos.

In all the old police dramas there might be photos, but video surveillance in the early twenty-first century was nothing like it was while I was growing up. People fought against being taped at all times, not realizing that even as they struggled against Big Brother, they were already being watched and controlled in frightening ways.

We have video and audio of everything.

Rich people pay to keep their stuff private, as long as they don't get caught. Poor people are always watched, and the government kept an eye on big time criminals, taking out who they could when they could. Slum justice still had to prevail, so many were born and then died never knowing that every second of their lives was recorded and then stored in the national archives.

You can watch those videos, though, and not truly know the people behind them. You can't get into their minds. You don't know what they're thinking of when they sigh, or when they walk off by themselves and start crying. You can't pinpoint the exact thoughts going through their minds.

Watching my videos, I can see it and remember it like it's all tagged inside my mind. I can pinpoint the moment I decided to kill myself, a sort of calm came over me. I can see it on my face when my brother dragged me into the contract room. I saw the rage in me when I was raped, and the longing when I saw Nathaniel for the first time.

But others, looking in, can still only speculate.

The human creature is predictable, but at the same time, the fact that we are all human and separate keeps our minds to ourselves. Some of us are more shallow than others. Some cannot be understood at all.

Video data proved that I was raped and tortured, but the difficult task was to prove whether or not I truly believed that I had been raped. Or if—because I was a sub and in no small part a masochist—I enjoyed what had been done to me and asked for, or wanted, it.

The other charges filed against Albert Edwards by the prosecution were mainly just dressing. They could prove all that easily enough, but if they could prove that I had wanted what was done to me, then all was lost. The debate would then change over to death contracts, and those people choose to be hurt, so obviously Albert had done nothing wrong because everyone he interacted with wanted it.

They also didn't tell me that at the time, though in their

defense, they were afraid the pressure would ruin me.

By Thursday I was worn out, and I think everyone but me knew it. I was still learning my boundaries at the time, so waking to find my door locked almost pushed me over the edge. Mr. Wrightworth arrived at ten and apologized, taking me to his rooms.

There he tucked me into bed and watched over me until I fell asleep once more. I woke sometime around one to an empty apartment and tried to make myself breakfast. I knew the basics, but cooking was something I was never good at. Mr. Wrightworth arrived at about two to find me crying over burned eggs.

Not because I had discovered something I wasn't good at, but because I had wasted food. He made me lunch, and we ate in silence before he sat me down in the living room and began dictating.

"Tomorrow night Nate will come here—you can still back out at any time, even afterward. You need to be here because as far as anyone knows, he's coming to spend the night to figure out some sort of what's going on."

"Will that be decided?" I asked, unable to meet his eyes.

"The decision has already been made," Mr. Wrightworth said.

"And?" I asked.

"Not right now, Isabella."

"Izzy," I corrected for the millionth time.

"Tomorrow night Nate will come," Mr. Wrightworth repeated. "You will be here. We will all eat, under my rules. You have been obeying those rules right off, so I hope you will continue to follow them tomorrow night."

"Yes, Master," I said glumly, picking at the leg of my pyjama bottoms.

"Don't get petulant with me, or I will give you orders for tomorrow night," Mr. Wrightworth growled out.

Hope flared, I dared to glance up at him, but didn't voice my question.

"After dinner, you will come in here, and I will put something on the television. Nate and I will go to the playroom. Do you remember what I said before?"

"Uh, I wasn't punished for spying?" I asked.

Mr. Wrightworth sighed loudly.

"Watching can teach us much about our cravings. The important thing is that the sub never catches you unless you are given permission beforehand. Nate is not a sub who enjoys public displays. He was lent out once by his Master and did not enjoy it. It was punishment. If you see anything, you will never say anything to Nate about watching him."

"Yes, Master."

"You will sit on this couch. You will watch the video I put on for you," Mr. Wrightworth said sternly, pointing first at me, then at the screen. "Once the video is done, you will be free to go to bed or take a bath. Masturbate if you please, but you cannot leave this apartment."

"Can I put what I want on the television?" I asked.

"As long as it's not a police procedural," Mr. Wrightworth muttered dryly. "I think you've had enough of that for the rest of your life."

"Fine, no police procedural shows," I said.

"Tomorrow night is not the time to be a domme," Mr. Wrightworth said.

"I wasn't planning on it," I said with a shake of my head and a frown.

Mr. Wrightworth frowned as well. It was only then that I realized that he could read me like most could read a book. Whatever he had read on my face said that I wanted to see Nathaniel tied and beaten.

Maybe that was true. Maybe I wanted Nathaniel underfoot even then. For fucking me over and jerking me about, for kneeling before Mayfair instead of hanging on for me. Maybe, just maybe, I wanted to see him suffer for what I considered the slights against me.

"Darling, I meant what I said," Mr. Wrightworth murmured as he leaned forward just slightly.

"What in particular are you talking about?" I asked.

"That I will hurt him for making you cry."

Chapter Eighteen

The next night I arrived at Mr. Wrightworth's before Nathaniel did. He had just enough time to touch the side of my face, fingers grazing over my cheekbone as he seemed to take me in. Even as I looked up at Mr. Wrightworth, I had to wonder how much I had changed since the last time Nathaniel and I were alone.

Even my features had changed, the scars were still marring my skin, though they were not as vivid then as they had been to start. My hair was slowly growing back but was still barely longer than the original pixie cut.

Our eyes locked as there was a second knock on the door. We stood like that for a moment. His hand on my cheek, the other hand settling on my hip as we stood in silence.

He pulled away without a sound and opened the door.

We greeted Nathaniel as one, then Mr. Wrightworth asked the question just as he had always asked me:

"Have you eaten?"

"No," Nathaniel responded as he closed the door and shrugged out of his suit jacket, which he handed to me.

"Tie as well, Nate," Mr. Wrightworth said sternly.

"Sorry, habit," he said, then removed the blue tie and handed that to me as well.

I took both and hung them up where Mr. Wrightworth put his outerwear, behind the door. Then I followed them both through the kitchen, into the dining room and sat. The food was already on the table, waiting for us. Salad, I'm not certain what kind. I doubt it was a 'kind' of salad besides something that Mr. Wrightworth threw together with items he had in his fridge.

We ate in awkward silence.

Nathaniel focused on the food, paying close attention to how much food was left on Mr. Wrightworth's plate. Once we were finished eating, Mr. Wrightworth set down his fork. We followed suit. My plate was almost empty, Nathaniel's about half-full.

Nathaniel stood and took my plate then his, then walked around the table and took Mr. Wrightworth's plate without comment. I frowned at him as he walked into the kitchen. I turned that frown to Mr. Wrightworth, who frowned back at me as if to ask why I was confused.

Mr. Wrightworth typically cleaned the table. He had also basically inhaled his food, which was abnormal for him. Generally he took his time and idled his way through dinner.

Nathaniel returned and knelt by the dining table. His face was lowered, hands placed on his legs, palms upward. Seeing him like that made me bite my bottom lip. I knew what that position meant. As much as I knew that Mr. Wrightworth had plans with Nathaniel, I wanted to be there, kneeling and ready to serve.

Though, Mr. Wrightworth had never asked me to be kneeling at the start of play. That seemed more of something a slave would do instead of a sub.

Masters have slaves. Doms have subs.

Mr. Wrightworth stood and tugged at his tie. He walked around the table and motioned to me as I stared at Nathaniel, wondering why he had done that and how he knew that he should have done it.

Mr. Wrightworth pulled me into the living room, sat me down and put something on the television. Then he walked back into the dining room. I kept my eyes carefully on the television as the video played.

It was ten minutes long.

What in the fuck is he playing at?

I had taken to keeping my journal at Mr. Wrightworth's because I trusted that he wouldn't pry. After finding several of my items moved, I knew someone was going through my belongings in the apartment. That had been when I shifted my journal to Mr. Wrightworth's place.

The journal sat in the living room on the coffee table at all times. While the first video played through, I filled out a few pages in frustration. The television automatically played through several more videos as I added to the journal.

Then I got bored. I cocked my head between videos and swore I heard something. Ever so slightly, I turned towards the playroom. I listened to the sound again and fully turned.

It was an indescribable sound. It took hearing it several more times before I registered what that noise was.

The strike of leather on flesh, and the small moan of need.

If he wanted me to stay put, why was the video only ten minutes long?

I stood and edged down the hallway.

The light from the playroom lit up the wall as I dared to move a little closer. Mr. Wrightworth had left the door open, something he had never done while playing with me.

I stood on the precipice and came to a halt.

Despite hearing the sounds, I knew that if I looked, I would be crossing into something else entirely.

As I stood there, I wondered if I would be breaching the trust between myself and Nathaniel. I didn't know what to think of the idea. After all, I had no idea where Nathaniel and I stood. He hadn't exactly spoken to me at church, and Mr. Wrightworth's so called hints had only confused me more.

I knew that Mr. Wrightworth had wanted this, he had wanted to have Nate at his disposal. He wanted Nathaniel to kneel to him and wanted it enough to arrange this little get-together, and I didn't know why. Perhaps I wanted to watch to see if what happened in that room explained why Mr. Wrightworth had wanted Nathaniel so badly.

Taking in a small breath, I stepped into the light that escaped the playroom's partially opened door.

I peered into the room and immediately bit my bottom lip.

Nathaniel was tied to the spanking bench, but not the way that Mr. Wrightworth had ever tied me. I had been tied and knelt on the step with my body over the uppermost portion. Nathaniel was bent over the other side of the bench. His feet touched the floor, his wrists bound to the step, which stretched him out over the upper level of the spanking bench. His left side and back were towards the door and utterly naked.

Anything that is uncovered is a target.

As I thought that very thing, Mr. Wrightworth struck Nathaniel's back with a cane. The cane broke on contact, causing Mr. Wrightworth to swear and throw it across the playroom, away from the door. I flinched at the swear.

"Well, I thought I taught you the value of a proper cane," Mr. Wrightworth snapped at Nathaniel.

"I'm sorry, Master."

"Did you want it to break?" Mr. Wrightworth demanded, walking to the wall that his toys hung off on.

"No, Master," Nathaniel said.

There was no fight to his tone, but there also wasn't the distance of someone too far gone to understand what he was saying. Nathaniel had served as a sub. He would know where the line was and know not to cross it. Being too distant was disrespectful, being too in the moment led to being bitter or snarky and resulted in discipline.

"I'll just have to use my own items, tried and tested, you'd like that, wouldn't you, Nate?"

"No, Master," Nathaniel said, almost pleading.

Mr. Wrightworth almost moaned.

"Say that again."

"No, Master," Nathaniel said, in almost the same tone he had said it in before.

Mr. Wrightworth selected the flogger and walked back towards Nathaniel.

"And one more time."

Nathaniel repeated it, once more almost the same as he had before. Mr. Wrightworth responded by smacking Nathaniel gently with the flogger, then dragged it up his back.

"Consent," Mr. Wrightworth crooned.

"No," Nathaniel said with a shudder.

Mr. Wrightworth struck him, then said, "Consent."

I should be clear.

This was not Mr. Wrightworth torturing Nathaniel. It was a scene between the two of them. Mr. Wrightworth would strike and beat Nathaniel, commanding throughout for Nathaniel to give consent. It culminated in Mr. Wrightworth spanking Nathaniel quite hard with a paddle and demanding consent.

Nathaniel's response was: "Never." instead of 'no.'

Mr. Wrightworth made a sound and walked towards the door, causing me to shrink away and hide to the side of the doorway, where he couldn't see me. I all but held my breath as he fumbled with something and then walked away from the door.

Daring to look again, I watched as Mr. Wrightworth growled as he approached Nathaniel. He tore something open with his teeth.

I was confused as he pulled the item from the package. He took the item and seemed to roll it out.

Before that moment, I had never seen a condom before. The slums didn't use condoms, as contraceptives tended to be drug based, not latex in nature. I was so baffled that I missed two things.

The first was the shape of Mr. Wrightworth when he wasn't directly in my view so to speak.

The second was that first thrust.

It was Nathaniel crying out, the yank and twist of chains that drew me back to myself. Mr. Wrightworth took a long moment, his hands on Nathaniel's hips, digging in tight. As Mr. Wrightworth hesitated, Nathaniel trembled under him. It was not the struggle of a man unused to what was being done to him.

Which surprised me.

It also wasn't the reaction that I expected from someone being made to submit to a man of Mr. Wrightworth's caliber. After the shudder, Nathaniel seemed to push backward, against Mr. Wrightworth.

I slapped a hand over my mouth and pulled away from the door. With my back pressed against the wall, I stared at the other side of the hallway, where a bunny picture was hung.

It was the oddest thing and something that I hadn't noticed until that moment. I stared at the picture as the sounds from the playroom tugged at me.

The first contractee will serve the second for a term of two years.

Nathaniel cried out, begging but not voicing what in particular he was pleading for.

After a term of six months, the second contractee will serve the first.

Mr. Wrightworth had been Nathaniel's master. That was how Mr. Wrightworth had access to the videos of Nathaniel's time as a sub. That was how he knew so many intimate details about Nathaniel, what bound the two of them.

I thought the contract had been about Mr. Wrightworth working as an aide. That was what they had said.

It had been Mr. Wrightworth's ring.

Purple was Mr. Wrightworth's colour, not Mayfair's. Her violet eyes were just a freak of nature, not something she had selected for her colour. Mr. Wrightworth had been the one Nathaniel had been concerned might claim me. He was also the same man that Nathaniel had all but delivered me to.

His Master, the man who had seduced him.

What had Mr. Wrightworth said of his sub? That he had seduced a straight man, and that he had trained his sub into responding and begging for homosexual activities. Taught his sub in a similar way that he had begun training me.

The trust between the two of them, the hesitance, the slight pauses when Nathaniel had answered anything regarding Mr. Wrightworth. It hadn't just been long-term friendship. It hadn't been the contract.

It had been this.

This indescribable thing that was a Master-slave relationship.

Nathaniel trusted one person in the whole world because that person had laid him bare and not used that information to his advantage.

In terms set forward by the contractor at the time of the start of the second period.

Nathaniel hadn't served as Mr. Wrightworth's sub because Mr. Wrightworth had wanted a sub.

Mr. Wrightworth was the first contractee, Albert, the contractor. By the time Nathaniel had to submit to Mr. Wrightworth, Albert had visited him at least five times. He had, no doubt, laid out in very clear terms what was to happen to Nathaniel and when.

Their entire relationship revolved around that damnable contract.

Did Nathaniel know that Mr. Wrightworth had encouraged me to press charges against his father? Did he know what was going on in the Program building? What would he say when he found out?

Nathaniel shouting out a sound, then begging drew my attention. It was a different sort of begging, something I almost recognized as I refocused on that bunny image across the hallway from myself.

Mr. Wrightworth, for his part, had been all but silent.

How long had it been since I had actual sex?

Four months and counting since penetrative sex with a man. The thought of that made me burn with need as I bit my bottom lip.

Nathaniel used to make me sound like that.

Which didn't help matters in the least. The proper upbringing in me demanded that I walk away and pretend that I had seen nothing at all. You didn't spy on one another on purpose, and if you were caught peeping the punishment was a day in the stocks.

But Mr. Wrightworth had all but invited me to watch. Just so long as Nathaniel didn't find me. And why?

Because the idea of tying a man down and being in control of him was so very, very appealing. Maybe it was the victim in me. Maybe that desire had always been there and had just grown keener over the past months, but I wasn't just interested in the sexual act.

I wanted to watch Nathaniel pull at the bonds and know for certain he couldn't get out. I wanted him under me as I gave the orders and he eagerly did my every bidding.

Pushing off the wall, I dared to look again. Nathaniel was begging for nothing in particular, at least nothing that I knew of as an outside observer. Mr. Wrightworth had his hand at the small of Nathaniel's back, pressing down in an attempt to control Nathaniel's movements somewhat.

"Please..."

"You know what you need to do," Mr. Wrightworth

purred out. His words sent a trembling reaction through Nathaniel, causing me to take a sharp breath. I had felt it so often I recognized the outward signs of being on that precipice. The cold tingle washed over me as I watched, anticipation making me writhe in my place at the door, "if you want to be good."

Nathaniel cried out as I gasped, the sound of his voice covering my surprise.

Mr. Wrightworth had said that final word in *that* tone. The one that all the Doms seem to have mastered, the one that they kept using around me.

Except Mr. Wrightworth was the only one who used it around me, wasn't he? The others used it whenever Nathaniel was present.

'Good' said just like that was Nathaniel's trigger word.

His reaction, despite not serving as a sub for years, was instantaneous, eager even. He did as his master bid him and Mr. Wrightworth responded in kind, rubbing Nathaniel's back affectionately.

"That's very good," he repeated in that tone, causing a shudder to roll through Nathaniel in response. Mr. Wrightworth chuckled and pulled away.

He half-turned in my direction, and I bolted. I rushed into the living room, grabbed my journal, then ran into Mr. Wrightworth's bedroom and closed the door as quietly as I could. Another three pages were filled as I strained for outside sounds.

Someone went to the bathroom, quiet voices just outside the door. Then someone went into the bathroom again.

My pen hesitated just above the page as the door to the bedroom opened. Fear made me tremble, a cold gripping me as Mr. Wrightworth opened the bedroom door and stared at me with those hazel eyes. No judgment, no anger, he just studied me as he leaned on the door frame.

Looking over his shoulder towards the bathroom, Mr. Wrightworth stepped fully into the room and closed the door behind him.

"He heard you," Mr. Wrightworth muttered.

"I'm sorry, I don't know what I was thinking," I babbled.

"You were thinking two attractive males would be

engaging in a sexual act," Mr. Wrightworth said steadily. "It was I who forgot how good his hearing is. No matter, he thinks you caught a peep at the beginning, and that was it. That was one reason the television is on autoplay, to help cover the noise in the apartment itself. Of course, I damned well forgot why I do that until after the fact."

"Is he mad?" I asked.

"Goodness, no, Darling. The last person to catch him and I together was a vanilla, Nicole. Now that pissed him off, but she had put her nose where it didn't belong."

"Are..." I glanced at the bed, then to Mr. Wrightworth. "Are you two going to bed now? I can sleep on the couch."

Mr. Wrightworth smiled, lips curling up slightly. It wasn't quite the smile he liked to use so much, but close enough that I wondered if it meant something specific and I just hadn't learned its meaning yet.

"I have him for the entire night, neither he nor I will be sleeping."

"Oh," I managed to get out.

"Come help me clean the playroom while he showers," Mr. Wrightworth said with a motion. "I used to make Nathaniel clean it for others I'd play with when I gave them a reprieve. I like having a clean playroom."

"I'll help," I said, closing the journal.

I followed Mr. Wrightworth into the playroom and came to a sudden stop. There was the distinct smell of rubbing alcohol mixed with a floral sort of scent. Edging towards the spanking bench, I noticed that the bonds that had held Nathaniel had been changed. The chains on these others were longer, the manacles hadn't been used before, the leather hadn't even been creased.

With a shiver, I turned towards Mr. Wrightworth, who smiled at me and handed me a wet cloth.

"There's blood on the floor," he said gently, motioning towards my feet.

I went down on my knees immediately and wiped at a couple of drops of blood that were there. Mr. Wrightworth left the room and then returned with another caddy of items. This one was pink, the caddy that I had seen so many times before. The one he had removed had been purple.

That was my caddy.

My heart pounded in my chest as my hand paused mid-wipe. I turned my attention from the caddy to Mr. Wrightworth, who quirked an eyebrow at me.

I considered running, what with having been warned about being alone with the two of them, but I was pretty certain I'd be caught and then I'd be in trouble. Part of me was curious, however. Curious as to what the pair of them did to subs that sent such a quivering need through half of the community even while it repulsed them.

"I need something from you," Mr. Wrightworth murmured as he approached me.

"I consent," I said clearly.

"Good," he responded, holding a hand out to me.

I took the hand, and he brought me to my feet. His free hand slipped around my waist as he brought me close to him.

"Red and yellow today, Darling," Mr. Wrightworth purred out. "Or in your case, yellow and banana. If we come to anything, *anything* that makes you uncomfortable, you tell me immediately, understand?"

I remember thinking to myself that a dom and a sub because Nathaniel was clearly still in sub-mode, couldn't push my limits that much. Mr. Wrightworth would be in control like he had always been in control, and he wouldn't cross any lines while Nathaniel was there because that wasn't the time to push my limits.

And then I wondered how that would work, two subs and a Dom. Two female subs and a Dom I would have understood, the rules would be the same as a threesome with two women.

"Here," Mr. Wrightworth said, snapping his fingers in front of my face. "I might let you slide into that soft little cloud, but that can't happen tonight. Alert and understanding can give consent. Floaty and stupid cannot."

"I don't get stupid," I grumbled.

"Not particularly no, but I like seeing that glazed look in your eyes and knowing I was the one who did it," Mr. Wrightworth said with a sigh. "Now, there is no plan, can't plan when there are three because there are too many possibilities. All that can be planned is the beginning. So, over here."

He drew me to the spanking bench, and I allowed him to arrange me. Just as Nathaniel had stood, I was bound to the bench. Mr. Wrightworth took my clothing, minus my underwear, and set the items by the door. He returned and came before me, holding a wide ribbon in his hands. Satin and oh so soft, the ribbon was purple, but it wasn't quite Mr. Wrightworth's shade of purple.

The ring was Mr. Wrightworth's, so why did Nathaniel give it to Mayfair?

"I know you've wanted this for some time," Mr. Wrightworth purred out, sliding the purple ribbon through his hands. "To wear my colour, to be mine. Tonight I'm going to let you wear it. What do you say to my gift?"

"Thank you, Master."

Of course, I had thought about it, though I hadn't quite realized that it was his colour. I should have, just as I should have realized that Nathaniel and Mr. Wrightworth had been in a dom-sub relationship. But it's easy to get caught up in the moment and ignore the truth.

He walked around me and slid the ribbon under my belly. I couldn't see it, but I'm told that he tied a very nice bow. Another of his many tricks.

After tying the bow, Mr. Wrightworth set the ends carefully down my buttocks, fingertips grazing down my legs before he walked back to me.

"The underwear will be lost at some point this evening," he whispered.

"Oh?" I asked.

There was that Cheshire cat smile.

"Well, he might preach play without sex, but he's still who I trained him to be."

I made a small sound, a squeak that was almost a moan. It had been months and months, and now the sex being offered to me—at least I thought it was being offered to me—was from the man who used to look at me, and I'd get wet.

Oh right, that's what that feels like.

For all Mr. Wrightworth could taunt out of me, I never had the 'oh shit' moment of being so aroused that I was afraid of what I would find if I dropped my underwear. It had been so long that for a moment, the barest moment, I thought I had done something embarrassingly inappropriate, and then it dawned on me.

And the distinction was clear.

Mr. Wrightworth ran his fingers over my cheek, chuckling quietly.

"My dear, he has that effect on everyone. I long ago stopped being jealous of it. You might shudder at the thought of his caress, but I am the one you call Master. Say it."

"You are Master."

His response was a huff of breath, half-annoyance, half-laugh. Mr. Wrightworth looked away and wiped his lips with the back of his hand.

"We'll work on that," he said, looking at the floor and away. His hazel eyes flitted back to me. "If you aren't careful, we might, what is Mayfair's term for it...?"

"Tag team," Nathaniel's dark voice said from behind me.

There was a quality to it that I couldn't quite put my finger on. Nathaniel was behind me, out of my view. My back was to the door, just as his had been. It wasn't lost on me that Mr. Wrightworth had placed me in the same position that Nathaniel had been in.

"That's right, tag team, why is it called tag teaming, do you think?" Mr. Wrightworth asked Nathaniel, ignoring me as if they were the only two in the room.

"I don't know, as tag teaming is typically one watching and the other tagging them back in," Nathaniel said, his voice coming just a little closer. "I would think Elaina of all people would understand that that is not how we work."

"Good to see you're feeling more like yourself, Nathaniel."

A cold washed over me.

Mr. Wrightworth had only ever called Nathaniel 'Nate' since the time at the church, except, of course, during the interviews with the police officers. He took the naming system seriously, separating the subs and doms by their names alone.

And he had just called Nathaniel by his Dom name.

Fuck.

Chapter Nineteen

The spanking bench was meant to keep a sub about hip level, though it wasn't exactly Mr. Wrightworth's hip level because the man was tall and lean. Because it was about hip level I could lay across the top level, and my feet still touched the ground, but it wasn't the most comfortable position. The bench had been padded and then covered in leather, a material which is relatively easy to keep clean but also had the smell of leather, something I've not always been a fan of.

It's grown on me.

The manacles had been replaced with ones with a longer chain and smaller cuffs, more suited to my height and size. Given the fact that Mr. Wrightworth had never placed me in that position before, I assumed he had some other female sub that was about my height tied to the bench in the past.

I couldn't lift very far off the bench, making looking around me difficult as I had to crane my neck. Craning almost immediately pulled muscles in my neck, which made me cringe and set my head down on the bench.

All I caught was a glimpse of Nathaniel's disheveled hair, and that cold look as his eyes traveled down the bow wrapped around my midsection. He wasn't wearing a shirt and there was still a towel around his neck, which he had been drying his hair with moments before.

"What's this?" Nathaniel asked.

"A birthday present."

"I thought we agreed, no presents," Nathaniel said, his voice right by my hip.

Mr. Wrightworth let out a dry chuckle.

"I thought playing with me would be considered a present."

"You aren't God's gift to all men, Mr. Wrightworth," Nathaniel muttered. "Playing with you is a privilege, but I'd hardly call it a present. At least not one for me."

"True, and I do enjoy it more than you," Mr. Wrightworth sighed out. "But little Darling here was snooping. I thought I'd wrap her up in a cute bow and have you unwrap her. Underwear optional."

"Do you just lend her to anyone?" Nathaniel asked, a cold edge to his tone.

"Goodness no, only you. I'm still trying to talk her out of playing with Mayfair, but she and I both honour our word, so it's been difficult," Mr. Wrightworth said. "I only agreed to the swap because I thought she'd back out. Besides, how much harm can she do in an hour?"

"She," I swear I saw a finger jab in my direction out the corner of my eye as Nathaniel walked past me. "Can do a great deal of damage in an hour."

Mr. Wrightworth's Cheshire cat smile returned.

"Do you want your present, or not?"

Nathaniel was quiet a long moment. He looked over his shoulder at me. I blinked back at him, wondering if this whole thing had been a mistake.

"Oh, for crying out loud, Nathaniel, she's not gagged, not fully trained, and I even made certain she didn't start enjoying herself early. The woman consents."

"Do you?" Nathaniel asked as he turned entirely to me.

His green eyes locked with mine and I lost all will to breathe. Struggling to get in air, I was silent for a long moment.

"Yes, Sir."

Both of them reacted.

Nathaniel shivered, Mr. Wrightworth, behind Nathaniel, twitched.

As I watched, a thumb grazed over index and middle finger of Mr. Wrightworth's right hand. A motion that I learned meant that he wanted to smack something.

When playing with another dominant, it's always best to

see to the needs of your Master before the needs of the second Dom. A Master agreeing to let you play with another, and then watching it happen, are two different things.

In my words I had been respectful, I had used the right title.

But in my tone, there was an entirely different story.

Mr. Wrightworth might have claimed that he was merely preparing me for another Dom, but there was no denying that he had made some connection with me. He had slowed down his so-called training to take more time with me. That he had crossed what he had thought were his own lines, to test the waters with me.

Nathaniel turned to Mr. Wrightworth. The two met eyes and seemed to have a silent conversation.

The result of that conversation?

"I would love to, you know I've wanted this for months."

Yeah, to be a Dom again.

I could be dense, let's just leave it at that.

"Underwear optional," Mr. Wrightworth repeated slowly.

"Oh, you've not?"

"Goodness no, I'm still gay," Mr. Wrightworth protested.

He seemed flustered.

It made me wonder if part of Nathaniel's allure to Mr. Wrightworth was the simple fact that Nathaniel could still elicit such emotions from the well controlled Mr. Wrightworth.

"Limits?" Nathaniel asked.

"When you reach one, you'll know," Mr. Wrightworth responded.

"You...you aren't putting limits on me?" Nathaniel asked.

"No," Mr. Wrightworth responded.

Nathaniel leaned down, suddenly acknowledging me.

"Mr. Wrightworth always puts limits on Doms who share his subs. This is quite a treat for me. The temptation to push you to your limits and then right over just to see if he'll let me go that far."

"Do remember who you are playing with," Mr. Wrightworth said.

"Mm, suppose," Nathaniel said, moving behind me.

I felt a tug on the ribbon, then another. Ever so slowly the bow shifted against my back and stomach as the bow came undone. Nathaniel pulled the ribbon free of my stomach in one motion.

The slick satin slid over my skin, causing me to shudder and move instinctively with the motion.

"I have a thought," Nathaniel said, to which Mr. Wrightworth made a questioning sound as he walked away from me and towards the wall of the room. "Have you...?"

Mr. Wrightworth glanced at Nathaniel before he sat in the dining chair he kept in the playroom at all times, and arched an eyebrow.

"We are all just now learning rope play. I wouldn't risk her limbs."

Nathaniel was silent a moment, whatever he did caused Mr. Wrightworth to smile just slightly and twitch the eyebrow. His hazel eyes drifted to me even though his face remained positioned towards Nathaniel.

"Well, that's an oddly eager sort of thing," Mr. Wrightworth purred out.

"Blindfolds," Nathaniel said.

The ribbon slipped down over my eyes. Nathaniel tied the ribbon behind my head, just tight enough for it to stay in place. The ends of the ribbon were draped over my back, then Nathaniel arranged them carefully, grazing my back with his long fingers.

I could see nothing.

Not Mr. Wrightworth's lips twisting up in a smile as he chuckled, not the warming of Nathaniel's eyes as his hands ran over the bare flesh of my back, down my hips and legs. Then back up again.

"Sweetheart," Mr. Wrightworth said, causing my head to lift. Nathaniel responded with a small sound. "You only have an hour."

"When did you start counting?" Nathaniel asked, panic edging his voice.

"When you untied the bow, I'm not cruel."

"Just a question—"

"In the toy box," Mr. Wrightworth said, I swore I could hear the smile in his voice.

Blind, I struggled to fill in what was going on with my

other senses. I heard Nathaniel walk off, but didn't know what exactly the toy box was. Mr. Wrightworth had only ever used the items hanging on the wall.

I heard the sound of something opening and closing and didn't understand what I had just heard.

There were no cupboards or storage items in the playroom itself. Not unless a piece of furniture had a cupboard built into it.

I tugged at my bonds, for some reason forgetting that I was tied down.

"And have you been—" Nathaniel asked.

"Orgasm training, but we haven't reached the part about not coming until she is allowed to. It's not an exact science, not for me and not when it involves a woman."

"Oh, well that's simple," Nathaniel said in a cheery voice.

I distinctly remember thinking, '*Ah, fuck*,' a moment before I felt a touch. I relaxed, thinking that it must have been some other sort of toy that Nathaniel was teasing me with.

And then he turned it on.

I definitely don't recall those first few moments. By the time I wrapped my mind around the multitude of sensations, Nathaniel had pulled away.

I panted, forcing myself to relax.

One arm protested, my back hurt down my spine. I had convulsed as the vibrator touched me.

"Now," Nathaniel said, setting his hand in the small of my back. "I'm going to use this again, and you are going to enjoy it. But you aren't allowed to come. Understand?"

"Yes, Sir," I whined out.

"Whiny," Mr. Wrightworth muttered.

"That's not whiny," Nathaniel said, even though I would have said it was a whining tone. "It's more frustration. She wants to come. Don't you, Darling? You want to come for me?"

Yes, I reacted because he used the right tone. Every bit of me leaped to obey the trigger word. The swirl in my stomach flooded my limbs with that wonderful feeling of pre-orgasm.

I'm not even fully trained, and I react like that?

"No, no, not yet," Nathaniel said, his hand pressing

tighter against my back. His tone promised more. "Not yet, just remember that."

I cried out as the vibrator pressed against me and turned on at the same time. The vibrations continued, causing me to writhe against the spanking bench. As the first wave came upon me, the first warning that my orgasm was nigh, the sensation was suddenly pulled away.

"What was the indicator?" Mr. Wrightworth asked.

"She went perfectly still," Nathaniel responded, his voice moving away from me and towards the toy wall as he spoke. "You're used to men, where we want faster and faster, more sensation. I swear every woman I've ever been with just stops. And that's not the orgasm itself. That's the pre-wave."

"And to bring her back down?" Mr. Wrightworth asked.

"Too soft and it won't divert her," Nathaniel said, moving back towards me. "Unlike with men, you can't beat her in rapid succession. The female mind—at least in my experience in dealing with them—can link the repetitive impacts to pleasure and it can push them over the edge."

"Is that why Nicole advises not taking up a rhythm when beating anyone?" Mr. Wrightworth asked.

"And making certain they're present," Nathaniel said.

I heard a whistling sound, then was struck by the many tails of the flogger. The very speed of the flogger sent a shock through my body. Then my mind caught up with the motion and my back bloomed in burning pain.

"Izzy," Nathaniel snapped.

"Fucking, Christ sake," I snapped out before I realized what I was saying and what he had said.

"And she's present and off the edge," Nathaniel said.

"Quick and dirty," Mr. Wrightworth said.

"Oh, there are subtle ways, but I don't feel like teaching you all the tricks."

"On the contrary, I think you do feel like it," Mr. Wrightworth said. "But this is your time, and I've only seen you smack her once. So why not show me what sort of a Dom you are?"

Nathaniel struck me again with a great deal of force. It was the kind of strength that I had grown accustomed to experiencing.

Over my time with Mr. Wrightworth I had learned the differences in each strike. Nathaniel was holding back with each strike, only hitting me hard enough to make it seem like he was putting effort behind it.

Unlike that first strike.

He traded off between the impact toys and the vibrator, tormenting me until I was on that edge and then beating me back down. Each time he beat me, it was a little harder to come back down. The edge stayed there and so close at hand.

"Please, Sir," I pleaded, unable to take it any longer.

Nathaniel tangled his hand in my still growing hair. It was just long enough to get a handful of hair and pull. He pulled my head back, but all I saw was a haze of purple through the ribbon. I couldn't see shapes, just the colour purple, or black if I closed my eyes.

The ribbon was a constant reminder of the fact that I didn't belong to Nathaniel, I wasn't his.

"Please, what?" Nathaniel asked.

"Please, let me come."

There was a sharp intake of breath from across the room.

"We aren't playing that game tonight," Nathaniel growled.

My mind struggled because no one had told me ahead of time how to react or what to expect. If it wasn't about me getting to come, it was about him. I made that connection thankfully.

After a long moment, I slid into the other conclusion in a startling realization.

"Please, Sir, fuck me."

Nathaniel sighed out with a chuckle.

"There it is. Such a fast learner. And what is the point of my fucking you?"

"For Sir's pleasure."

One of Nathaniel's hands roved down my back roughly. I felt him shift above me as if he were looking across the room. Then he pulled away entirely. I was left, devoid of sight and touch, not knowing where he was.

I didn't like it.

"Easy," Nathaniel said, setting a hand on me as I twitched. "Easy, I'm right here. Just needed something."

I felt cold steel slide against my hip and heard the snip, then the second snip a moment later. My underwear fell away.

That's the way underwear should be removed. I've also had it yanked upon, apparently expecting it just to rip. It doesn't do that, it's made of fabric and meant to survive the washing and the drying, and the randy bouts of sex.

I heard the scissors be set on the floor.

I felt Nathaniel's hands moving up my back.

The heat of him was oh so familiar and welcoming, even over my already bruising flesh. Nathaniel leaned down against my back, his hot chest against my aching muscles. Even the weight of him was a comfort.

And then he shifted and thrust into me.

I moaned, my voice higher and just a little louder than I meant it to be. To be filled by the man after months of fantasizing about that very moment?

What Nathaniel proceeded to do was definitely fucking. Hard and fast and...oh, just what I need at least once a week, or I'm just not satisfied.

Bent over the way I was, the spanking bench put pressure on my front while Nathaniel's chest put pressure against my back. Pressure in the right places during sex is delightful. Nathaniel held me down as he pounded into me and I loved every minute of it.

"Come for me," he said.

I shuddered at the sound of his voice in my ear. He slammed into me and hesitated, his body trembling against mine.

"Come for me, Darling," Nathaniel begged.

And I did.

It was not like the times at his estate, where he teased it out of me and my world melted away entirely. It was good, yes, it was marvellous, but we didn't have the time to play the way we both liked. I was used to longer sessions, and Nathaniel had been working each session longer.

It was good, but it wasn't really what either of us wanted.

Nathaniel moaned as he pulled away from me. I was left in darkness a moment and then the blindfold was removed and tossed to the side. He knelt before me, and I finally saw the warmth in his green eyes as he smiled.

"Tell me that you're all right," Nathaniel whispered.

"I'm all right," I responded.

He released first one, then the other of my wrists. With Nathaniel's help, I stood. He plucked me off the floor was if I weighed nothing at all and carried me out of the play room. Nathaniel took me into Mr. Wrightworth's bedroom and set me on the bed gently.

He climbed in beside me, almost atop me.

His lips met mine, tongue thrusting into my mouth. We were tangled together in a moment. I rolled and pinned him to the bed, huffing out my triumph.

"You've been working out," he managed to get out before I kissed him again.

Nathaniel's hands roved up me and back down, feeling every bit of me. The playroom and bedroom were always kept in a kind of twilight, never the full light that the overhead fixtures offered. There was something sharp and even medical about full light that Mr. Wrightworth seemed to avoid. In the twilight of the playroom my scars were faded, in the darker dusk of the bedroom, the shadows would have hidden most, if not all of the damage.

So while Nathaniel's hands seemed to search for the damage, to inspect my body, all he would have felt were muscles under whole skin.

As his hands moved over me, I writhed against him with need. The only thing that stopped me was his manhood, hard and at the ready once more, poking me when I lifted slightly and moved back down.

With a squeak, I lifted off of him.

"Take me," Nathaniel said.

"How?" I asked.

Nathaniel went still, gripping me tight as he frowned at me.

"Seriously?" he asked. "How many positions do you know?"

"No, I mean... I meant..." I dropped my head glumly.

"I just meant take control," Nathaniel said, his hands drawing me upwards. "To have me," he drew me down, spearing me upon his rigid flesh. "As you please. That's it.

Enjoy me."

I shuddered at every word he spoke. I writhed against him and moved this way and that until I found just the way I liked it. As I found that position, my fingers dug into his flesh. I went taut as I brought myself down again.

"There you go," Nathaniel said, his hands moving over my stomach and down my legs. "Mm, Darling."

I slapped at his chest gently. It was an idle motion of someone who wasn't entirely paying attention. I was focused on the pleasure and that building, frustrating feeling just out of reach.

The name Darling startled me out of the delightful cloud that I had been building. It wasn't right. Darling would never do this to her Sir.

Suddenly his hands hardened.

He turned us, pushing me into the bed as he slammed into me.

With hot breath against my ear, he said, "Sorry, Izzy."

My hands locked onto his shoulders, legs wrapping around his hips. Nathaniel thrust into me with what little space I granted him. With each thrust, I was brought a little closer to the precipice. I moaned under him, hardly believing what was happening.

"Come for me, Izzy," Nathaniel said, thrusting a little faster. "Please, Izzy, come for me."

Again, I came.

I swear I saw stars.

Not the ones painted on the ceiling, but the real thing, falling from the sky. The whole world seemed to fade away to nothingness as Nathaniel stilled over top of me. With a small sound, Nathaniel slid down on the bed, head settling on my stomach.

Sex the second time seemed to make everything heavy. I was weary in a pleasant sort of way, but as I was about to fall asleep, I remembered the contract. Sleepily I pulled on Nathaniel's shoulder. The man made a small sound and lifted his head, his eyes meeting my own.

"Mr. Wrightworth was your master," I said to him, though I meant to phrase it as a question.

"Yes," Nathaniel said, setting his head back on my

stomach. His fingers traced circles on my still hot flesh. "Yes, I'm the sub that he refers to often."

"You said you were auctioned off," I said. "That was how you came to your master."

"I was, it was also how we found out that my father has nearly everyone in their pockets. We thought it'd be a way around the contract. Technically it was, but they didn't bid, so Mr. Wrightworth had to. I went for a whole fifty cents because that was all he had in his pockets at the time."

"Mr. Wrightworth is the one who owns purple," I grumbled.

Nathaniel almost laughed.

"Yes, yes he is. He takes it very seriously. Lit someone on fire who dared to wear it. Though she was standing by a fountain, and once the fire took he pushed her in. But still, the warning got out quick enough."

"Then..." I struggled to come up with what I wanted to ask.

Nathaniel pushed off of the bed and then moved upward, adjusting so that he could wrap around me. The man sighed out slowly.

"The ring?" he asked.

"Yes."

"Mr. Wrightworth was supposed to use me as my father saw fit, not to claim me as a sub. When it came time for me to be collared, we had to come up with something random. Something no one in the outside world would think that a man like him would give another man. Then one day we found the ring. Still utterly in servitude to him, I took it. I was his slave, not a sub. He made every decision for me while he was my master."

"If it's a mark of that, why do you still wear it?"

"I rarely do, but when I do it's because I want him back. We didn't want to do it at the time, but we both came away from that changed men. It's so freeing to have someone else making the decisions for me."

"Fair enough," I grumbled because I knew the feeling. "Why is Mayfair wearing it then?"

"I had to give her something," Nathaniel said. "I held out long enough for her to think she had broken me. Then I whimpered and cried some and told her where it is, that I wanted her to wear it. She thinks I'm completely subservient to her. Thankfully she doesn't know my trigger words, so I don't have to fake anything awkward."

"You weren't exactly good in the church," I said.

This time, Nathaniel did laugh.

"That's a sign, to Mr. Wrightworth. If he ignores me then I'm on my own, if he doesn't and points out my misbehaviour, then we're ready to go."

"And you'll swap subs?"

"Not... no. Mr. Wrightworth doesn't lend his subs. There's too much trust that has to go into it. For discipline? Yes, he would, but you've done nothing wrong. It shouldn't even be happening and you should back out. I'm not broken, but I do go into subspace."

"What's subspace?"

"The mind basically shuts off, and you'll do whatever you're told. A proper Dom cultivates that so that whatever you do brings you pleasure. Pleasing him is your only goal."

"So you'll do whatever she tells you to."

"At all. I like being there, but I don't trust Mayfair not to take advantage of that."

The fact that my gorgeous Dom wanted to be in subspace scared me. He wanted to serve someone else, and that terrified me. I had no experience being a domme and didn't know if I could pull it off, let alone if I would like it.

If we're both subs, can we even have a relationship together?

The answer is yes, but neither of us was subs. We were switches, myself a natural and Nathaniel trained.

"Don't do it, Izzy, don't go to Mayfair."

"You serve her. I serve him," I said.

Nathaniel sighed and nodded once.

He kissed my cheek and laid down, pressing himself as close to me as possible. With his warm body pressed tightly against mine, I was asleep in moments.

Chapter Twenty

"You serve her. I serve him."

I had said those words to protect myself from the pain. I still didn't know where I stood with Nathaniel. With the community, it can be difficult to tell.

Each scene is different. Each interaction could be like love at first sight.

When I woke in the morning, I was confused. Very, very confused. Not about my own feelings, but about my sexuality. I fell asleep beside Nathaniel and woke to a cold bed as Mr. Wrightworth closed the door. The man tiptoed towards the bed and slid in beside me, wrapping an arm around my middle.

He kissed my cheek, then my neck, then my shoulder, causing me to sigh out a breath as I bent my head to give him better access to the delicate flesh of my neck.

Mr. Wrightworth pressed himself close to me, his hand sliding down my belly. His warm fingers slid between my legs as I shuddered against him. It wasn't until they caressed my folds that I stiffened, eyes going wide.

I had had dreams that began just like that...

He made a questioning sound, his lips still against my throat. I knew that not answering quickly enough, or not giving a full answer, would result in being bitten.

"Your hand's position suggests something we have not done," I said, my voice quivering.

The anticipation stoked a fire in my belly that I thought had long been put out.

Mr. Wrightworth wasn't just taboo. He had no interested

in women. What little interest he did have was in passing, and only involved the playroom. He was not one to chase after or fantasize about. He would beat any woman who made a comment of more than jealousy for the men he paid attention to.

Even making such a comment was dangerous.

"It was brought to my attention that it is believed I want something," Mr. Wrightworth said, lifting his face from the crook of my neck. "It was also suggested that I should simply take what I want, that perhaps getting it out of my system is the only course of action."

"You aren't afraid that it's a trap?" I asked.

"The door was open last night, the two of you were not plotting against me," Mr. Wrightworth said. "Not that he is capable of plotting against me."

"I meant," I struggled to turn in his arms, surprised when his hand followed me, "you aren't afraid that my vagina is a trap, and you'll never want a man again?"

Mr. Wrightworth laughed as if it were a joke.

I couldn't help but wonder why he wasn't taking me seriously.

Nicole's words were ringing in my ears. There was something odd about how Nathaniel and Mr. Wrightworth treated me, and I didn't know why. I had been with Nathaniel for a whole of two weeks and yet he had visited the night before as if we had been together the past four months. He had behaved as if we had shared secrets and I would understand what his hints were.

"There's no way that what's between your legs is going to turn me off men forever," Mr. Wrightworth said. "Not unless you remain mine. Forever. The moment you are gone, I'm going to find myself a lithe little thing that enjoys consensual non-consent, I'm going to pretend to rape them, and then I'm going to find myself another lithe little thing, this time, blond with blue eyes. A vanilla creature from one of the slums, or perhaps a rich younger son who has never known anything but mummy's love, and I'm going to seduce him slowly to the lifestyle until he begs me to give him pain."

"And while I'm yours?" I asked.

"Right now, you aren't," he responded quietly. "You are

Izzy, and I am—well, you know who I am."

Him.

Mr. Wrightworth wasn't my master, was what he was saying. He was a man who had been born in the slums and had risen to a high position.

Dear Lord, it was my ritualized fantasy come to life.

He bent to kiss me, tongue darting into my mouth briefly.

It wasn't the world-altering kiss of Nathaniel, but it also was not Mr. Wrightworth's usual fair. The kiss was gentle, kind, even hesitant. We kissed like the man and woman we were, connected by the past, yes, but neither of us in control of the other.

His hands caressed down my sides, leaving trails of cold in their wake. I shivered and moved with every motion of his fingers.

On our sides, we explored each others' bodies. I dared to touch first his arm, then his side. His flesh was so much warmer than mine and rough to the touch.

Here was a slum boy, grown to a man with thick skin.

Nearly everywhere I touched, I felt the raised lines and marks of scars years old. Lines that hadn't been tended to as mine had. There were some that were more prominent than others. My doctors had told me to watch for that sort of scar tissue, that it meant the new tissue was infected and needed to be seen to.

That was just the kind of scar tissue I was used to seeing in the slums. Raised, prominent, rarely seen to by a medical professional. Mr. Wrightworth had apparently received many scars in the slum before he was raised up.

It was no wonder Nathaniel thought he could sum up my damages with his hands in the dim light.

The only time Mr. Wrightworth took off his shirt was for play and during play, I wasn't exactly paying attention to the condition of his skin. With it under my touch, I came to understand a little more about the man I was in bed with. It wasn't just the past eight years that had been rough on him. Surely, if someone else had been deliberately destroying him every six months, the scars would have been more visible.

I rolled onto my back, pulling him with me.

I wanted the feel of a man over me, the push of the bed

behind me. He followed obligingly, sliding a knee between my legs. Holding himself off of me with an arm, he reached past me to the nightstand and picked up a little package.

"What's that?" I asked.

"A condom," he said.

"What's a condom?" I asked.

He stiffened, frowned slightly, then muttered something under his breath. What he muttered, I discovered later, was the name of the slum that I had been born into. We didn't know the names unless we travelled between the slums for work.

"A condom is a type of birth control—"

"I still have that thing in me," I said.

His tongue stuck out slightly. Biting it to keep from saying something, from slipping into the Dom that he was so used to, the man looked down at me.

"I have the male version of that," he said. "Condoms also help with transmitted diseases."

"It's been in my mouth before."

"It's also been in someone's ass since then. I'd rather be safe."

"Ohhhhh," I said.

"You're so adorably naive," he grumbled in response, capturing my lips with his own. "You probably have no idea what I'm talking about, just nodding and going along."

"Anything so you'll kiss me again," I said with a grin as I bit my bottom lip.

"I don't want to risk your health."

"If you want to use it, and it's not going to hurt me, I'm not going to say no, I was just wondering what it is," I said with a shrug. "Do those come flavoured?"

"They do," he said, setting the package on the pillow and just to the side. "But to me, the flavour has always been... powdery or chalky. It's not right. There are even some that glow in the dark."

"So... the whole room would light up?" I asked.

"No, it just glows."

"I know, but the larger the glow stick, the more light it gives off."

"I don't..." Mr. Wrightworth frowned and pulled away

from me slightly. "I'm not using a glow stick on you."

"Anyone who calls that a glow stick obviously has never seen one before," I said. "That's not even a flare. That's like a flashlight."

"Oh," Mr. Wrightworth sighed out. "I get it. You devious little creature. I thought mincing words was beyond you."

"It's not beyond me. I just don't understand what you two were trying to say. And that's just frustrating."

"Knows we were trying to say something, but not what," he said quietly, a hand sliding up my neck and caressing my cheek. "Most hear it and just don't know what to think, but the fact that you picked up on that? Your mind was wasted in the slums."

And then he kissed me again.

Who knew a brain could be so arousing?

It wasn't just a kiss this time. It was possessive, needy even. As he kissed me, his hands roamed over my body. His chest pressed close to mine. This was only the second time a man had pinned me with his body, something that made me writhe even as his fingers made me shudder. My hips ground against his leg, still between my legs.

I whimpered with need as he turned his lips to my throat. When he turned back to my lips, a hand wrapped around my throat possessively. The hand was tense but didn't tighten. It was my anchor point in a storm of emotions that I didn't know how to handle.

He would caress me and, when the motion elicited a shudder of response, would explore the area. With tongue and tooth and nail he brought me to that edge but never gave me enough to push me over. I never could decide whether he was just that skilled, or if he was inept in a way that was oh so good. He balanced me on that cliff as he took his time exploring my body.

His hand settled on my breast.

You know how, growing up, you hear all these stories about young men touching the breasts of women? How boobs are like man-magnets?

Well, before that point no one had just full on grabbed a handful of breast. It was like men were afraid I'd eat them if they did.

Ass? Sure, handful of ass by the...ass...who ran me over.

But my breasts just never ended up getting involved in sex.

Thankfully, he didn't just grope. His hand was almost large enough for my breast to be held. The fingers of his hand worked gently into my breast, eliciting the most disturbing, delicious feeling I had ever had. He kissed downward, surprisingly me even more as his lips, then teeth, found my nipple. His teeth grasped me firmly, tongue darting over my flesh.

When I moaned, he pulled away.

For just a second I wondered if making sounds was a bad thing.

And then he blew a cold breath over my nipple. The wet flesh reacted, hardening and yet so sensitive. That one little breath was wonderful and yet tortured me all the same. As I writhed and whimpered, he turned his attention to the other side.

My breasts are one thing that does not have to be 'even' as it had been called in the past. However... making them even made me cry out loud enough that the hand around my throat moved to cover my mouth.

"Shhh," he said. "No one's heard you before, hearing you now might raise questions."

His hand shifted back to my neck as his leaned forward, capturing my lips with his own. This time, I thrust my tongue into his mouth. The kiss deepened as we pressed tight against one another. He slipped between my legs, pushing against me. He ground as I writhed. I could feel his arousal through his sweatpants.

Hard, long, needing release. But he didn't go right for the goal. He took his sweet time.

I was already on that edge and needing release, willing to do whatever was necessary to be given what I needed. With every kiss and caress, he pushed me just that fraction closer.

Yes, I needed this man, I wanted him to slide into me, but our little tryst changed.

I was no longer in control. I could not drive us forward any longer. We were working at his pace and not because we had agreed to it beforehand, but because that was the way things had gone. He pressed tighter against me, an action that I believed impossible.

"Please," I begged.

"Not yet," he whispered back, untangling my hands. "Put them above your head and keep them there."

Back to dom and sub?

I did as I was bid, clutching my hands together. He kissed my collar bone, then down, between my breasts. I watched as his head moved ever downward, biting my lip to stop from moaning as he reached my hip. After a moment of consideration, he took my hips in his hands and pressed them into the bed.

He glanced up, his hazel eyes flashing in the dim light as if daring me to ask him what he was doing.

There was no way I'd ask, no way I'd interrupt.

I wanted to know what he had in store for me, what was so important that he would put off sex?

His lips brushed over my hip and downward, causing me to have a frightened moment where I wondered when I had trimmed last was. Thankfully I hadn't chosen shaved, or my forgetfulness would have been a lot more noticeable. He moved over that area as if it was an everyday thing, no comment or hesitance.

Head lowering slightly, his tongue darted out experimentally. I shivered at the heat and slickness of it.

"So wet," he grumbled. "Do you want me that badly?"

"Yes," I moaned, almost lowering my hands.

His eyes narrowing as I looked down at him was the only reason my hands stayed above my head. He waited as I panted, getting my breath under control, before he shifted closer, tongue darting out as we met eyes.

How a tongue can have that much strength, I don't know. It wasn't sloppy in the least. It was careful and almost practised.

I was surprised.

Not only by his skill but by my own reaction.

"Oh, oh, what was that?" he said, licking his lips as he pulled away.

Afraid I had done something, I tried to close my legs. Only, he had his hands locked on my legs, keeping me from closing him off.

"The *sound*," he said sternly. "That came from your mouth. What was that?"

"What sound?" I demanded.

He was quiet for a moment, then smiled lopsidedly.

"You don't recall making a sound? Let's see if I can make you do it gain."

Did he make me do it again?

"Oh yes!" I cried out.

He pulled away and slammed my legs back onto the bedspread. I had been attempting to headlock him in just the right place. As he sat up, he wiped at his bottom lip and glowered at me.

"That's not a nice thing to do to someone who is doing you a favour."

"I'm sorry," I whined out.

"But your hands stayed where they should," he responded, reaching for the package on the pillow. "Perhaps I should reward you anyhow."

"Please," I pleaded, my hips shifted in an attempt to ease the throbbing between my legs.

He kissed me again, tongue probing my mouth as he fumbled with his pants. I heard the rustle of his pants, but I was so focused on what his tongue was doing, a promise of so much more. The kiss was a distraction, of course. He's the only man I've ever met who actually managed to put on a condom without stopping and stripping the activity of the sexual tension. When he was ready his hands roamed over my body. His mouth turned to my throat as I bent my head eagerly.

There was a hesitance, then his hand slid between my legs, probing me gently. I spread my legs willingly, needing more as he settled between them. He continued to kiss as his hands shifted my legs further, giving him more space. The hand on my hip shifted between us.

I made a very uncomfortable sound as he penetrated me.

Recall, though, he was not a small man by far. Even ready and willing, he was almost too much for me. He hesitated just there, on the uncomfortable side of penetration. As he slipped deeper into me, the discomfort almost entirely vanished.

He filled me, and in filling me, brought on those first waves of release. Buried to the hilt, he hesitated. As if wondering what sensations he was feeling, or perhaps waiting for me to adjust.

Which was kind of him, if that was what he was doing.

The first thrust made me gasp in a breath. The second brought forth a whine as the breath left me. The sounds I made? Dear Lord. I could have competed for a porn star, except I wasn't acting. I did try not to make sound, but it was difficult. Just picture your own sounds of pleasure, except mine were better because this is my story.

I bit my lip by the third thrust and tried to move with him. I shifted my hips down with each thrust.

... which did not help the sounds coming from my mouth.

He made a small, almost desperate sound against my neck.

The sound was my only warning as he sped up, thrusting faster, hesitating as he was buried deep inside me, then withdrawing and doing it all over again. With one arm for leverage, he used his free hand to pin me to the bed by my wrists. His face was buried in the crook of my neck as he thrust into me.

I locked my legs around his hips, which kept him from thrusting quite so hard but did nothing to slow him down. Short and fast was just what I needed. I tugged at my hands, pressed into the pillow above my head, but found his hold steadfast. I wanted to drag my nails down his back, to dig them into his shoulders. I wanted to latch onto this Adonis and never let him go.

"Please," I shuddered out with a breath.

He didn't slow, didn't change pace, as he raised his head and looked over my face. His eyes were half-closed, pleasure clouding his vision as it made me whimper with need.

"I'm going to come," he whispered.

"Please," I begged.

The cold came over me, the tingling getting worse.

"Please," I begged, my voice getting a little higher.

"Come for me," he whispered in my ear.

Why do those words have such control over me?

I cried out but didn't come. I was almost there. It seemed I balanced on that point. That back and forth moment, the almost but not quite.

Would I ... wouldn't I... why couldn't I...?

"And I'll come for you," he added after a long moment.

Everything reacted as one.

My body tensed, pleasure rocking through my veins as I tried so hard to meet each desperate thrust. Even as I came, he continued.

That's not a bad thing.

As each wave of my own pleasure slammed through my body, he thrust into me. There was no stopping it. Everything was just stuck on 'come.' It didn't leave, and it didn't subside. That moment of oh so much delight continued as he did. It didn't stop the way it had in the past.

No, my release was not just momentary, it lasted for what seemed like forever.

And then he stilled and groaned out, a tremble rolling through his body.

He withdrew and dropped to the side, tucking himself almost immediately against me and around me. An arm draped across my midsection as his face tucked back into the crook of my neck. His breath was coming in quick, shallow gasps. It slowed, as my own did.

I stared up at the ceiling, wondering what the fuck was wrong with me. Sex with two men in less than twelve hours? Did that make me a slut?

I had come from a vanilla slum, as they put it. One that said sex with one man, one's husband, was what was necessary. Sex before marriage, yes, it could and did happen. No one judged for sex before marriage as long as it was one man at a time.

Two though. I had had sex with two men in less than twelve hours. Who could boast that number? Why boast that number?

Who is better in bed?

I found myself suddenly wondering that question and couldn't decide.

The difference clearly being that Mr. Wrightworth was larger and had my full attention. Nathaniel, months before, had had my full attention. The night before was not any less than my time with Mr. Wrightworth.

Certainly, it takes a lesser part in this part of my story.

But never mistake my being short as saying that Nathaniel performed less amiably than he had before.

In the half-dark of the room, I stared up at the ceiling and wondered.

You know that half-dark? Of curtains being drawn but light still filtering in through the curtains. It wasn't bright daylight but it certainly wasn't darkness either. Nor was it twilight.

It was the laziness of a mid-day nap. The solitude of an afternoon masturbation session.

The startling realization that I was a person I existed, I had just done something that my family, my slum, and numerous other people and beings would condemn.

And no one would ever know.

"What are you thinking about?" Mr. Wrightworth asked.

"Nothing," I said.

He sat up suddenly. I could feel his glare even though I didn't meet his eyes. With a sigh, I stared up at the ceiling, not wanting to ask.

"What's wrong?" he asked.

"Last night—" I started.

"You had sex with Nathaniel, I know," Mr. Wrightworth said. "Oh, oh... you're having an awakening."

"A what?" I asked.

"You think you're a slut for having sex with two men in less than a day."

"W-how did you...?" I asked.

"You're not the first, let's just leave that at that," Mr. Wrightworth said. "But I counter your problem with a question: do you care for us both?"

"I do, yes," I said without hesitance.

"Then you aren't a slut, who has sex with anyone for any reason," Mr. Wrightworth said. "At best you might be considered polyamorous. You have the capability of loving, and therefore having sex with, more than one person."

"Oh," I said, suddenly put on a worse tangent. The one that asked how many people I would have to love before I was content enough to love no more than those in my life.

"Thank you," Mr. Wrightworth said suddenly.

"For what?" I asked.

"Being my first."

There was a long moment where my mind stumbled over what he said.

Then I said, "Your first woman."

"My first vanilla."

Well shit, he has fucked a woman before.

Chapter Twenty-One

We fell asleep in each other's arms.

I awoke sometime later and all but fell out of bed. It took a moment to get my legs working properly. There was a raw ache between them and a twinging deep in my belly.

If that's what happens when you poke a sadist, I have to do it more often.

I gathered up a shirt from the floor and slipped it on as I left the bedroom, headed for the bathroom. I had a pressing need.

"Shower," Mr. Wrightworth called from the kitchen as my hand settled on the doorknob. "Then dress, Nicole is coming over."

"Okay," I called back and walked into the bathroom.

I relieved myself, sighing out as I did so.

That was what had awoken me.

After flushing the toilet, I went directly to the shower. The hot water helped relax my muscles but reminded me that my body hadn't exactly been treated carefully. My back and legs ached as I pulled muscles that had been smacked the day before. The flesh of my back had been recovering from the whipping I had taken a week previously but hadn't completely healed.

This was a side effect of my choice of lifestyle. There were days when I didn't like the pain, times when the aching muscles were too much, and all I wanted was a fluffy blanket and a pat on the head. Over long periods of time, the best way to approach things was to alternate the type of play or the area that was used for impact play.

In the end, only rest and due care will help a body recover. Doing impact, abrasion, or knife play every day will result in a continually damaged body. Not my cup of tea.

I washed thoroughly, enjoying the feeling of being rubbed all over. Out of the shower, I dried everything and wound the towel around my hair.

I brazenly walked out of the bathroom with only the towel in my hair.

Nicole and Mr. Wrightworth stood at the door, which was thankfully closed.

Mr. Wrightworth turned towards me as Nicole's mouth fell open. I shrugged as he raised an eyebrow and walked back into his bedroom. My clothing was on the end of the bed, where it hadn't been when I had woken up. I dressed and towelled my hair dry.

The one plus side of it being so short was that I didn't necessarily have to brush my hair after a shower. I simply ran my hands through it to tame it in some fashion, then walked back out and into the kitchen.

"How is she still walking?" Nicole demanded as I walked in.

Mr. Wrightworth made a sound and handed Nicole a plate of food.

"I don't know, why don't you ask her?"

"She poked the sadists, she spent the night with the two of you, didn't you..."

"He had an hour with her," Mr. Wrightworth said. "I also spent some time with her. Darling, food."

I took the plate and went immediately to the dining room. The other two followed after me. We sat and ate our food. Then Nicole removed the plates and other dishes. Once the table was cleared, she returned to the table and sat. She looked pointedly at Mr. Wrightworth, which drew my attention to him.

"I thought it best if we talk about this with you before anyone from the Program does," Mr. Wrightworth said quietly.

"Is it about the cover for Nathaniel's visit?" I asked.

"That wasn't a cover," Mr. Wrightworth said. "It just happened that there were two reasons for his visit."

"Why didn't you tell me that last night?" I asked. "He was here to make a decision, and you didn't even give me a warning."

"If I had, you might have over thought the whole thing, or panicked."

"What did he decide?" I asked.

"Nathaniel Edwards has decided to extend a one-time contract, a blank slate document with standard lines offering protection and the ability to keep you from abuse by others," Nicole said.

Relief swept through me, then terror. I felt faint. A hand went to my head as everything just seemed to slip away.

Why wasn't my response simple and straightforward?

Slowly everything came back into focus. I looked up at Mr. Wrightworth, who sat quietly, without judgment. His hazel eyes roved over my face, then turned to Nicole.

"It seems I didn't need your services after all," he said.

Nicole rolled her eyes, then glared at Mr. Wrightworth.

"You're a fucking idiot," she said.

"What's it pay?" I asked, hardly believing those words were coming out of my mouth.

Mr. Wrightworth looked surprised as he said, "Emancipation."

No debt. No name either, but no debt.

I would be free to build whatever I could of my life. I would need to choose a new surname, but my debt would be entirely erased. My family would take on the debt that was linked to my name, debt which would have passed on to my children.

"The term?" I asked.

"Six months," Mr. Wrightworth responded.

"That's not long at all," I said with a frown.

"No, not long at all," Mr. Wrightworth said.

"Why?"

The man frowned, glancing at Nicole. She responded with a shrug.

"What do you mean, why?" Nicole asked.

"Why is it six months with emancipation, a blank slate but offers protection? The judge ruled that a contract would protect me from Albert, which means that Nathaniel doesn't need to hide anything from his father any longer. Taking me back on, it's obvious what would be going on. So why a six-month blank contract offering emancipation?"

"For protection, sweetie," Nicole said.

Mr. Wrightworth held up a hand to stop her from speaking. His eyes narrowed as he considered me, lowering his hand slowly until it was sitting on the table top.

"She's too smart for that," he said, hazel eyes locking with mine. "Six months, because that's about how long we expect the trial will take. At the end of that time, you would be free to do as you please.

"It's a blank slate, not because we want to hide what Nathaniel might do to you, but because that was what was offered to you before. Also because it is a blank slate. You, me, him, we don't know what's going on, and we don't want to put terms to it. Signing this contract does not mean that you need to be his sub, or that you need to sleep with him or be subservient to him in any manner or form. It means that you will be under his protection and live in his estate for six months in exchange for emancipation.

"Emancipation needs to be cleared by the government. Having heard of the charges we want to lay against Albert, they agreed readily. They think this is Nathaniel's way of soothing his ego. They believe he holds himself responsible and that he wants to make amends, so they have allowed him to. Don't take that as an offhand thing either. Emancipation requires a hundred thousand dollars be paid to the government by the contractor as well as your entire debt. In this case, they demanded twice the debt, a payment for them as well as repaying the portion of your debt that you would have passed on to your children."

"But that's not what emancipation is," I said.

"As I said, they believe he wants to make amends. They gave him a way to do so. So Nathaniel took it and paid. This has already been paid. Whether you take the contract or not, the government retains the fee."

"And why emancipation, why not make another payment to my family?" I asked.

"So that you won't be returned to the slums," Nicole said. "Emancipated poor folks are found jobs outside of the slums.

You also can't take another contract after you've been emancipated unless you have a poor person representing you, or you sign a contract before your contract with Nathaniel is up."

"If we lose the trial, we believe Albert may try to strong arm you into signing a contract with him," Mr. Wrightworth said.

"Protection, he's offering protection," I said.

"For six months you would live with Nathaniel, learn all you can. I strongly suggest you take the contract, but I can't make you."

"You want me to go away?" I asked.

He must have known about the contract when Nathaniel left.

Mr. Wrightworth had sex with me, then told me about the contract because he knew what my answer was going to be. Even though I didn't know it, he did. He knew what I wanted better than I ever could. He could anticipate every move I made during play, of course he knew me well enough to know what I actually wanted from life.

"Don't view it as going away," Nicole said.

"Nathaniel's estate is only an hour drive," Mr. Wrightworth said. "I would still have my visits with you at least once a week, as well as church on Sundays. Nicole could also visit. You will not be alone."

"But..." I said.

"No buts, no maybes," Mr. Wrightworth said. "You know I don't take this lightly. You know that I normally keep to myself and let others come to the decision they want without telling them what I think they should do."

"But he's still with Mayfair," I protested.

"She's got a point," Nicole muttered.

"The charges are being laid on Albert on Monday. Nathaniel will be coming in for the interviews which contractors need to go through. He will be here most of the day, and Mayfair thinks he has business meetings. Once he's done there, Tuesday and Wednesday will be for reviewing. If you take the contract, you will wear the black plug, if you decline, the purple."

The black plug was smaller than the purple. Mr.

Wrightworth had just purchased the purple plug, and it had never been used before. If I chose to wear the purple one, I'd be highly uncomfortable throughout because of the upgrade in size.

"Fuck you," I snapped.

Mr. Wrightworth smiled in response to my outburst.

"I'm not wearing a fucking plug while that cunt beats on me!" I added.

"If you don't, she might peg you," Nicole said.

"Or have Nate do it, and he doesn't want to," Mr. Wrightworth said. "By wearing a plug, I can set a limit. It stays in, or so help me. Nate is very well trained."

"So well trained," Nicole muttered. "Use the right word or tone, and he'll react."

"Mayfair has arranged for her time Wednesday night," Mr. Wrightworth said. "So Thursday morning you be formally offered the contract. If you choose to take it, you will need to go through the interviewing process again. The board is up in arms about everything that has happened revolving around your retrieval. There's an entire review of our policies because, as you've said, you slipped through all the cracks. They will not allow you to sign a contract without following due process."

"Church tomorrow?" I asked.

"No, because Mayfair may be there," Mr. Wrightworth said. "And if I see her again I might just bend her over and give her the fucking she's been telling other people I've offered."

"She wants vaginal," Nicole said idly.

"She's not getting vaginal from me," he said sternly. "She'll have to settle for Nate if she can figure out the triggers to make him hard."

"What is that trigger?" I asked.

Mr. Wrightworth stared at me, frowning slightly as he seemed to process what I had just asked.

"I beg your pardon?" he asked in response.

"What is Nate's trigger word for what you just mentioned?" I asked. "I already know his trigger for orgasm. Though I'm not sure I can imitate the tone yet."

"And what do you believe is Nate's trigger?" Nicole

asked.

"Good," I said, trying to imitate the tone.

Nicole went a funny colour, Mr. Wrightworth choked, apparently on air.

I watched the two of them as they seemed to struggle to cover their surprise.

"What?" I asked.

Mr. Wrightworth cleared his throat before he countered with a question of his own.

"Where did you learn that?"

"You said it last night," I said, motioning towards the play room.

"No, that tone, where did you learn that tone?" Nicole asked. "You some sort of mimic, hear it once and can imitate it?"

I blinked at them, not understanding why they were asking that. Ever so slowly it dawned on me.

The doms in the community weren't saying the word to torment Nathaniel. They didn't know they were doing it. It was something they heard Mr. Wrightworth say, and it was a tone of voice that implied a pride and something deeper.

"You all use that tone, on that word. A lot. I learned it from you all. And Nathaniel."

"He uses that tone?" Mr. Wrightworth asked, sounding amused with himself.

"Yes," I said.

"Interesting," Mr. Wrightworth muttered.

"She should pull out of the time with Mayfair," Nicole said. "As of Monday, she'll know something is up. Especially if they take Albert into custody. She might take advantage of that hour and actually try to kill Izzy, say it was a play accident or something."

"No breath play, no strangulation," Mr. Wrightworth said.

"She knows that, Mayfair knows that, would Nate know that?" Nicole asked. "She should pull out, damn it."

"To gain access to Mayfair's records I need someone either on contract or being watched in her house. Izzy is being watched in case Albert has someone threaten or attack her."

"Which Mayfair will do. If she wasn't in cahoots with

Albert, Izzy's given plenty of reason for Mayfair to want to cause real, actual damage, lasting damage."

"She hasn't got the balls to attack Izzy," Mr. Wrightworth said.

"After Izzy attacked her at church? You really think she wouldn't take action after that?"

"I'd like her to," he said sternly. "At least if she did, I wouldn't have to press to find evidence connecting her with Albert to subpoena her records and have her charged with whatever I can. Or bring her down. Or... something."

"Vengeance isn't the answer," Nicole said.

"She broke the trust. The tenets and almost outed us to the whole world!"

"You're outing us to the whole world!"

"Oh, I'm sorry that you haven't lost someone to that man's fucking appetites," Mr. Wrightworth snarled back at Nicole. "We aren't outing anything but Izzy and me and Nathaniel. The prosecution has asked about the community, and no names have been, nor will they be, given."

"You're risking us all to take down one man."

"Well, I would kill the bastard, but if I do it voids the contract and results in all of us either being killed or outed!" Mr. Wrightworth shouted. "Isabella Martin is the one pressing charges, not me, not him, no one but her. So don't you fucking sit there and tell me that I'm wrong for doing what's right."

"You are a master manipulator, of course, she's doing exactly what you want her to."

"He is a rapist and a murderer. He has destroyed numerous lives, killed tens of women, and gotten away with it all because of his damned money. We finally have him. He's stuck. There's no amount of money that can save him from the evidence we have."

"Except them proving that she's a masochist. Which clearly she is."

"It's not whether or not she's a masochist. She's already admitted that she is. It's whether or not she consented to him doing what he did."

"Which is made easier by the fact that she's a *masochist*. A fact that you told them, and then outed the community."

"Law enforcement knows about the community. What they don't understand is the consent."

"Which is what they'll be debating!"

Awkwardly, I stood and left the dining room as the pair of them began arguing at a louder volume.

In the bedroom, I closed the door, which drowned them out a little bit but not completely. I sat at my journal and wrote about the night before and that morning. After finishing my writing, I went back and tried to read, but couldn't focus.

I stood and went back to the dining room.

"Can I borrow a phone?" I asked.

Nicole pulled hers out and handed it to me. I looked at it, then back up at her.

Holding it back to her I added, "make it call Nathaniel."

"He might be busy," she said, typing in the number before she handed the phone back to me and rounded on Mr. Wrightworth as he growled something under his breath.

The two of them ended up shouting again as I walked back into the bedroom.

The phone rang several times in my ear.

"Nikki, not now," Nathaniel growled.

"Nicole gave me her phone," I said.

"Oh, because only Nikki calls from this number," Nathaniel said, there was a flurry of something, and he growled something at someone else. "Give me one second. I'll call you back."

"Wait! How do I pick up the phone?"

"Hit the green button when it pops up and slide your finger the way the phone tells you to."

The line went dead.

I sat in the half darkness until the phone went off. I almost dropped the phone trying to answer it.

The name that lit up the screen?

'Sir.'

Nicole and Nathaniel hadn't been involved in years, yet he was still labelled as 'sir' in her phone. For all her proclamations, I don't think even Nicole fully understood what she wanted from life or where she stood. Even though she had been in the community for years, she was still very confused about what she wanted out of the fetish lifestyle that she participated in.

"What's going on?" Nathaniel asked.

"Are you alone?" I asked in response.

"Yes, I'm in my study, you remember that room?" he asked.

I could almost hear the smile in his voice.

"Yes, I do."

"Your book is still sitting on the table, waiting for you to return and finish reading it," he said. "I've desperately wanted to reread *Paradise Lost*, but thought I should wait until you came and read it to me."

My God, I think he still likes me.

Dense, I was so dense back then. But a man waiting to do something until I was there, that I understood.

"I'd like that," I said. "But Mr. Wrightworth and Nicole are arguing about the..."

"About the charges, you're pressing," Nathaniel finished.

"Yeah," I said sadly.

"Who's debating what?" he asked.

"The, uh, consent issue," I said. "She seems to think that we'll fail in proving that I didn't give consent. Mr. Wrightworth seems pretty confident."

"I'd rather not talk about evidence, it might tarnish the case somehow," he said with a sigh. "I wish I could, Izzy, but I can't. I can't risk there being a mistrial because you needed someone to talk to. It's too important. It's bigger than us."

I sat in silence for a while, struggling for something to say.

"Suppose I'll see you Wednesday," I said quietly.

"That you will," he said, sounding happy again. "It'll only be an hour, and it won't just be us, but I look forward to any time we spend together."

"That's, um, that's good."

"Are you looking forward to it?" he asked.

"Nicole thinks I should withdraw consent," I said.

"That's up to you. You can withdraw at any point during as well."

"But what if I withdraw consent, and she keeps going?"

"That would change the play to assault, the community

takes that very seriously," he said. "I've never known Mayfair to ignore consent. I trained her for crying out loud."

"Not very well," I said. "She's already broken one rule."

"That's true, but consent isn't the same as sharing an image," Nathaniel said. "And besides, from what has been said, I'll be participating in the event. She's, well, Mayfair is like a wet noodle. Rich woman arms."

"So she's going to use you?" I asked.

"Yes, and I'm going to beat you senseless," he said, then chuckled. "My only regret is that I can't fuck you afterward, make you come for me, then use the vibrator on you until you beg me for release."

I whined out, desperately wanting that.

"Would you like that?" he asked. "Would you like me to tie you up and pleasure you until you beg me for release?"

"Yes," I said.

"Perhaps if you're good, I will even grant you that release."

I bit my bottom lip as the door of the bedroom opened, and Mr. Wrightworth walked in. Our eyes met, and I realized, in a startling moment that I still recall years later, that I knew what my answer had to be.

"Mr. Wrightworth is here," I said.

"That means you need to go, and I need to get to work," Nathaniel said.

"I'll see you Wednesday."

"See you Wednesday," he said, then hesitated. "And Izzy?"

"Yes, Nathaniel?"

"I feelings you."

I smiled and lowered my head. "I feelings you too."

Chapter Twenty-Two

Wednesday came up very quickly.

Going in I knew that Nathaniel had been approved for the contract, but not whether or not the Program board would allow me to sign it.

The rules for the hour I would spend with Mayfair were set while we were at her second home. It was said with all four of us in her sitting room so that there'd be no question as to who said what and what the rules were.

Two homes, like she's queen of the world or something!

Once the rules were set out, we went into the playroom. The rules had been relatively simple, and Mayfair had gotten suspicious because Mr. Wrightworth always had very strict rules for those borrowing time with a sub. He claimed the rules were simple because he needed her to obey what he said. It boiled down to no sexual activity, which Mr. Wrightworth passed off as my being frightened after the attack months before.

I wasn't afraid, but the look on her face when he said that?

I was glad that he brought it up. I didn't want that woman anywhere near my genitalia, and I certainly didn't want to be anywhere near hers.

In the room, she commanded me to strip, which I did. Happy to do so because I didn't want the dress getting damaged. In underwear, I stood before her with my eyes downcast.

"Those as well," she demanded.

I slipped off the underwear, kicking them to the side. The

only reason I had left them on was to make her feel like I didn't want them off.

After baring myself to Mr. Wrightworth and Nicole, I had brazenly walked around Mr. Wrightworth's apartment completely naked. There was something so freeing about being bereft of clothing and then denying Mr. Wrightworth the ability to touch me. I knew the man wanted to. I saw the way his thumb grazed over his fingers, the way he eyed my legs.

I also knew that he granted me the ability to stop him. His rules stated that anything not covered could be struck. He was my Master, which meant that I was breaking the rules by denying him.

Taking control from him was exhilarating.

Which meant that standing naked before Mayfair wearing nothing more than a plug, I felt strong. I could see the judgment in her eyes, but at my core, I was still solid as a rock. While I may have been playing the part of Darling, Isabella was fully aware, at the back of my mind.

Making snarky comments about how she would have used a female sub properly.

Mayfair walked around me, humming and hawing and even scoffing at what she saw.

I knew I was supposed to feel little, being judged by this plastic doll of a woman. Her disgust was evident as she grimaced at me.

"You're too fat," Mayfair growled out, flicking my back with a crop. It didn't hurt. It just irritated me because it wasn't what I had come to expect during play. "Look at that fat layer under your skin. Who could be attracted to that? Wrinkles already on your face, scars on your back. Nate, what do you think?"

"She needs to work out more, Mistress," Nathaniel responded reverently from the door.

"Honesty, Nate, we've talked about this."

He moved away from the door, stripping off his shirt as he did so. The shirt was tossed to the side as Nathaniel stopped in front of me, his hands clasping behind his back.

When I dared to glance up at him, there was pity in his eyes.

I got it, I did. She wanted to tell me all about how I sucked. She wanted to point out all my flaws to make herself feel better.

Nathaniel had to participate in the ritual to hurt me and to show his loyalty to her.

"Calling her fat would be kind," he said, his voice cold. Suddenly he was no longer my Nathaniel. He was Mayfair's Nate, and I didn't like the man she had made him into. "The cellulose in her legs alone is disgusting. Veiny. Blotchy. Slum scum, really."

I told myself that it wasn't what he believed. There wasn't anything wrong with my body, damn it. My strength from moments before withered under Nathaniel's words.

"Hit her," Mayfair said.

Nathaniel reached out and struck me in the face. It hurt, it made my whole face hurt, not just where he hit. The strike would leave my face reddened, but wasn't hard enough to bruise.

Bruising the face was on the no list, it was one of the only things that Mr. Wrightworth had reiterated in front of Mayfair. Nothing had been said beyond that for damage and repeating several times that sexual activities were off limits.

While Nathaniel might have broken Mr. Wrightworth's rules, the sub that was Nate would never disobey his master.

"Again."

The next strike was to the stomach.

I bent over and almost hit the floor as my stomach threatened to empty its contents. Mr. Wrightworth insisted I eat before playing with Mayfair, despite the fact that I hadn't been hungry. Getting air in was difficult. He grabbed a fistful of hair and dragged me back to my feet.

Over the next twenty minutes, I took one of the most brutal beatings of my life. That was why I was there, though, to be used as Mayfair saw fit and this was how she wanted to see me treated. It hurt, I hadn't been struck with a closed fist since puberty.

Even Nathaniel's father hadn't used his actual fists.

After the second strike, I no longer heard Mayfair's commands, but I knew she was giving them. I'd be pulled to my feet every time I tried to stay down.

"Hold," Mayfair barked as Nathaniel's hand wrapped around my neck.

The woman approached us, her violet eyes flashing as she smiled.

"You cost me tens of thousands of dollars in reconstruction."

"Maybe you shouldn't have abused your face so much that a punch or two needed reconstructive surgery."

Mayfair's smile grew wider.

"Be snarky. But by the end of this hour, you're going to be broken. You will kiss my feet and beg me for forgiveness."

"I tend only to kiss the feet of the one who gives me the pain I crave," I snarled back.

She struck me on the face with an open hand. Her fingers each had heavy rings on them, one of the rings broke the skin on my cheek. I felt the fiery pain and revelled in it. Finally, she managed to do something I liked. The delightful fog was setting in.

She had just broken Mr. Wrightworth's rules. But breaking his rules didn't mean she broke the law. It did mean that I'd get to see Mayfair under Mr. Wrightworth's foot, literally. He had been very clear as to what would happen if there was any damage to my face.

"Why don't you give consent?" Mayfair asked, her hand locking onto my chin, yanking my face upward. "He said no non-consent, he said nothing about you consenting. Consent to my sub fucking you."

"Not a hope in hell."

"Hit her again," Mayfair snapped, pulling away from us. Nathaniel obliged. "Now grab the belt."

I was released, my legs going out from under me as Nathaniel walked towards the door. He opened a box by the door and pulled out a leather belt, the kind that a man from the slums might wear. It was wide and thick, unlike the things rich folk tended to wear.

"And the whip," Mayfair said.

Nathaniel pulled out a whip. He moved to Mayfair and handed her the whip handle first.

The belt remained in his hand as he turned towards me.

"Face down position," Mayfair commanded of me.

I was a little surprised that she hadn't commanded me not to speak, or hadn't chosen to pull out a gag. Easing to my knees, I leaned forward and assumed the face down position.

"Beat her, if I don't hear her whining in five minutes, you'll be bleeding."

Unlike the hour he had with me at Mr. Wrightworth's apartment, Nathaniel did not hold back. The first bite of the belt's leather across my back drew out the barest sound, but it was so low that neither Nathaniel or Mayfair heard.

I gritted my teeth, trying to make no sound at all as the belt felt four more times.

There was a pause as Nathaniel walked around me to the other side. He brought the belt down with all his might. It struck a spot that he had bruised during our play session four days before. When the belt came down on the same spot, I knew he was desperate.

My making sound versus his bleeding.

He had given something he loved to Mayfair in order to make her think that she was in control. I didn't want to do that, I didn't think I could do that, and I think he knew it.

Which was why he used those carefully honed skills to cause me actual pain, real pain.

I cried out through my gritted teeth, and the belt hesitated.

"Keep it up."

The belt continued to fall, across my back and then my backside, which remained in the air. That belt on my backside was the only thing that kept me going. He layered his strikes just so and managed to catch both sides as one. It was a kind of relief as if the words of earlier were being washed away by the pain.

"Stop," Mayfair said in a disgusted tone. "She's enjoying it too much now."

"Yes, Mistress," Nathaniel said.

He sounded out of breath.

I would have looked up, but I was more than a little worried that she would tell him to use the belt to strike my face or head.

"She hardly seems phased, what the fuck is wrong with

her?" Mayfair snarled.

"Mr. Wrightworth says she's a masochist waking to her nature, Mistress," Nathaniel said reverently.

"A masochist? There are no true masochists. But if he's training her to accept pain, then this isn't going to work, now is it?"

"No, Mistress, the pain will not work," Nathaniel said.

"Take her by the throat," Mayfair said.

That worried me, but I didn't dare speak out as Nathaniel reached down and took me by the throat. Kneeling down, he turned his attention to Mayfair.

"Tighten," she commanded him.

Fuck.

Nathaniel's hand tightened around my throat, closing off my air. Instinct kicked in after only a few seconds. I grabbed his wrist and tried to get my fingers on his hand. There was no way for me to get a hold of his hand. Darkness clouded my vision. The strength went from my limbs.

"Release," Mayfair said.

He released me, and I dropped to the floor, gasping for breath. The darkness receded as I struggled to regain control over my body.

"Again."

Fuck.

Which, in all honesty, was something a great deal cleaner and friendlier than what ended up in my journal about the event.

Again he took me by the throat and squeezed. Again the darkness encroached on my vision. Still, I fought to grasp his hand as if that would make any difference. She held it longer the second time.

I was out of it, but not so out of it that I couldn't tell that I was held for a longer period.

"Release."

I dropped to the floor and gasped in several breaths. Daring to look up, I made eye contact with Mayfair, and I knew.

"Again," she said, smiling slowly.

I dragged in another breath as Nathaniel's hand wrapped around my throat. I struggled against him, not understanding what I could do to break through to him.

Mayfair would see me dead, and she would blame Nathaniel being in that place where subs went during play.

I tried to get my tongue to work, but it felt thick.

To call out, to beg for release.

There was only one word that came out: "Banana."

Nathaniel's grip loosened. He leaned in close to me, hand remaining around my neck, but loose enough for me to drag in a breath of air.

"What was that?" he asked.

"Banana," I said, then laughed at the ridiculousness of the idea.

That a word, that a banana might save me.

It made me laugh, which didn't help my breathing problem. There were tears in my eyes, and I must have laughed for a full thirty seconds before I realized what had happened.

Nathaniel had released me and retreated.

"What are you doing?" Mayfair shouted at him. "Continue!"

"She withdrew consent, Mistress," Nathaniel protested.

The whip cracked. Nathaniel cried out as I struggled to my knees. He was between Mayfair and me. She had struck him in her attempt to strike me.

"Get out of the way!" she bellowed.

Nathaniel obeyed. No, Nate obeyed.

Nathaniel wasn't present.

Nate retreated from his angry Mistress because he was in that place. He was a sub, and he was serving her, his mind wasn't present, he wasn't thinking rationally because Mr. Wrightworth had trained Nathaniel to shut that part of his mind off.

Mayfair cracked the whip, bringing down on my shoulder.

I had given my safe word, and still been struck.

The pain that flooded me was beyond compare to anything I could recall. Every bit of me sung out in agony as she snapped that whip back.

"You will obey!" she shouted, cracking the whip again.

I couldn't get my feet to work. I couldn't get my body to

move.

The whip came down three more times in rapid succession. She may have been rich and weak, but Mayfair knew how to handle a whip. The force of a whip isn't always about strength. It's also physics.

The door was thrown open and men with weapons flooded into the room. I dropped back to the floor, having been in the middle of attempting to stand. I laid my hands on the floor where they could be seen and kept my eyes on the floor.

I wasn't stupid. I had been raided before.

Some rival of my eldest brother had claimed we were dealing drugs. We had been raided by police four times before actual evidence had been found that showed the rival had been trying to frame my brother.

"Drop the weapon! Drop the weapon!" one of them shouted.

"I don't have a weapon!" I sobbed in response.

A blanket fell over my back, warming me even as it hurt my tender back. Mr. Wrightworth knelt, an arm draping over my back as he shushed me gently.

"You're all right," he whispered.

"Elaina Mayfair, you are under arrest for assault with a weapon. Anything you say can and will be used against you in a court of law."

"What?" she demanded as she was handcuffed. "You don't understand this was—"

"Mr. Wrightworth told us all about what this was," the arresting officer barked out. "Right before he explained what a safe word was, what hers was, and we took access to your systems, as per Marian Law."

Marian Law has been altered a great deal and now goes by another name.

At the time it, at its very basic, stated that anyone who had signed a contract or was under the Program's protection was protected by the law. This meant that any rich person who had a contractee with them gave up their right to privacy when it came to surveillance.

Mayfair's security systems had been hijacked by the government at Mr. Wrightworth's instruction. The moment she had struck me the first time with the whip, they rushed in to stop her.

That same law stated that if a rich person was found abusing a poor person, their records for up to the past year could be reviewed to search for other criminal activity. The idea being that, if causing damage to a human didn't stop them, they were probably doing all sorts of other things wrong.

They had watched the entire thing, waiting for her to break the law.

If they found any evidence linking Mayfair to Albert, especially Mayfair to the events that led to my being taken, she could be charged with accessory to anything he was charged with in relation to me. They would then search everything she had ever done that was still on record.

Basically, Mayfair was fucked.

In Mr. Wrightworth's arms, I watched as they physically dragged Mayfair out of the room.

"Nathaniel Edwards," one of the remaining men said, producing a pair of cuffs.

"Whoa," Mr. Wrightworth was on his feet in a moment. "No! He's not—" the man stepped between Nathaniel and the officer. "He stepped back immediately."

"Until the tapes are reviewed, we need to take him into custody as an accessory. You want to do this by the book?"

Mr. Wrightworth swore, then glanced back at Nathaniel, who was cringing away from the officer. Nathaniel was still in that place. Not all subs, but some who were trained in a certain way had to be released from sub space. He was one of those subs, and release from that place wasn't as easy as a word.

Without that release, he would go through a bad drop.

"He's a victim in this," Mr. Wrightworth said quickly.

"He still needs to be in custody," the officer insisted.

"Uh... uh..." Mr. Wrightworth actually seemed to struggle.

"He needs to be treated as a psychologically unstable person," I managed to get out. "He's dropping."

Groaning, I stood, pulling the blanket with me. I wrapped it around myself and hissed out as I walked around Mr.

Wrightworth, to Nathaniel.

With a small smile, I reached up and touched his cheek. I tried not to show the pain on my face as he looked down at me.

There was a cloud over his eyes, but I knew somewhere in there, my Nathaniel was still alive and well.

"You need to go with this man," I said to him. "You need to do everything he tells you to do. And you cannot drop. Understand?"

"Yes," he said quietly.

"If you need to call a lawyer, do so," I added.

Procedural shows didn't make me an expert, but I understood that rich people probably wouldn't want to speak to the police without a lawyer present.

"Yes..." he said with a small whine.

"Nate?" I asked.

He made a small sound.

"I feelings you," I said.

For a moment I saw Nathaniel, and then he was gone again. He moved away from me awkwardly, holding out his wrists to the officer. Nathaniel was handcuffed and taken away.

Mr. Wrightworth slid an arm around me, then bent and plucked me off the floor. He carried me out of the estate and deposited me in a car, sliding in beside me.

"Will he be all right?" I asked.

"He'll be fine," Mr. Wrightworth said. "It may take a day or two, but he'll get out once the tapes are reviewed. There's no way Nathaniel agreed to do that to you, and I'm sorry for not letting you in on my plan. If you had known, you might not have done what was necessary."

"I hurt all over," I groaned, pushing against him.

He draped an arm over my shoulders, causing me to hiss out in pain. The man made an annoyed sound.

"And to think, all this time I could have been whipping you until you bled," he grumbled.

"No," I said stubbornly. Then thought about what had just happened. "What did just happen?"

"I took a meeting with the prosecution and told them who Mayfair was. When she asked for time with you, I told them that as well as my fears as to what she might have planned for you. They agreed to tap into Mayfair's security, which took relatively little on their part to arrange.

"We watched what happened and when she struck you after breaking consent, they moved into place. We still needed a judge's order, however, to interrupt anything. That was why there was the hesitance, but because I told them the exact time and place, and they had gone to a judge to get the right to touch the footage in the first place, they had the same judge waiting in case this did go wrong.

"On the one hand, I'm upset because it did go wrong. On the other hand, I'm happy that it did."

"He's suffering."

"From a misalignment, yes," Mr. Wrightworth said. "Having a sub strike another sub tends to cause a backlash. That's all that was. He'll recover quite well, but what you did? That might cause a problem."

"What did I do?" I asked.

Mr. Wrightworth placed a hand on my cheek and drew my face towards him. His hand was so warm and comforting against the dull ache of my damaged face.

"You... you took control of him. You need to act on your promises and commands. But we'll have a few days to get you on track and on the mend. Your poor face."

"And body," I groaned.

"And body," he sighed out. "Wish I had thought to use you like that. Mm, I could see bending you over and having my way with you after you took such a beating for me."

"Not sure I want to do that again," I groaned.

"You just need to make it to the building. Nicole is standing on guard. She'll deliver a sedative and then there'll be pain killers available to you while you heal. I've made certain everything is arranged. A hot soak, some pain killers, and lots of sleep. No work either, because you need rest."

"Want this thing out," I said, shifting uncomfortably.

"Which did you choose?" he asked.

"Black," I said sadly.

"Don't sound sad, Darling. We knew what this was when we started."

"That's not what it turned into, though," I said, tears

filling my eyes as I raised my head. "That's not what we are now. What if I'm making the wrong decision?"

"As humans we always question, but our first choice is usually the right one."

"I don't even know what my first choice was," I said.

"Well..." Mr. Wrightworth murmured. "You have six months to figure out whether or not you made this choice based on your feelings, or because I told you that it was a good idea. At the end of it all, you'll still benefit whether you stay with him or not."

"What if I still don't know what I want?" I asked.

"Then we'll cross that road when we get there."

"I don't know what I want," I said, wanting him to understand.

"No, that's not true at all. You know exactly what you want. You want a Sir or a Master to tie you up and beat you, then make you come. That's the easy part. What you're afraid of is taking control, of being a domme, something that both of us will insist you learn.

"The thing that you don't know is who you want. And I don't think there's a person in the community who would judge you for being on the fence. No one is going to think twice if you walk away from both of us, even. At the end of it all, you'll have six months to decide. Just think of how far you've come in the last six months. How far might you go in another six months, or a year?

"Ah, we're here. Thank goodness she lived so close to the building."

"Uh... Mr. Wrightworth?"

"What?" he growled.

"Did anyone at the building—besides Nicole—know where we were going and what might be happening?" I asked.

"No, it's none of their damned business," he said.

"Mm," I said, looking down at the blanket that covered me.

He looked down as well, then looked up and met my eyes. For a long moment, I saw his mind trying to make the connection. When he did, his eyes went a little wider.

"You're naked," he said.

"Yes, yes I am."

"In only a blanket."

"Yup."

"Shit, I didn't think this through."

Despite the events of the day, I laughed.

He poked me between the eyes in response and then laughed with me.

"Well," I said as the car pulled to a stop. "Good thing I like strutting about in the nude."

"That's not just an in the privacy of my apartment thing?" he asked. "Wait, Izzy—"

But it was too late.

I was already out of the car. The blanket left on the seat I had been occupying.

I'm comfortable in my body, but strutting about naked wasn't just about showing off. It was about taking control. And walking out of that car, past the board members who had come to meet Mr. Wrightworth to ask about what had happened?

I was very much in control.

Introduction From: CONTRACT

Contracted Book III

I have had many younger people ask me as to whether or not the contract was real, and for those who knew that it was, what it actually said. There seems to be a belief that this particular contract could never have existed. It's true that in the modern day and age, it couldn't exist. However, the reason why it cannot exist is because the Program helped bring about laws which protect the poor from the rich.

We were never quite the serfdom that many countries reverted to, the rich were not able to own the poor for life, but the government was made up of rich folk and one of them, surely had a need for odd contracts. So long as a poor person was involved and signed the contract, a rich person could do whatever the poor person agreed to, even if the poor person had been tricked into signing.

The contract was very real, and Albert could do all those things to Nathaniel and Mr. Wrightworth, if they disobeyed, they would forfeit their lives. The lives of those around them would be shattered by association.

Albert couldn't attack anyone in the lives of Nathaniel and Mr. Wrightworth, which was why the first time he caught Nathaniel with a sub, he had sent the woman home and taken Nathaniel instead.

The Program changed the laws to prevent new contracts like that from being made. They were a regulatory body, not the first and only ones to bring up contracts. From the perspective of the the slums, however, they were. Unless a rich person forced you to sign a contract before the Program, you had no idea that such contracts could exist.

All the old contracts were grandfathered in. As in, because they existed before the laws, they were allowed to continue to exist, despite the harm they caused to poor folk.

Many have even suggested that due to the nature of the contract—which kept Mr. Wrightworth or Nathaniel from mentioning the event at Mayfair's to anyone—and the seclusion of the community that there were no repercussions to my being beaten and almost killed, or to her being arrested for assault.

There were repercussions, of course.

Mayfair wasn't just some rich woman. She was the heiress of the largest manufacturer of parts that every vehicle needed to run. They dabbled in other things as well, but her family was known as automobile royalty.

Paparazzi were not what they are now, the vultures circling anyone of notoriety at all times. It took them three days to publish the story, but it hit all newspapers and even some of the rich peoples' news broadcasts. By Friday every rich person knew who Isabella Martin was—that she was a part of the community and a poor person from the slums. They even got a hold of some of the videos from Mayfair's estate, which I'm pretty confident she leaked.

She was painted as both victim and aggressor. She was the awkward woman put in a position by a damaged and deluded person.

Politicians—Oberon and so many others—were seen on the broadcasts and even stepped up at the Capital to both condemn and defend those involved. Someone from the Capital called for all those law enforcement officers to be disciplined. Another called for the Program to be shut down, for Mr. Wrightworth to be stripped of his duties and returned to the slums where he belonged.

The politician caught saying that suffered backlash like no one could believe. He had to resign in disgrace. When those in the slums heard, they rioted. His servants, even those under contract, quit. No one would work for the man because he was, in the eyes of poor people, everything that was wrong with rich folk.

He wasn't everything wrong with rich people, but he was pretty damned close. The division of class should never have been pointed out in such a way. Most politicians knew that, and knew that the debtees didn't outnumber them, but those straddling that line and the poor commoners did outnumber the fabulously wealthy.

Debtees didn't have a vote, but those others did. They were the deciding factor for the Progam's funding and the laws that protected poor folk.

Those words from that moron started the first riots, though the debtees didn't know who Isabella Martin was. Those poor folk involved in the first fights only heard rich people denouncing slum folk. They worried that the rich would take everything from them, would take the way out.

Some even worried they would shut down the Program in its entirety. I'm guessing that was the goal of making that announcement, as the man and those who he worked with were a driving force behind the laws which attempted just that. He and his were paid by rich folk who wanted to drive the wedge between the classes, to raise themselves to a position that lords of old held over their fiefdoms.

The riots resulted in violence, of course. Several people died. A debt was added to the slums involved, to pay for the policing.

When all was said and done, it was decided. There would be a moratorium on Program contracts from anyone who participated in the riots. Nearly an entire slum was cut off from the very thing they wanted to keep.

Other slums grumbled in protest but were too afraid of costing their families the bounty that was a Program contract. A few didn't care, but their family set them to rights pretty quickly.

In the slums, you stood with your family, or you suffered slum justice. I don't think a single one of those who were strung up ever received more than a casual glance from the police forces. The troublemakers were dealt with, and the officers didn't have to do anything. Slum justice caused more fear than the government proclamations and new laws.

The government wasn't there, after all. The poor folk

didn't think they'd ever set foot in the slums, didn't think life could get worse. Family members were there, however. They were there as you slept, there as you showered, there when you thought you were alone.

As for myself, I was painted the whore.

Or the virgin twisted by rich people.

I was the black sheep. My history was paraded across the screen for rich people to judge and pick apart. My face on every screen.

They talked about my family, my history, my work in the slum and their supposed reasoning for why I went to the Program building. The Program itself released absolutely no information, they believed in full confidentiality except when participating with law enforcement. An officer once leaked information. They charged him with everything they could come up with, and then the prosecution added on endangerment.

The first of the riots were subdued.

And then Albert Edwards was found and arrested.

Let me be clear. The warrant was issued before I went to Mayfair's place. Officers were told first and foremost to catch Albert and bring him in. They weren't to waste time searching his estates or lands. Every house was under surveillance, but the man was slippery.

The police made it seem like they weren't interested in searching his home because they wanted to catch him walking in.

When they did catch him, it was as he was headed to his private plane. That plane was bound to the only free country left on the planet, the last of the old nations to still be alive and well. The only place to never extradite to another country, who had never lost the technological advances that the rest of the world had lost and recovered.

He was charged with kidnapping, sexual assault, assault with a deadly weapon—eight counts—and premeditated murder—seven counts—amongst a plethora of others which I don't rightly recall.

Why, you might ask, were there so many counts against him? Remember when I said karma is a bitch?

Well...

Seven bodies were found buried on the grounds of estate Albert had taken me. Bodies that were found because the prosecution reviewed the tapes with a psychologist, who said that Albert was ritualizing what he did to me.

With that and a second opinion, they had all the evidence they required to search the other tapes.

There were none. Albert had erased them. The act of erasing surveillance tapes over two years old is not, nor has it ever been, illegal. At some point, room has to be made in storage for other tapes. The only reason he hadn't deleted the videos of his time with me was the fact that the moment they went in to rescue me, they took control of the systems.

He always kept the tapes. His usual ritual was to show the tapes to the next one. It was just that no one knew where he kept the copies, and I didn't remember that. Perhaps he was evolving with me. That is what the psychiatrists call it, I think. Evolution of a serial killer.

Upon finding everything erased up to the moment I was taken into the building, the prosecution approached a judge. It didn't take much to get a hold of a search warrant. The building was searched, everything was stripped apart, trophies were found. He hadn't just cut my hair to make a point. He had done it to keep the hair. That was his trophy.

Suppose it could have been worse, and bloody. He could have removed all my teeth, or taken a finger.

They tore apart the grounds and found seven bodies and one hand.

We never did find out the history, or owner, of the hand.

He was given no bail and was kept in solitary confinement, for the safety of all. He was assigned a team of psychiatrists, to keep him from manipulating one.

You have to understand; he was the first serial murderer of the modern era. The courts were well aware of the serial killers of the past and were afraid that they were somehow super-human. They took necessary precautions and unnecessary ones.

From Mayfair's I was taken back to the Program building and left the car naked. Those in the building kept their eyes to themselves and never brought it up again. Except for

Nicole, who would never let me forget that walk, the baring of my skin and the physical damage from the hour I had spent at Mayfair's.

They made me stay in medical until I was fully healed. After that, I received a full psych evaluation. So many problems, I'm sure, but it was determined that I had gone in of my own free will and that I was a willing participant.

Outside the building the riots began again as the names of Albert's victims were slowly released.

I watched them with Mr. Wrightworth and Nicole, afraid of what would happen to all of us if the riots broke out in the nearby slum. The government couldn't trace the information or how people in the slums were all finding out about the riots. They kept strict control, and these incidents showed them that something was very, very wrong.

The slums where Albert's victims came from did riot, and that was understandable. After the first two names, police enforcement changed their approach and the riots weren't as bad. A few were entirely avoided. But then slums not involved in Albert's case began rioting over the victims, having never known that the victims were women from the slums.

We worried then. The power went out more than once. There was the sound of explosions in the parking lot. Program buildings were both a sanctuary and the enemy. The slums involved in the riots might have been far off, but the poor folk weren't contained by walls, not then. We stayed in the slums because we knew there was nothing for us outside of them.

Poor people were free to come and go as they pleased, and they did.

All the buildings were targeted. Each slum had a small outpost building. For some that saw few contracts, the building was small, little more than a rented office space.

We were in the main building, which had high fences and security. The main building had the mainframe, the original paper contracts, the controllers—who had access to all the buildings that had been upgraded to their standards—and the recovered contractees who had to be protected at all costs. Our security was doubled, special procedures were brought in, no one was allowed in or out without special permission.

I couldn't even go to church most Sundays because they were afraid that I would be attacked either by protestors from the slums, or Albert sympathizers.

Despite all the precautions, we had plenty of reason to worry as well.

Being in the main building made us the primary target of a group of terrorists that chose the riots as the time to strike.

Funded and founded by rich people, but hiring poor people to do their dirty work, these terrorists wanted to destroy the Program in its entirety.

The Program offered contracts to the poor, raised them up and delivered up to three emancipations a year.

Their reasoning was simple: rich people were born rich, poor people were born poor. Both should remain separate.

They didn't just view themselves as better than poor people, but honestly believed that they were above poor people, that those in the slums were content with their lot in life and that not everyone can be rich. They didn't see the long-term view that Nathaniel had shared with me, or if they did, they didn't believe it was the way the world should go.

They wanted to retain control.

Of course, they didn't just attack us.

They had spent years undermining everything we did. None of them held contracts, so it was easy for law enforcement to find them, once they stopped a poor person who had been sent to bomb the building.

Morons.

But they did a lot of damage, and they started the whisperings amongst the slums, which put a black mark on the Program.

It's important to note that history does not recall Mayfair's arrest as the cause. Nor do they mention Albert Edwards being arrested as the reason why the riots began again. The books don't say, "So Isabella Martin took a beating, and then Elaina Mayfair violated consent, and the whole world lost their fucking minds."

Which from my point of view, was basically how the events happened.

History tends to say something more like:

"Robert Cavell was recorded, on national television, as saying that the head of the Program, a man who had been born in the slums and had been raised up by the very contracts he was overseeing, should be stripped of all he had earned and be returned to the slums. Where Cavell believed all slum people belonged, no matter their hard work or skills. The tenuous trust between the upper and lower class was broken in a moment, and those from the slums nearest the capital rioted.

"Sixteen hundred people lost their lives. Numerous were wounded in the first riots. The cost of putting down the riots was in the millions, but the cost of the rebellion it would birth in later years is still being felt.

"Cavell resigned in disgrace after the first riots ended. He would later take his life in a motel room on the outer edges of a slum, having lost his family's fortune trying to regain his position at the capital."

The rebellion took place years later, but those who rebelled claimed the riots as when they began planning. The government cracking down on surveillance, going public with the fact that we were always watched at all times, didn't help matters. Building walls around the slums was just a stupid idea, but politicians weren't exactly known for being intelligent in their decisions.

A week into the riots, martial law was enacted.

For the poor people, realizing that there was a third class was surprising. The military was made up of men and women who were taken as children. Orphans, mainly. Unwanted children whose mothers were convinced to carry to term and give up for adoption. There were some few poor rich who sold a younger child to the government to get our of debt, or to give an older child the education they needed to bring in wealth.

Those in the military didn't carry debt, per say.

But they knew how and from where they came.

They held no love for the slums.

They were mainly reserves, trainees who hadn't seen fighting yet. We were fighting wars overseas for control of black lands, but no one in the slums knew that.

None of us were told how badly the collapse hit other countries or the fact that we were waging a war over what was once France.

I was terrified.

There was no way for me to know how my family was doing because no one was allowed access to what was going on inside the slums. My previous contract with Nathaniel had stated that I couldn't contact my family. It had ended and then the whole problem began. No one had ever taught me how to use the surveillance system. I couldn't look into it myself. Mr. Wrightworth was far too busy for me to bother with such a silly request. So I just never saw them.

The Program didn't know, the other slums didn't know, the rich people didn't. Everyone just lived their lives and was either happy nothing was trying to kill them, or just trying to survive until the next day. The news stations would have snippets, but didn't report the whole story, just vague generalizations as to what was going on. Military officials would give statements and talk about a successful operation like they were doctors excising cancerous tissue.

No one talks about what did happen. Like it never did happen.

Rape and war crimes are what happened.

Each slum was brought to heel. Even those who had no involvement in the first riots saw military on their streets. Starting a fight, even protecting a wife or sister, resulted in debt being added to one's genetic profile. It became a crime to protect your family. Protesting rape? Well, fuck you. And your sister and your mother and your aunts, any daughters you might have as well.

Of course, there were women in the military, but they didn't see slum women as people. We were an infestation to them. Each woman would mean a multitude of more poor people in the next generation. Each of us was the mother that abandoned them.

So they didn't care.

That cold-hearted, borderline sociopathic behaviour is what won us a war. Doesn't make it right, though.

Somehow life went on.

A month after the riots began all word of them just stopped.

I was still in the Program building because all of us were on lock down for our safety. During that month I had no idea what was happening with Nathaniel either. Mr. Wrightworth did his best, but the government had put a gag order on pretty well everything, especially anything that might have led back to the riots.

It was another three weeks before I was pulled in and formally offered a contract. I made certain who the contract was from, then accepted without reading the terms. I trusted Nathaniel and Mr. Wrightworth not to screw me over.

For a majority of the country, life simply went on the way it had before the riots. Perhaps a little stricter, with more scars, but everyone was getting up and going to work in the morning, eating the same food as before, living in the same places.

And then there was me.

Accepting a contract with Nathaniel and getting ready to face the biggest fight of my life. The same day I took the contract, I was contacted by the prosecution and told of the impending trial of Albert Edwards.

Life had never been so complicated.

How I yearned for the days when I could just be tied up and spanked.

***

The story continues in *Contract Renewed.* Get your copy today

Coming Soon:

MASKED INTENTIONS

Daughters of the Alphas

Book One

My name is Rachel.

In my world, genetically 'superior' humans are called Alphas. They spend their lives trying to outdo one another and accumulating wealth in the form of property, money, and companions.

What's a companion you ask?

I am.

We're humans who carry what the Alphas call the G14 genetic marker. That particular sequence of genes means that under the right conditions we will break and form an everlasting bond with the one who breaks us, Alpha or human.

Women were once excluded from the selection and breaking process, but when the Alphas overthrew the government, everything changed.

I was been caught, charged with a ridiculous crime, and they've decided it's time to break me.

I won't go down without a fight.

At Death's Door

Wraith's Rebellion Book 1

I was chosen to interview a man who claimed to be something more. I expected the usual drabble about culture and art and history that all the other interviewers received. With a little fluff and maybe just the slightest hint of intrigue.

I don't think any of us truly believes they are what they claim they are: vampires. None have witnessed feeding, no hard evidence of their lives throughout history are given.

I personally believe it's a giant con, perhaps a huge PR move before a movie is announced or something. This is the real world, vampires and supernatural creatures don't exist. If they did, we'd know about them long ago.

In one night, my whole world was turned upside down. It's a story that spans centuries, of secrets no mortal has ever been told.

The other vampires hadn't been telling pre-approved stories constructed by the Council, they had just led really boring lives. Quin, on the other hand, has spent his immortal life near the Council, running from his Maker, yet unable to escape the man's grasp.

This is *his* story.

Prototype*

An Aurora Novel

(*Working Title)

My name is Maggy Doyle. I have a three-year-old daughter, a husband, a home, and an extended family. I work a secretary job for a lawyer's office and spend my days just trying to fly under the radar of pretty well everyone.

See, five years ago, I was found wandering around a field. I don't recall anything before that moment. I had no idea who I was. If it weren't for Harry, if not for how much he loved me before the incident, I would have probably been lost forever.

Imagine my surprise when I opened my front door one day to find men standing there, demanding my daughter and me go with them. They wouldn't answer my questions or tell me where they were taking us.

There's this nagging at the back of my mind telling me that it has to do with Aurora. The still new, third world we were linked to, ruled by a woman who is said to have not only created the world, but also animals, and who knew what else.

What could she possibly want with twenty people ranging from late teens to middle-aged? The only thing we have in common is amnesia. Our lives before a certain point were erased. We didn't do anything wrong, none of us know each other and our incidents were months or even years apart.

We're completely harmless.

I think.

About the Author

Aya DeAniege wrote for years, first to please herself then writing stories for free—believing no one would ever pay to read her stuff—before pursuing indie publishing. She still writes mainly for personal pleasure, with topics ranging from romance, fantasy, science fiction, on to whatever takes her fancy in the future. World creation fascinates her, and when she finds one she likes, she dabbles endlessly.

Connect on:
Facebook: Aya DeAniege
Twitter: @DeAniege_A
Wordpress: A Little World with a Big Story
Email: deaniege@gmail.com

Made in United States
North Haven, CT
06 July 2023

38597810R00171